FÊTE

Beech Grove's Annual
FOUNDER'S DAY PROGRAM
ART FESTIVAL

and

Summer Solstice
CELEBRATION

Also by Daniel McVay

The Baggy-Kneed Camel Blues

Fête

Daniel McVay

Stamford, Connecticut

Designed by Able Reproductions, copyright © 1985
Published by Knights Press, P.O. Box 454, Pound Ridge, NY 10576

Library of Congress Cataloging in Publication Data

McVay, Daniel.
    Fête.

    I. Title.
PS3563.C9F47   1985   813'.54   85-4270
ISBN 0-915175-11-8 (pbk.)

Printed in the United States of America

To Vicki

The characters in this book live only in the imagination of the author. Likewise, there is no town called Beech Grove in Southern California. In fact, there isn't a town like Beech Grove in the USA, possibly the world. The author apologizes for this; he, too, would like to live there. Sorry.

FÊTE

Beech Grove's Annual
FOUNDER'S DAY PROGRAM
ART FESTIVAL

and

Summer Solstice
CELEBRATION

1. Queer Night At Respighi's

My mother always hated Queer Night at Respighi's. She should've preferred it: It was quieter than Bowling Night, friendlier than Dad Night aka Poker Night, less bitchy than Mom Night, a lot less rowdy than Music Night, better tips than Art Night, and it was the night before her day off, Monday, which was Family Night and the bar at Respighi's was closed.

My mother, Edwina "Eddie" Russell, was the bartender at Respighi's. And she hated Queer Night.

It was not officially called Queer Night. The little sign over the bar—the sign that listed who got half priced drinks on which night—simply said "The Regulars" in the Sunday night slot. And if any of us had cause to refer to it, we called it Gay Night. It was the gay clientelle who called it Queer Night.

Although a California native, my mother inherited a midwestern robust figure, corn fed, you might say. Definitely healthy, she was fairly tall, big boned, ample breasted, wide hipped and whiskey voiced. My father is—well, Dad looks like what he is: a cabinetmaker. But he could just as easily be a cobbler, a house painter, a plumber; he has that look of the American tradesman. He's ruddy, thin, getting old too soon, an inch shorter than Mom.

As far back as I can remember, Eddie was always a creature of routine. And as our lives were irretrievably interwoven with hers, the rest of us in the family were held to that routine as well.

Especially Sundays. We were on our own till ten:

At our house, my wife, Elizabeth, and I would always get up early to bake muffins—blueberry on my weeks, bran on hers—which we would devour with about a gallon of coffee out on our front porch, doing a crossword puzzle and watching the birds, squirrels and neighbors.

At my family's house, my father, Carl, would always be up at dawn. He'd start the first pot of coffee, then jump in the shower for a quick rendition of something, anything, from Gilbert and Sullivan, much to the dismay of those of us who ever had to share a household with him. Shower and song once completed, Carl would grab some coffee and go out to his workshop to meditate over a spinning lathe until breakfast was on the table.

Mom equals breakfast equals cholesterol: a dozen eggs, a pound of sausage links, home-fried potatoes, and biscuits with butter and jam. Eddie always waited until Carl got out to his workshop before she got up to start cooking, even if she had to lie in bed awake for an extra half hour. For some reason which I could never grasp, Carl thought his Sunday morning ritual was a secret and Eddie was determined not to destroy his delusion.

My brother, Donny, who was still living at home, would stumble blindly from his room to the kitchen, stuff three or four of Mom's homemade chocolate chip cookies into his mouth, pour a mug of coffee and then stumble back to his room where he would encase his head in a Sony Walkman stereo headset and scramble his brains with the latest and loudest heavy metal rock and roll.

It was always the same.

Then, just as the last plate of food was set on the table and Donny was forced out of his room and out of his earphones, Carl would walk in the back door and take his place at the kitchen table. Eddie would refill his cup with fresh coffee, asking: "Where did you go, dear?" To which he would reply: "Oh, just out for a little walk." Same words every week.

After breakfast, Eddie would send Donny to his room to change from his cutoff pants and tank top shirt into "anything else." To which he would reply: "I don't see anything wrong with what I'm wearing." "March!" Same words every week.

About once a month, they'd spice it up a little:

"Well, you let him go like that!" Donny would start.

"Him" meant Dad. "Like that" meant dressed in Sears and Roebuck catalog green or khaki work pants and shirt, and construction boots.

To which Eddie would reply: "Your father's clothes are clean. He doesn't have those scraggly threads hanging from the bottom of his pants, and he certainly doesn't have his underpants pulled down below the fringe for the whole world to see. Now march! If you have to wear short pants, why don't you wear those nice safari shorts I bought you?"

"Mother!"

"I think they're nice."

"You would."

"Put on anything you want then. Just go do it. Now. I will not be late for the service."

I will not be late. He will not be late. We will not be late.

Sunday Service began promptly at ten. At about nine-forty-five, Donny would be sent ahead to our house to make sure Elizabeth and I were ready, which we always were, and we'd all meet on the road to walk the last few blocks to the hotel where Sunday Service was held.

Sunday Service in Beech Grove is very informal. An inspirational gathering would be a more apt description. There is no minister. People bring things they want to read to the others—anything they want to share, usually poems or something from one of the world's many bibles. The Brownings and Walt Whitman seem to be the most popular in our group.

After the meeting, we would always take the long way, over the hill and through the woods, back to Mom and Dad's house, where the remainder of the day would be spent in family comraderie and overindulging.

Coffee and cookies were first. Then two beers each with pretzels. Lunch was at two. Honey-basted ham or fried chicken. Mashed potatoes or rice. Gravy. Green beans or peas. Squash or corn or carrots. Sweet pickles. Bread-and-butter pickles. Dill pickles. Green olives. Black olives. Homemade dinner rolls. Apple pie *and* chocolate meringue pie. Coffee on the veranda.

The men would go out on the porch first. Each letting the screen door slam after being asked not to. Each patting a bloated stomach while faking manly belches and asking the mythical deity why He let us eat so much.

Then the women would join us so that Elizabeth could start the argument about who should do the dishes.

"Matt," she would always say, "you do them at home. Why can't you do them here?"

"Queenie," I always reply, "it's not the same."

(My wife's mother was a loyal subject of Elizabeth II, worshipped the ground the Queen walked on. Named her sweet little daughter after that blessed monarch. My mother-in-law was not English, just strange.)

"It just isn't the same," I would repeat.

It isn't the same. It's one thing to be a modern husband, doing things around the house, sharing the work load, being a partnership. It is another thing when you're at your mother's house.

Carl always ignored that part of our Sunday afternoon festivities; always turned his hearing aid off, as a matter of fact. Donny always pretended to be lost in thought so he wouldn't have to get into the argument. And up until a couple of years ago, Eddie would always end the fight by going in to start the dishes alone, shaming Elizabeth into helping. Then something happened. The change was so gradual, one hardly knew he was being maneuvered. At first, it was something as simple as, "Matt, can you put this up on the top shelf for me. I can't reach it." Then it progressed to, "Would you mind putting these back in the hutch for me, honey?" And, "Don't put them away wet, dear!" And, "Oh that hot water burns the cut on my hand, the cut I got while I was fixing *your* typewriter." And finally, "Matt, don't splash the dishwater all over the floor!" And to my equally miserable baby brother, "Donny, you're getting behind. Do you need a dry towel?"

Carl managed to elude their charms, so while Donny and I did KP, he got to sit out on the porch with Mom and Elizabeth and listen to them pat their bloated stomachs, fake womanly belches and ask Him why they ate so much.

Five o'clock. Time for Eddie the Mother to become Eddie the Bartender. And time for our weekly "Why can't Donny go to the bar?" argument.

"Mom . . . ?" Donny begins.

"No!" Eddie says.

"Mom!" Donny shouts.

"Don't you take that tone with me, young man."

"Mother, he's twenty-one-years-old," is my weekly contribution.

"Matt," Elizabeth warns me every time.

"You stay out of this, Matthew," Eddie scolds me. "As long as he lives under my roof, he does as I say."

Carl looks at Eddie every time she says "my roof," but he says nothing.

"And I say," Eddie concludes, "that Donny doesn't go to the bar on Sunday nights."

Sunday night is Queer Night at Respighi's. And my mother always hated it. And Donny wasn't allowed to go.

So Donny would stomp off to his room, encase his head

in Sony Walkman earphones and scramble his brains with the latest and loudest heavy metal rock and roll.

Mom would always change from her blue smock to her red smock, keeping the navy blue slacks and sensible shoes.

Then she, Dad and I would walk Elizabeth back to our house, leaving just the three of us to continue on to the bar, which was in the hotel.

Respighi's Bar and Restaurant is the entire east wing of the Beech Grove Hot Springs Hotel. All the way up front is the one-lane bowling alley, then the bar room, then the dining room and then the kitchen is all the way in the back. Every room, including the bowling alley and the kitchen, has big, double French doors leading out onto the veranda/dining patio. The veranda used to run all the way around the building, all the way around the entire hotel, until the bowling lane was added. They put it right where the veranda used to go around the front end of the east wing. Just walled it up! So now there are weird-looking and inconvenient dead ends on either side.

Eddie was the manager of the bar; Hugh Vance was the manager of the restaurant. Mom and Hugh had been dear friends since their school days. He owned three-quarters of the business; Eddie owned a quarter.

Respighi's bar is a genuine relic and beautiful. It has, of course, a bar which is hand carved oak, L-shaped and accommodates eight bar stools, also oak. There are four oak tables with matching chairs and, between the French doors on the back wall, there is a magnificent hutch. It's about eight feet tall, seven or eight feet wide and at least two feet deep. Hand carved. Mahogany maybe. All the stuff is from the Twenties, when the hotel was built. Then there are some noisy, ugly, mood-spoiling electronic games along the wall that separates the bar from the bowling lane. Eddie used to put "Out of Order!" signs on the games. Hugh used to have to take them off the next morning.

Five o'clock on Sunday, a few months ago: It was Mother's Day, May 13. The walk to Respighi's was especially pleasant that evening. It was balmy after a hot day. Mother's Day dinner had gone smoothly; more than smoothly: beautifully. Elizabeth and I did our barbecued steak and lobster for the family. Delicious. Donny and Carl did the dishes! Donny didn't ask if he could go to the bar. It was a special day. Mom wore her new yellow smock. We dropped Elizabeth off at our house a little early that night because she was working on a new watercolor and was anxious to get back to it. Then Mom, Dad and I took the long way, over the hill and through the woods, *to* the bar. First time we had ever done that. We all commented on how different everything looked when you're coming from the other way.

When we got to Respighi's, we found that Hugh and the day bartender, Gordy (another Beech Grove relic), had conspired to decorate the bar for the occasion. A banner offered a "Happy Mother's Day!" and there were a half-dozen large bouquets haphazardly placed about the room. It smelled like a florist shop in there. The largest bouquet, white and red roses, graced the back bar. The card said, "To Eddie, with Love. Hugh and Gordy."

Dad had his own little surprise for Mom. He disappeared into the kitchen for a minute, then returned with one yellow rose, which he gave to Eddie with a kiss. She got a little teary-eyed, kissed Carl on the cheek, then set about putting those bouquets into some kind of tasteful arrangement. Dad and I began our once-a-week, six-hour eight-ball marathon.

It wasn't that we loved pool playing that much. It was just that we had to keep Eddie company at the bar on Sunday nights. Sunday night was Queer night at Respighi's. And Eddie hated it.

She started hating it around eight when the Sunday Night Regulars started showing up. Until then, there would usually be a couple of stragglers around, usually people who'd gone out for a Sunday afternoon drive and then had forgotten to leave after three or four drinks. But they always left by eight.

Dennis was usually the first to arrive. And Mother's Day was no exception. Dennis is a drunk. A fairly good artist, too. But a drunk nevertheless. He walked in sober, keeping with the trend of strange happenings we seemed to be experiencing. He set up two of the tables for bridge, even before ordering his first drink. Eddie was so taken aback she had to look to us for confirmation. We nodded.

Pat and Gwen came in arm in arm. Pat is my assistant-everything on the Beech Grove Clarion and the mother of a fourteen-year-old whirling dervish by name of J.D. Her lover, Gwen, is Beech Grove's only nurse. When she first moved here a few years ago, Gwen was Beech Grove's only black. Now there are, I think, nine.

Aunt Gloria and Rae arrived next. Aunt Gloria is not really my aunt, just a really good friend of the family; she and Mom grew up together. She used to be married to Hugh, who used to be called Uncle Hugh even though he wasn't really an uncle. For some reason, Hugh lost his uncle status when he and Aunt Gloria got divorced. Rae used to be a semi-famous Hollywood actress. Rae and Gloria operate the town's only hairstyling shop—unisex—which is located in the hotel.

Then came Kurt and Terry, but they never walk into the bar together. They have a little game they like to play. Terry comes in first. He's mid-twenties, too thin, sort of effeminate, bleached blond. He always goes to the pinball machine, whether or not it's "Out of Order!" and stands there posing. Then Kurt, owner of the Junque Shoppe, saunters in casually, glances around the room, then inches his way toward the games and tries to pick up the cute boy at the pinball machine. He, of course, scores and they join the others.

Dennis' partner, Jack, was the last to arrive that night. Jack is Beech Grove's senior teacher and school principal.

Jack's been around a long time. He taught both Donny and me, from seventh to twelfth grade. He's the most levelheaded of the Sunday Night Regulars and the unofficial leader.

After hugs and kisses, they all sat down to begin their bridge game.

Eddie had set up the glasses for their first round of drinks, but they hadn't ordered them yet, so she just stood there wondering whether or not to start pouring.

They were waiting for the ninth and newest member of their club: my best friend, Josh. Josh is often late, but not usually that late. It was almost 8:30. I looked over at Dennis to see if he was getting anxious, but he was calmly dealing the first hand at his table, seemingly unconcerned about the fact that he'd been in a bar for thirty minutes without having a drink.

Josh walked in.

"Sonofabitch!" Dennis screamed, as he dropped his cards in mid-deal. "She's finally here! I officially declare Queer Night in session. Let's drink!"

The nine thirsty members of the Sunday Night Regulars hit the bar en masse. No table service in the bar. Eddie was prepared for them; all their drinks were lined up on the bar: each in the size and shape glass preferred by the individual drinker; each made with the customer's favorite brand of poison; and each to the exact proportions, as once specified in their bartender-client relationship. Dennis downed his in one gulp and ordered another before rejoining the others at the tables. Josh, Dad and I alternated at the pool table.

About an hour later, I had just beat Carl with an incredible two-bank shot—so he had to buy a round of beers—and Josh and I were about to start a new game . . . when Donny walked in the front door!

I missed the cue ball entirely.

Josh chipped a tooth with his beer bottle.

The Sunday Night Regulars, who had already begun

their first screaming argument involving both tables, snapped quiet in unison as though the Maestro had tapped his baton. They knew. They had often pleaded Donny's case, sometimes rationally, sometimes emotionally. If any of them were offended by Eddie's stance, they never showed it. A mother's prerogative, they called it. It didn't prevent them from trying to change her mind from time to time, but it didn't upset them either.

The Regulars watched silently—first Donny, then Eddie. They looked to Carl for guidance. He nodded them back into their game.

Donny walked slowly up to the bar.

"Gin and tonic," he said, just as though we hadn't fought about this every week for the last six months.

I thought Mom would break a bottle over his head. She was calm, though, as she told him to get the hell out of there.

He didn't leave.

We were all on the edge of our seats. Even Dad.

Josh went up to the bar and stood next to Donny.

It was an old-fashioned standoff, both of them repeating the same old arguments about why he should and why he should not be allowed in there . . . until Donny dropped his bomb.

Eddie played right into his hand: "You can drink at home. You can drink in here any other night. Give me one good reason why you think you have to be in here on Qu . . . on Gay Night."

"Because, Mother, I am gay," Donny announced. And to top it off—or twist the knife, if you prefer—he turned to Josh and kissed him on the mouth.

There were a few cheers from the Regulars, the ones who were too drunk to realize they ought to have been wary of what Eddie might do next. Eddie wasn't a mean woman, but she was strict. And she didn't like having her orders countermanded by anyone, especially her two boys. Dad got away with it once in a while; Donny and I never did. At that particular moment in time, I think Dad and I were about as quiet as we had ever been, or ever would be, in our lives.

Eddie mixed Donny's gin and tonic, squeezed a fresh lime into it, then placed it on the bar in front of him. She didn't say a word. She poured herself a double shot of bourbon, straight with no ice, then opened two bottles of beer and brought them over to Carl and me at the pool table.

She looked very much like she was about to explode.

Donny looked very much like he was about to faint. Josh put him into a chair.

Eddie just stood there, staring at me. Accusingly.

Someone dropped money in the juke box and started punching up some noise. That room needed it desperately.

A few notes into Creedence Clearwater Revival's "Bad Moon Rising," Mom finished off her bourbon and asked Dad and me if we knew about Donny. Why the hell was she looking at me if she was talking to both of us? Carl got away with a grin because her eyes were glued to mine.

"Yeah," I said and she looked away. "But only for about a week," I lied.

It wasn't a total lie. I'd known since we were kids that Donny was gay, but it had only been a week since he and I actually talked about it. He had also told me what he was planning to do that night, but I did not admit that to Eddie. Besides, I didn't think he'd really go through with it.

My disclaimer of only having known for a week did not placate Eddie's anger. And she didn't even wait for Carl's answer. She went behind the bar, mixed a round of drinks for the Regulars, and took them to their tables, on the house! Then she washed dirty glasses, the same ones twice, I think. She spent the remainder of the evening repeating that sequence. Free drinks and table service for the Regulars, and then washing dirty glasses—twice. Dad, Josh, Donny and I had to pay for our drinks. And we had to go up to the bar to get them. Dad and Josh did most of the getting, though, because Donny and I thought we'd better keep our distance.

At about ten, the bridge game ended and Gloria and Rae fed the juke box. Dennis was too drunk to get out of his chair, but the others were up and out on the little dance floor before the downbeat. Pat and Gwen invited Jack to be a threesome with them so he wouldn't have to just sit there. They said. Meaning they were hoping to prevent Jack and Dennis' weekly fight by separating them.

Donny grabbed my elbow. "Will you dance with me?" he asked.

I stood there like an idiot.

"Matt?"

"I can't."

He was hurt. I was hurt. I don't know why I couldn't dance with him, I just couldn't. I'm not usually that insensitive; too embarrassed, maybe.

Carl nudged Josh. Josh smiled, then took Donny by the hand and led him onto the dance floor. They looked good together. I was really pissed at myself for letting him down. I guess Carl sensed it, because he put his arm around my shoulder. Together we watched my little brother and my best friend, in each other's arms, dancing to Jane Olivor's "Stay the Night."

Respighi's closes at eleven o'clock. Usually Eddie has to push, scream and threaten to get the Sunday Night Regulars out of there. On Mother's Day, May 13, nothing had to be said. Everyone had been watching the clock for the last half hour and when eleven hit, they quietly filed out the front door with a few subdued and polite good nights and see you laters.

Josh walked Donny home. Carl and I lagged behind, as usual, expecting to be given our cleanup orders. Eddie waved us out, still not speaking.

Dad and I walked home together, in silence. What the hell was there to say?

Donny told me later that Eddie didn't get home for over an hour. She slept on the couch in the den—A first. Dad thought it was funny: "Maybe now she'll believe me about the lump in the middle of the sofa."

Donny said the last thing he heard before he finally fell asleep was sort of a thud-whack-tinkle-crash, to use his words. He lay there in the dark, a few last tears still wet on his cheeks, and tried to identify the sounds.

Thud. Heavy piece of pottery hitting wood. The only thing made out of clay in the den was an ashtray—an ashtray Donny had made for Mom in his seventh grade Arts and Crafts class. The wood, he guessed, was the mantel over the fireplace.

Whack. Pottery against glass, he thought, the glass in a picture frame.

Tinkle. The glass falling to the tile hearth.

Crash. Ashtray to hearth.

There were three photographs on the mantelpiece at that time. One was of the four of us taken at the zoo. The second was a picture of Eddie's father and his twin brother taken the year Eddie was born. The third was a copy of an old tintype of their father, Eddie's grandfather, taken with Buffalo Bill and Annie Oakley on the night the twins were born.

2. Twins

My great-grandfather shook hands with Buffalo Bill and Annie Oakley on the night my mother's father and his twin brother were born. He even had a tintype to prove it. The photographer had written the date across the bottom: February 29, 1896. A leap year.

The Gay Nineties, they were called. The end of the horse-and-buggy era. Vaudeville. The Palace. Minstrel shows. The Gay Nineties were Lillian Russell, Art Nouveau, the first moving pictures, the first automobiles, Edison, Freud, H.G. Wells, Mark Twain, Toulouse-Lautrec, Tchaikovsky, Tolstoy. The last of the Gilbert and Sullivan operettas debuted in London in 1896.

The Spanish-American War. Remember the Maine. Teddy Roosevelt and the Rough Riders charged up Kettle Hill, erroneously reported as San Juan Hill.

The Gay Nineties were the youthful days of Truman, Eisenhower, MacArthur, Churchill, Hitler, Khrushchev, Einstein, Dempsey, Picasso, Hemingway, Huxley, Faulkner, Prokofiev. And Jack Benny.

"The War of the Worlds." "Cyrano de Bergerac." "The Adventures of Sherlock Holmes." "The Jungle Book." "The Picture of Dorian Gray." Oscar Wilde wrote his masterpieces, buggered the son of the Marquis of Queensberry, and went to gaol in the Gay Nineties . . . then died with them. Walt Whitman also died. Arthur Rimbaud died. Vincent van Gogh died. Paul Gauguin went to Tahiti.

The firt modern Olympics were held in Athens in 1896.

Eddie's grandfather raped her grandmother. He said it was the only way he could get a fuck out of that icy little bitch. That's what he said to his wife. That's what he said to Esther, their black maid, their *negress*, when she was putting cold packs on Eddie's grandmother's bruises that next morning. That's what he told his twin sons when they were eight-years-old. That's what he told his cronies down at the saloon—a Pendergast saloon.

Kansas City, Missouri still had gas lighting in 1896. And dirt streets, open sewers, disease, and the beginnings of a powerful political machine. Alderman Jim Pendergast was making his climb from precinct to county politics, establishing a regime which would last for almost half a century. Grafty and corruption. It started with illegal gambling upstairs at his saloons. Eddie's grandfather was a bartender in one of those saloons.

He was a big man, burly, over six feet. Over two hundred pounds, strong, broad shoulders with a short, red neck. His name was Dick Delaney. Never just Dick; never just Delaney or Mister Delaney. Always Dick Delaney. Even his wife called him Dick Delaney.

She was tiny and frail, Mary Delaney, not even five feet, not even a hundred pounds. Small bones; small hips.

"That po' li'l baby jus' din' have the size ta be birthin' no twins," Esther said that night, and repeated it every night in her prayers for the rest of her life.

Mary Delaney spent her entire pregnancy in bed. Esther said it was 'cuz of the rape. Dick Delaney said it was worth it if he got a son out of it. Dick Delaney also said he didn't see any reason to hang around the house just because Mary was going into labor; there was nothing he could do anyway. So he went to the fairgrounds to see "Buffalo Bill's Wild West."

The labor pains had started at dawn that day and Dick

Delaney had gone to work about mid-morning. The doctor came to the house twice that day. Said to wait; said Mary wasn't ready yet; said he'd come back around eight that night.

Around six that night, Dick Delaney left the saloon to go to the fairgrounds. Around six that night, Mary's water broke.

"Lordy, I don' know. Maybe I should'na took her there. Them folks din' seem ta know wha' they was doin'," Esther said a thousand times over the next sixty years.

Esther carried Mary Delaney to the clinic. Esther wasn't a large woman herself, only a few inches taller than Mary and only twenty pounds heavier. But she was strong and hers was a labor of love. The nurse at the clinic said the long walk to the clinic probably didn't hurt Mary. She said it probably kept Mary from giving in to the pain. Kept her fighting.

"Birthin' started righ' there in the hall. I cou' see tha' baby's hiney a-comin' out. An' they was askin' me questions. So I says, 'Don' you see that?' An' they's runnin' over theirselves 'steada helpin' Miz Delaney. I tol'em so, too! An' I stay with'em for the birthin'. Don' trus'em ta do it alone!" Esther said.

Matthew Delaney backed into this world at 6:53 p.m. on February 29, 1896. All but his left arm.

"I can't get his arm out!" the young doctor shouted over the mother's screams. The baby choked on his first breath; the doctor pulled. He pulled very hard, then the arm came free.

"Lordy!" Esther declared.

"What the hell is that in his hand?" the doctor shouted over baby Matthew's first screams. "It looks like part of an ear!" the doctor shouted over mother Mary's last screams.

"Doctor!" the nurse shouted over the silence. It was seven o'clock.

"What?" the doctor muttered as he pried the bloody cartilage from the baby's fist.

"She's dead," the nurse said.

"Oh Lord, my Lord," Esther cried.

"I've got to go in there," said the young doctor. And he cut the mother open.

"My Lord, my Lord," sang Esther.

"Jesus Christ! There's another one in here!" the doctor shouted.

Mark Delaney was released to this world at 7:04 PM on February 29, 1896.

"Bless these babies, O Lord," Esther chanted. "O Bless these po', po' babies."

At seven o'clock that night, Dick Delaney had his picture taken with Buffalo Bill and Annie Oakley.

Teddy Roosevelt won the presidential election in 1904. A leap year. The Olympics were held in the United States for the first time. Anton Chekhov died. Graham Greene was born. Work began on the Panama Canal. A woman was arrested in New York for smoking a cigarette in public. Anton Dvorák died. George Balanchine was born. Jack London wrote "The Sea-Wolf." James Barrie wrote "Peter Pan." Charles Looff built the carousel for his first west coast amusement center. Caruso and ragtime played on new phonographs.

There was no leap year in 1900, so it wasn't until 1904, at the age of eight, that the twins celebrated their first real birthday.

Esther was living in the Delaney house by then, moved in right after her husband died in '98.

"You've been livin' over there anyways," her husband used to complain about his wife's nursemaidin'.

"Well, I hasta raise my boys," she tol' him.

"Have to raise *my* boys," Dick Delaney corrected.

Well, Matthew was his boy anyway. Dick Delaney didn't much care for Mark. Mark cried too much as a baby, his father thought. Esther spent a lot of time rockin' tha' po' baby back to sleep.

When the twins finally got out of diapers, Dick Delaney started taking Matthew down to the saloon with him. The boy was cussin' like a sailor before he was five. Mark stayed home with Esther.

When they were old enough to go to school, Mark loved it. He was very bright, a quick learner. But he had to turn his good ear toward the teacher, so it always looked like he was staring out the window. After a few run-ins, and his being able to always answer the questions, new teachers got used to Mark's cocked head; they even spoke up when they saw him turn toward the windows.

Matthew hated school and seldom went. He like the saloon better. Dick Delaney didn't care. The boy did his chores around the saloon and he sold the afternoon paper out in front every day. "The boy's getting all the schooling he's gonna need. And the Church'll teach him anything else he needs to know," Dick Delaney often said. He took Matthew to Mass every week.

Esther took Mark to the Baptist Church with her every week.

Then there was the problem of that ugly ear. The whole top half was gone and what was left of the bottom part had folded over and grown back into itself, covering the opening. Only the lobe resembled a normal ear. And it was stinging red all the time from being pulled by his brother. And from being slapped by his father. But Esther loved him, ear and all. Esther would always love him.

Esther loved both of the boys, and she made that first real birthday of theirs extra special. For two weeks, she counted down the days. Only ten more days, boys. Only six more days. Next Monday's the day! Two days, Mattie. Tomorrow is it, Markie.

She made two little cakes. Each with a great big *1* on top. She learned how to write their names just so she could put them on their cakes. Then she sent Dick Delaney out to the store to buy some ice cream for their party. He came back with the ice cream, and with a new cap for Matthew; the store had gift wrapped it in a shiny red box with a big red bow.

Esther saw Dick Delaney come in the back door with that shiny red box in his hands. She knew what he had done, and she wasn't gonna let him get away with it. She took a shiny blue box out of the cupboard and she marched out to that living room, right behind Dick Delaney. And as he handed the red box to Matthew, she handed the blue box to Mark, telling him it was a gift from his father. And with her eyes, she flat-out dared Dick Delaney to say one word.

The Titanic *sank in 1912. A leap year. Woodrow Wilson captured the presidency. Europe was rehearsing for WWI. The Piltdown Man hoax began its forty-one year run. Stockholm hosted the Olympics. Zippers, fountain pens and the "weekend" were gaining in popularity. People were talking on the telephone, listening to the radio, reading comic strips and dancing the tango.*

The sixteen-year-old twins celebrated their third real birthday on February 29, 1912.

Mark ran home from school, leaping trash cans and dodging the Model T's that raced the streets of the West Bottoms district of Kansas City. The streets were paved. The sewers were underground. The lighting was electric.

Mark ran because that night would be the last chapter of Jack London's "The Call of the Wild." At age 52, Esther was learning to read and write; Mark was teaching her. He had started her with Beatrix Potter's "Peter Rabbit," then they did Kipling's "Jungle Book" and "Just-so Stories." Esther almost got through "The Wind in the Willows" by herself and she was reading Jack London without too much help from Mark. "Moby Dick" would be next. But that night was the last chapter of "The Call of the Wild." So Mark ran.

Esther was waiting for him. She had made him a cake with a great big *3* on it. And she made a birthday card for him. She wrote the message herself, looking up each word in Mark's dictionary:

> To Mark,
> Happy Birthday to a wonderful
> boy—man—from the only 52 year
> old woman who was ever taught
> to read and write by a 3 year
> old.
> > Love,
> > Esther

She made his favorite dinner that night—beef ribs, the real short and fat ones, creole rice, the green beans with almonds and sauce, and homemade bread. The chocolate fudge cake. They split a beer and made a toast. "To Mark! And to Readin' and Writin'!"

"Chapter Seven: The Sounding of the Call," Esther read. "When Buck earned sixteen hundred dollars in five minutes for John Thornton, he made it possible for his master to pay off certain debts and to journey with his partners into the East after a fabled lost mine . . ."

Matthew lay with his head on Jake's shoulder, watching his lover blow smoke rings—one inside the other, a series of small rings racing through a larger ring. His hand made slow circles on the older boy's chest and stomach, stopping periodically to tug gently on the reddish-brown hairs around the nipples and below the navel.

Jake Halloran was a pretty eighteen-year-old, tall and thin with an Oklahoma Indian chiseled face; smooth; tanned; green cat eyes. It was those eyes that had fascinated Matthew two years before when Jake walked into the saloon and asked

Dick Delaney for a job. It was those eyes that led Jake from bar boy to runner for the Pendergast Machine in only two short years. It was those eyes that brought Matthew to Jake's bed on his sixteenth birthday, his third real birthday, on February 29, 1912.

If Dick Delaney knew about Jake and Matthew, he said nothing. Matthew was a tough kid. That's all Dick Delaney cared about. He wanted his son to be able to fend for himself; that was what was important in Kansas City in 1912. He let Matthew skip Mass most of the time, but made sure the boy went to confession regularly.

Dick Delaney owned the saloon then, and spent most of his time there, working both the day and night shifts. Couldn't trust a hired man with that kind of money, he said. Matthew worked in the bar, Delaney's Bar, then. Jake had gone to work for Pendergast, but he worked out of Delaney's.

Big Jim Pendergast died two years before, leaving his political position to his brother, Tom, and leaving one of the saloons to his loyal worker and friend, Dick Delaney.

" . . .his throat a-bellow as he sings a song of the younger world, which is the song of the pack. The End," Esther read.

"My oh my," she said and lay the book on her lap, clucking her tongue and shaking her head.

"You really liked that, didn't you?" Mark said.

"Tha's the bes' one yet, honey."

"Wait'll you read Moby Dick."

"Tomorra?"

"Tomorra!"

"Mark?"

"Yeah?"

"Mark, how come you don' come ta Church no more?"

"Any more," he said, looking away.

"Answer me, son," she was still his mama, sixteen years or no.

"I don't need it anymore, Esther. I know what I want. I know what I believe."

"You don' believe in the Lord?"

"Not the way you do."

"Lord, bless this boy's soul," Esther prayed for him.

"Thank you."

"Don' thank me. Thank Him!"

"Thank you, just the same," he said as he kissed her on the cheek.

"Your brother, he still go ta his Church," Esther said.

"Matthew goes to confession. He does not go to church. And that has nothing to do with me!" he shouted in a tone she knew well.

She regretted saying something like that to her boy, her angel. He'd be all right. He was a good boy, the best. He was kind, gentle, smart and giving. He was loving and was loved. God would take Mark to heaven even if he never set foot in a church for the rest of his life.

"Well, you still walk me ta church ever' Sunday and come ge'me after. And tha' oughta coun' fo' somethin'. Don' you think?" she said, laughing. And she kissed him on the cheek. "Le's you and me have another o'them beers. I's still yo' birthday," she said and ran off to the kitchen before he saw the tears that had started to roll down her cheeks.

Prohibition went into effect in 1920. A leap year. The Roaring Twenties. Flappers. Sacco and Vanzetti. Hitler was moving up in German politics. Jazz was hot. The Nineteenth Amendment gave the vote to American women. The American Legion. Dadaism. Agatha Christie. F. Scott Fitzgerald. Eugene O'Neill. The Olympics were resumed after a hiatus for the War. World population was nearing two billion. The Tommy Gun was invented in 1920.

When Mark came home from the War, Esther stood in

the doorway for the longest time without saying a word, without crying, without moving. She just stared at him. Then she was all over him, making sure he had everything he left with and scolding him for going off to the War in the first place.

"If they'da knowed abou' that ear, they'da never took you in the firs' place," she said when he left in 1917, and said again when he came home in 1919.

Mark had pulled his cap down over his ears that cold April morning he enlisted in the army. No one seemed to notice it during the physical. The training sergeant didn't care.

"It's all over, Esther. I'm okay! See?" Mark said.

And she hugged him and kissed him and she babied him for a week . . . until he finally had to beg her to stop. She stopped babying him, but she did not stop fussing over him and worrying about him, driving him crazy with questions about where's he goin' and where's he been and how come he has ta go out so much, anyhow?

She prayed for him every night. Twice on Sundays.

Mark wrote about his war experience for the Kansas City Star, but it paid very little and it was only one article every other week. When he tried to include something about the adjustment problems his fellow veterans were having, they cut it all out. They wanted war stories; they wanted heroes. It was the only work he could find since he refused to work for Pendergast.

Matthew didn't go to war. He knew the right people. His service was to Kansas City, helping Tom Pendergast's politicians stay in office. He helped them do that by paying off voters and by driving bums from one precinct to another and telling them which names to vote with, the names of people who couldn't get to the polls. Dead people. And Matthew tended bar at Delaney's.

By 1920, with the advent of Prohibition, the bar at

Delaney's Restaurant had moved upstairs with the gaming tables. Dick Delaney stayed downstairs in the restaurant. Dick Delaney entertained the police department.

Jake went from one Pendergast speakeasy to another, checking on things. Around election time, he was a precinct boss.

By 1920, Matthew had developed a weakness for prostitutes, which was a constant source of aggravation for Jake. Jake would wait up half the night, pacing the floor of their hotel room, knowing Matthew would stumble in about four in the morning with one or two whores from upstairs at Delaney's. Jake paced, knowing what their fight would be like, knowing the words they would scream at each other, knowing the words he would use in the morning to beg his lover's forgiveness.

On February 29, 1920, Jake waited and paced. But Matthew wouldn't be home that night. He would be at his father's house, having dinner, celebrating his twenty-fourth birthday with his twin brother. Their fifth real birthday.

Esther beamed as she watched the twins together. Such handsome young men they were. It was all she could do to keep from committing the sin of pride—pride that she was the one who got them together for their birthday after all these years. And with their father, too.

She missed Church that morning to get the turkey started. It was the first time Esther had ever missed her Church on Sunday. Not even for illness. But this was mos' special, she had told herself, and she knew the Lord would understand and forgive her.

Dick Delaney was still at work when Matthew arrived at the house that Sunday night, so it was just the two brothers standing there in the entryway at six o'clock on February 29, 1920. Their twenty-fourth birthday. Their fifth real birthday.

Esther beamed as she watched the twins together. Such handsome young men, she thought. Piercing blue eyes, strong, solid. Dark hair from their mama. Mark's hair was longer, covering his ears, but that and their clothes were the only things that were different between them. They were identical.

She had to prompt them to speak. But even with her filling in the gaps, they had little to say to each other. When Esther had to run off to the kitchen to check on dinner, Mark followed her to get two beers from the icebox, and Matthew went to the bathroom. It was much the way it had always been with them. It was much the way it had always been between Mark and his father.

Dick Delaney arrived as Esther set the last plate of food on the table. The three men sat. Esther did not; Esther would eat in the kitchen as she always did when either the father or the brother were there. Only she and Mark ever ate together, despite his urgings to get her to the family table. It was her choice, not Dick Delaney's; Dick Delaney didn't care one way or the other.

Esther brought out two cakes: each with a big 5 on it. The words "Happy Birthday Mark" and "Happy Birthday Matthew" were expertly lettered on the thick, creamy fudge frosting. There were no candles. There were never candles on the cakes Esther made. She said candles outside the Church were Devil sticks.

"Why don't we eat mine and you can take yours home with you?" Mark offered, cutting his cake.

"I'll pass," Matthew said. "I don't care much for chocolate."

Esther leaned forward, a multitude of sins ready to leap from her tongue, but God and a look from Mark closed her gaping mouth and she banished herself to her kitchen and her repentence.

"Dad?" Mark offered.

"No."

Dick Delaney excused himself to return to work, leaving the brothers to face each other in silence across the dining room table. Mark ate a second piece of cake as Matthew watched, grinning.

"So, brother, have you found a job yet?" Matthew asked.

"Nope," Mark answered, using his finger to get the last glob of fudge icing off the plate.

"Oughta get in with Pendergast, Mark. That's where all the money is these days."

"That I know. And no thank you."

"Why not?"

"Because he's a crook."

"You sayin' I'm a crook, too? And Dad?"

"Are you?"

Mark started to stack the dirty dishes, which brought Esther running from the kitchen, with a stern reprimand and a suggestion that the boys go have brandy by the fireplace in the living room, which they did.

"You asked if I was a crook," Matthew began, as he poured two glasses of brandy.

"It was a rhetorical question."

"What?"

"Never mind."

"Maybe I am. But Pendergast does a lot of good for Kansas City. Streets. Schools. Factories. A lot of money comes into this town with those contracts he gets out of the capital."

"I know," Mark said.

They sat in the large, overstuffed chairs on either side of the fireplace, facing each other."

"Cold tonight," said Mark. "Brandy warms you up."

"Good brandy, too. Last of Alderman Jim's private stock."

"He wasn't so bad," Mark admitted. "Not like his brother, Tom."

"It ain't bad against good, Mark. Big Jim died before he could get it all together. Tom just took up where Jim left off. They came out of the same mold."

"I guess."

"No guess about it," added Matthew.

They sipped their brandies, and enjoyed the heat of the fire. They mellowed.

"What do you do for them?" Mark asked.

"You don't want to know."

They laughed.

"I think you hurt Esther's feelings when you wouldn't eat her cake," Mark said after a moment.

"I suppose I did. At the time, I think I wanted to. This whole things was gettin' to me. Dad sittin' there like a stranger. You playin' Birthday Boy for the neg—for her, for Esther. And her bouncin' all over the place like we was still little kids. Besides, I don't like chocolate. I really don't."

"Neither do I, Matthew. Neither do I."

"But you . . . ?"

They laughed.

They sipped their brandies, and enjoyed the heat of the fire. They continued to mellow.

"Let me show you something," Mark said. He led Matthew to the large bookcase at the far end of the room and took a cigar box from its hiding place on the top shelf. He removed a stack of cards and papers from the box and spread them out on the floor, picking them up one by one to show his brother.

"This one, she gave me when I was five. You were at the saloon. She didn't even know what it said—just liked the picture, she told me. See the "E?" She couldn't write her own name in those days. These, she gave me after she learned to read and write. See, she made up her own verses. She's been my mother, Matt. I eat her chocolate cakes."

Mark made his brother read every card and every letter

that Esther had given him over the years. All the birthday cards, the Christmas cards, the Easter cards, the letters she wrote to him during the war, but never sent. The notes she left on his pillow on Sunday nights, blessing him for the week to come.

At dawn, they returned the cigar box to its hiding place on the top shelf of the bookcase. Then Mark looked at his twin brother and they stood in front of the fire staring into each other's eyes. First Matthew smiled, then Mark. They shook hands. They embraced. Then they marched off, arm in arm, toward the back of the house to wake Esther in the hope of getting some breakfast. They found her in the kitchen, singing and cooking—fried eggs, fried potatoes, bacon, homemade biscuits with homemade jam.

Herbert Hoover was elected President in 1928. A leap year. The Olympics were held in Amsterdam. Fleming discovered penicillin. Amelia Earhart flew the Atlantic. Ravel wrote his "Bolero." Gershwin wrote "An American in Paris." Lawrence wrote "Lady Chatterley's Lover." Mussolini wrote his autobiography. Thomas Hardy died. Mickey Mouse was born. The radio sang: "Am I Blue?" "Makin' Whoopee," "You're the Cream in My Coffee" and "Button Up Your Overcoat."

The wedding vows were only half taken when the word came that Dick Delaney had died. It was February 29, 1928. The man had thrown the doors open and shouted it from the back of the hall. The minister stopped in mid-sentence. He looked at the two sets of twins standing before him, expecting someone to tell him what to do. Matthew and Mark, the Delaney Twins, both nodded for him to continue.

Amelia and Sarah, the MacMillan Twins, both shrugged their shoulders. They'd only met the boys' father once, and it had been brief and awkward.

Everyone said how beautiful it was to see twins marrying twins like that. People still say that, and have to look twice when they see the wedding picture.

"We do," the MacMillan Twins said, and they extended their left hands to receive their wedding bands from the Delaney Twins.

Esther cried. She cried all the way to the Church, all the way through the ceremony, all the way through the reception and she cried all the way back home again. But she laughed when she got Mark alone in the kitchen and gave him the piece of chocolate cake she had saved for him, knowing he wouldn't like that white cake they had at the reception.

Dick Delaney's heart attack had come that morning as they were all getting dressed for the wedding. Matthew went down to the hospital for a while, but the doctor said they wouldn't know anything for several hours. Matthew made it to the Church just in time to see his bride and his brother's bride walk down the aisle.

Matthew and Amelia inherited the saloon, Delaney's Bar. Mark refused his brother's offer of a half-interest in the business because Matthew wouldn't break his ties with the Pendergast Machine.

Mark and Sarah inherited the family house, which they shared with Matthew and Amelia. And, of course, Esther.

That summer, Esther was as happy as she'd ever been in her sixty-eight years. The boys were friends; they were both living at home. They both had lovely wives, though a might lazy, she thought. And, praise the Lord, Mark got the prettier one. Mark got the pregnant one, too. That's why the wedding had been held on the Delaney Twin's birthday instead of the MacMillan Twin's birthday, as originally scheduled. Now Sarah was due in two weeks, July 20 or thereabouts, and Esther had plenty to do gettin' ready for a new baby in the house. *O thank you, Lord.*

"She's wonderful!" Sarah said of Esther.

"And at her age," added Amelia.

"Best mama a boy could ever have," Mark told them.

They were having a picnic lunch in the backyard. Esther had packed a basket with cold chicken, potato salad, cheeses, pickles, olives and four quart bottles of beer. Just for the hell of it, they drank right from the bottles. Sarah said she thought it made her look silly. She was right, judging by the photograph Mark took.

"Has your ear always been like that?" Amelia asked.

"Sh!" Sarah scolded her sister.

"It's all right, honey. I don't mind. Your husband did it, Amelia."

"Matthew!" Amelia cried.

"I wasn't even born yet, for Christ's sake!"

"You said you were going to stop swearing," his bride scolded again. "And how could you have done that if you hadn't even been born yet?"

"He was holding on to my ear when they yanked him out."

"Part of his ear was in my fist."

"That's horrible!" the née MacMillan Twins agreed.

"Hey Mark, remember that night we spent readin' the letters Esther wrote to you?"

"Sure."

"I was just thinkin': That changed everything. Up till then, I was figurin' you and me wouldn't see each other again. How come we didn't like each other all that time?"

"Probably because Esther and Father didn't like each other."

"Yeah. Then I saw more of you than when we was kids. It changed the way I felt about Esther, too. And . . ."

"Jake?"

"Yeah."

"Who's Jake?" Amelia asked.

"An old friend. Lost track of him about that same time."

"He's around," Mark told his brother.

"I know. I heard he goes to the capital all the time for your friend."

"Who?" Sarah asked.

"He means Pendergast. And he's no friend of mine."

The rain, as it is wont to do in Missouri on hot summer days, let loose without warning. The picnickers quickly stuffed everything back into the basket and hurried toward the house—as hurried as you can get when your baby is due in two weeks. Matthew and Amelia gathered up all the picnic paraphernalia, while Mark gathered up Sarah. He shielded her eyes from the pouring rain with one hand, holding her stomach with the other hand, as though that would somehow protect their baby within.

3.   Eddie

The Lindbergh baby was kidnapped and murdered in 1932. A leap year. The Great Depression. The Dust Bowl. Hitler became a German citizen. The Olympics were held in Los Angeles. Erskine Caldwell wrote "Tobacco Road." Dashiell Hammett wrote "The Thin Man." Shirley Temple made her first film. Johnny Weissmuller made his first "Tarzan" movie. The neutron and positron were discovered. Vitamin D was discovered. Flo Ziegfield died. Kenneth Grahame, author of "The Wind in the Willows," died. Prokofiev wrote his fifth piano concerto. Cole Porter wrote "The Gay Divorcée." Over thirteen million Americans were unemployed. In November, FDR beat Hoover by a landslide. In June, 17,000 veterans of the Great War— the doughboys—marched on Washington to urge congress to allow them to cash their bonus certificates, their only veteran's benefits. Congress and President Hoover refused the Bonus Marchers, offering to pay their expenses home instead. Many accepted the token payment, but over 2,000 of them stayed behind to demonstrate for their cause. In July, army troops under the command of General Douglas MacArthur stormed the camps and drove the veterans out of the capital.

Mark Delaney was part of the 17,000-member Bonus Expedition Force. He was one of the 2,000 Bonus Marchers who stayed behind. He was one of the doughboys who were driven from the nation's capital by MacArthur's troops.

Mark felt he had to go to Washington. They all had to go.

How could they have waited until 1945 to cash their bonus certificates? In 1932 they were broke and out of work. There was a worldwide depression in progress.

Mark hadn't wanted to leave his family behind in Kansas City; Sarah was pregnant again. Their darling little Caroline was four; she was just becoming a person to him. He had wanted to take her along to Washington, but Sarah wouldn't hear of it. Matthew had finally begun to work his way out from under the Pendergast Machine. He had sold the saloon, thinking he and Mark could go into some other kind of business together. But City Hall wasn't issuing business licenses to "sheep who had left the fold," and the Delaneys would probably have to leave Kansas City. Mark went on the Bonus March, hoping to collect his veteran's benefits.

The army had cleared a swamp for the huge camp. Tents were provided for families; single men, men who were alone, had to forage for themselves. Mark built a small lean-to against a hill at the edge of the dump site and it collapsed during the first heavy rain. One of his fellow veterans helped him rebuild it the next morning, but the sliding mud from the hill destroyed it again that night. Mark and his newfound friend surveyed the damage and said the hell with it. Mark moved into his friend's tent.

Donald "Big Don" Russell, his wife Ginny and their seven-year-old son, Little Don, had been in camp for two weeks when Mark moved in with them. They had managed to put together a real homestead by scavenging from the dump and from other tents that had been abandoned by less hardy or less dedicated Bonus Marchers. The Russells had two cots and a cushionless easy chair. They even had a table and eating utensils. They were rich in comparison to most in the camp—those who ate with their hands, and sat and slept on straw or a single blanket spread out on the mud floor.

The Russells came from Pennsylvania. Big Don had been a house painter before the Great Depression. He had been a mess sergeant in the Great War.

Big Don was big. Ate too much of his own cooking, he said. Ginny Russell was big, too. Fat. Ate too much of Big Don's cooking, too, she guessed. Little Don was skinny, like most of the children in the camp, like most of the kids in the depression.

The Russells stayed until the very end, too. What good is it to go back home? they asked, along with the 2,000 voices that stayed behind, the 2,000 voices that were silenced by MacArthur's army.

They were tired when it was all over, when they were *forced* to leave the capital. They had spent almost two months in that camp, in that swamp. They had been harangued by their congressmen, they had been harassed by the police and by the army. The had been labeled as radicals and as communists. They had been called traitors; two of their comrades had been killed. They had gained nothing.

Big Don's '28 Chevrolet backfired as it roared up the driveway of the Delaney family home in the West Bottoms district of Kansas City on a very hot and muggy day in July of 1932. Mark invited the Russells into the family home, to make it their home.

Esther was in the kitchen, sitting quietly at the small table. She didn't rise when Mark and the Russell family entered. And when Mark asked her where everyone was, she said nothing as she handed him the letter she had been clutching in her hand.

The letter was from a Mr. Leonard I. Briggs. It was postmarked San Diego, California.

> Hey Mark!
> Congratulations Papa!
> You've got another little girl.
> Sarah named her Edwina. She
> was born the day we got

here—the 21st—the Solstice.
How about that? Should be a
special kid.

We found a great little
abandoned resort way out in
the middle of nowhere. It's
perfect! I'm going through the
county records now to see who
owns it and buy it from them.

Get out here as soon as
you can. I'll pick you up at
the Santa Fe depot in Riverside. I think that's the easiest
place. Just send me a note to
General Delivery in San Diego
and let me know which day.
Bring Esther! And burn this
letter!

> Your loving brother,
> Leonard I. Briggs

P.S. Your new name is Richard
Henderson.

Matthew had pleaded with Esther to go with them, but she
wouldn't budge. "Somebody's gotta be here when Mark ge's
home. I ain' jus' leavin' some ol' note," she said. "'Specially
the way you was talkin' ta tha' man this mornin'."

Jake had called.

"Heard you're leaving town, Delaney."

"Yeah. The place ain't too friendly anymore."

"Rumor says you've got some paperwork that isn't
yours," Jake said.

"Oh, it's mine all right."

"Delaney, what the hell are you trying to do?"

"I'm trying to stay alive, Jake. I got my insurance—now they better leave me alone."

"They won't."

"They better, or the feds'll get 'em."

"Don't do this, please."

"Bye, Jake. You tell 'em to stay away from me—away from all of us!"

"Matthew . . . ?"

Matthew jammed everything he could into his old Packard, a gift from Tom Pendergast back in '28. He left just enough space for him and Amelia in the front seat, and for Sarah and Caroline in the back seat.

They set out for California, leaving Esther to wait for Mark.

"Esther! What the hell does this mean?" Mark shouted, waving Matthew-Leonard's letter in the air.

"Don' you go yellin' at me," she said.

"I'm sorry. What happened?"

Esther rose from the table, indicating that the Russells should make themselves at home, and started to prepare dinner.

"Mattie, he got all mad 'cuz them folks wou'nt give 'im no license and he tol' tha' Pennergas' man he was gonna do somethin' t'im. An' nes' thin' I knowed, they's packin' up the car!"

"Goddamnit!" Mark screamed. He wadded the letter up in his hand and threw it across the room. It landed under the dough table. Esther would pick it up later, smooth it out and put it with her other letters and keepsakes in the top drawer of her bureau.

Mark and the Russells left for California the next morning, leaving Esther behind to wait for death. Said she spent the first seventy-two years of her life in the South, couldn't see no reason not to spend her last years there, too. Said the money Matthew had given her would be more than she could ever spend, what with her being able to live in their house rent free and all.

Matthew stayed off the main roads all the way from Missouri to California. Seemed like the whole world was heading out to the Olympics. People everywhere, cars jamming the highways with too many Missouri license plates on those cars. Pendergast might have sent someone to follow them.

They turned south when they got to Riverside and followed the isolated highway toward San Diego. They were out in the middle of nowhere when Sarah went into labor, so Matthew got off the road and headed for the first sign of civilization he could find.

The sign had said: "Beech Grove Hot Springs Hotel, 5 miles that way."

The small resort town was nestled into the foothills, hidden from the world. It was deserted, the houses dark and empty, the hotel boarded up. Matthew grabbed the tire iron from the trunk of the car and broke into the hotel, where Edwina "Eddie" Henderson was born five minutes later. It was the Summer Solstice, June 21, 1932.

"Why the hell did you have to call me Richard?" Mark-Richard asked his brother, Matthew-Leonard.

"It was the first one to come into my head when I filed Eddie's birth certificate," Leonard Briggs answered.

"Okay then, but keep it Richard—no Dick," the new Richard Henderson said.

"You got it, Richard."

"You're an asshole, Leonard."

"C'mon, let's get back to work."

"Will we ever get used to it?"

"What?"

"The names."

"I dunno."

They were opening the town. Leonard's town. The new Beech Grove. Leonard got the whole place, hotel and more than a dozen houses, for the back taxes, bought with the money he had left from the sale of the saloon. Dick Delaney's legacy to his boys.

The hotel was completely furnished. The houses were only about half furnished, so they chose which houses they wanted to live in and took the furniture out of all the others. Leonard and Amelia Briggs moved into the big stone place on top of the knoll. Richard and Sarah Henderson, with their two daughters, Caroline and Edwina, took the Victorian home closer to the hotel. Big Don, Ginny and Little Don Russell got the ranch-style house down near the creek.

Just on the other side of the creek, on a grassy, sunlit slope, there were two graves—new graves. A single marker spanned the heads of the graves. The marker said: Here lie Matthew and Mark, The Delaney Twins. Born on February 29, 1896. Died on July 24, 1932.

The F.B.I. shot John Dillinger in 1934. The New Deal was under way. The Dionne Quints were born. Max Baer was heavyweight champ. Fitzgerald wrote "Tender Is the Night." Cole Porter's "Anything Goes" debuted. "Good-Bye Mr. Chips" was a best seller. Movie houses were showing "Of Human Bondage" and "The Thin

Man." Clark Gable bared his chest in "It Happened One Night" and ruined the undershirt business. The S.S. Queen Mary *was launched in 1934. Marie Curie died. The radio played "The Continental" and "Blue Moon." Jack Benny skipped his fortieth birthday for the first time.*

Amelia got to play midwife again when Ginny Russell gave birth to her second son, Carl. Big Don was "proud as a peacock—two boys!" Little Don didn't like it at all.

"Damn thing cries all the time," Little Don, age 9, said to his only playmate, Caroline, age 6.

"Do what I do," she told him. "Just ignore it. That's what I do with Edwina. She's been up there sick for three weeks now . . . and that takes a lot of ignoring. But, it's the only way. Ignoring. Go crazy if you don't."

"Think Eddie will die?"

"Maybe. Doctor told Daddy they sometimes do with the fever."

"Do you want her to die?" Little Don asked.

"No. I don't know," Caroline replied.

"I wisht Carl would die."

"You do not, Donald Russell. Don't you say anything like that!"

"Do too!"

"Do not!"

"Do!"

"Don't!"

"Well then, I wisht he'd stop crying."

"He will. You just have to ignore him, like I told you in the first place."

Eddie had rheumatic fever. It was the second time in less than a year. The doctor said it would probably affect her heart. That she probably wouldn't live past eleven or twelve, maybe thirteen.

Everyone took turns looking after Eddie during her

illnesses. Amelia and Ginny helped Sarah with the housework and cooking. Big Don planted a vegetable garden for them and even kept the weeds out until the family got back on its feet again. Leonard came every night to read to Eddie.

Leonard's days were taken up with getting the hotel ready for the Grand Re-Opening.

Beech Grove Hot Springs Hotel had been one of a dozen or more thriving resorts in Southern California back in the twenties. Some of them, including Beech Grove, died with Wall Street. The ones that did survive were closer to the cities, only fifty or sixty miles inland from Los Angeles or San Diego. Beech Grove was out in the middle of nowhere, another two hours drive up or down the highway, depending on which city you came from. So it died and stayed dead until Leonard I. Briggs found it on June 21, 1932. The Summer Solstice—Mom's birthday.

When Eddie's second bout with the fever finally ended, everyone turned their full attention to getting the hotel fixed up. Big Don did all the painting, and as he was also a good woodworker and cabinetmaker, he got stuck with most of the repair jobs as well. Leonard and Richard did the plumbing and electrical, and cleaned up the hot springs facilities. The kids got to drag the rock, wood and trash out of the mud bath. Amelia and Ginny worked on the hotel kitchen while Sarah mended drapes, tablecloths, and anything else she could find while she minded the children.

But it was slow going. Every time they got one thing working, something else would break down or just plain fall apart. The stove vent in the kitchen fell on Ginny while she was trying to scrub it. Big Don tried to saw his left thumb off when he was repairing one of the stair rails. Richard fell through the deck next to the small spa. Dear little Caroline pushed Little Don into the mud bath with all his clothes on. The drapes from the lobby disintegrated in Sarah's hands and almost smothered Eddie, who was napping at her mother's feet, still weak from the fever.

Tempers flared often. The only ones who weren't fighting with each other were Leonard and Richard. They had found something they wanted to do, something they wanted to do together. They were perfectly happy, even when things fell around them. The worst fights were between the other set of twins, Amelia and Sarah. Sarah complained that Amelia was getting too bossy. Amelia complained that Sarah wasn't doing her share of the work, that she was spending too much time playing with the children. Privately, Amelia complained to Leonard that he loved the hotel more than he did her. She complained to Leonard that he spent more time keeping his old Packard shiny than he spent with her. She complained to Leonard that he hadn't given her a baby.

Cole Porter opened still another musical comedy on Broadway in 1939, "Du Barry Was A Lady." The English translation of Hitler's "Mein Kampf" was published. John Steinbeck received the Pulitzer for "The Grapes of Wrath." WWII was under way without us. England was singing war songs: "The Last Time I Saw Paris," "Roll Out the Barrel," and "Lili Marlene." The U.S. was singing: "Three Little Fishes," "Over the Rainbow," and "God Bless America." The popular films were: "The Wizard of Oz," and "Gone With the Wind." FM radio was invented. Sigmund Freud died. Nylon stockings first came on the market in 1939.

Eddie chased that squirrel from the bottom of the gully where the creek ran, over the hill where Uncle Leonard and Aunt Amelia lived, and all the way across the meadow to where the road split off to go out to the highway. That's where she lost him. That's where she thought she saw Uncle Leonard walking back up the hill toward the hotel. That's where she saw that car. The big, blue car. It was just sitting there by the side of the road. At first, she thought there was no one in it, but then a man sat up in the front seat. She ducked behind a tree, but he saw her. He started the car and sped away.

Carl pumped his little five-year-old legs as fast as he could, but he still couldn't keep up with Eddie. She was the fastest runner he'd ever seen. By the time he got across the meadow, even the dust from the stranger's car was gone, and Eddie couldn't make him believe there had ever been a car there. He said her uncle or his dad coulda made those tracks. He said she was just 'tending about the big, blue car with the strange man in it.

"You're dumb," Eddie said.

"And you lie," Carl said.

"I'm older than you."

"Big deal. Seven's not old."

"Race you back?"

"You just wanta win me again."

"C'mon!"

"No."

They walked. They looked for squirrels. They called his older brother and her older sister all the nasty names they could think up. They hid on the ridge overlooking the creek, watching Little Don, age 14, and Caroline, age 11.

"Look at those two down there," Eddie pointed.

"Yeah."

"Yechy."

"Yeah."

"All they wanta do is kiss and touch each other."

"Love."

"Yechy."

"Yechy."

They each threw a handful of twigs, leaves and dirt on the would-be lovers below. Then they ran like hell.

Beech Grove's population had quadrupled in five years—from ten to forty. The initial population explosion came in '35 with the opening of the hotel. The chef, his wife and their two children were the first to arrive. Then the barber and his family. Leonard hired a director for the hot springs facility, and an assistant to do the spa maintenance. He found a married couple to be the janitor and the maid in the hotel. They all worked for room and board the first couple of years. Then as business increased, he started paying dividends to his employees.

No one paid any rent to Leonard. Not his brother, not the Russells, not the two artists who came for a weekend and stayed thirty years. Not the hundred or so other people who became part of Beech Grove over the years, either by birth or relocation. When something needed to be built, if one of the houses needed repair or painting, if anything needed to be done, the people did it. That was their rent. No one went without, unless everyone did.

Their separate gardens became a community vegetable garden. The laundry room at the hotel was available to anyone during certain hours. They shared the teaching responsibilities, based on their education and backgrounds.

They shared their happiness. They shared their sorrow.

Eddie burst through the front door at home. She had to tell her Daddy about the big, blue car. He was talking on the telephone. He told her to shut up for a minute.

"Esther! It's me, Mark!" Richard said.

"Who's Mark?" Eddie wondered aloud.

"Esther? Are you all right?" He paused, then laughed. Eddie watched a tear roll down from his eye. It frightened her to see him cry. She ran to find her mama.

She found Sarah in the kitchen. Eddie blurted out everything at once: the big, blue car and the squirrel and the tear in Daddy's eye. And who was Mark? And that dumb ol' Caroline and Little Don down by the creek. Before Sarah could calm the child, Richard came in to tell about Esther.

Esther had been in the hospital. That's why they hadn't

been able to reach her by phone last week. It was nothing serious, Esther had said. She was okay now. She was very happy the boys liked the birthday card she had sent.

Esther was worried about one thing, though. While she was in the hospital, somebody had broken into the house. She couldn't see as how they took anything, but they sure did make a mess. They went through all the bookcases and the desk and the cupboards . . . even her room. She said all her keepsakes and letters—letters from Mark, too—were thrown all over the place. Lordy, people are strange, she had said. She wasn't going to worry about it anymore. The Lord would take care of her. And no, she would not move to California, Richard told Sarah.

"I even tried to tell her we'd sell the house out from under her, and she still wouldn't come," Richard said.

"You have to keep trying, dear," Sarah consoled him, kissing him on the cheek.

He took her by the arm and pulled her into an embrace. They kissed. Passionately.

Yechy, Eddie thought. And then started in again about the big, blue car and the squirrel and the . . .

"Not now, Eddie," Sarah said.

"Come with me," Richard pulled Sarah by the arm, toward their bedroom.

Eddie followed.

"Darling, don't you want to run out and play some more before dinner?" Sarah asked her daughter.

"I have to do my homework," Eddie lied.

"Why don't you go out on the porch to do it, honey? It's cooler out there," Richard said.

"I have to do it in my room," Eddie lied again, as she pranced one door down the hall to her room.

Richard waited until Eddie was all the way into her room before he led Sarah, on tiptoe, back through the kitchen and out into the yard, across to the garage.

"What's Mat . . . Leonard's car doing here?" Sarah asked.

"He's fixing that back wall this week. Asked if he could leave it here."

Richard picked up a piece of wood from the shelf under his workbench.

"See what I found this morning?" It was a large, flat shingle. Words had been burned, branded into it:

> Give me but one yellow rose . . .
>   it will be our life's bouquet.
> Give me but one yellow rose . . .
>   for it is our love today

"Corny, huh?" he said.

"I think it's pretty. Did you make it?"

"No. It's old. See?"

Some of the letters were worn away, as though for years someone had been rubbing their fingers across the words. But there was that lingering smell of the wood-burning. She loved that smell. She knew that it wasn't old, but she wouldn't say that to her husband.

"I guess it is old," she said. "Where did you find it?"

"Over here," he replied. He reached into a box at the end of the bench and pulled out one yellow rose. He gave it to her with a kiss.

A passionate kiss. He opened the back door of the old Packard and pulled her onto the seat with him. He wrapped his arms around her.

"Eddie was almost born in this back seat," she said.

"Let's see if we can make another one," he said, laying her back and nestling into her neck.

Eddie sneaked across the yard and hid behind a bush next to the side door to the garage. She heard something about a yellow rose. It sounded nice. Just as she was about to make her final move, into the garage, she saw that car again. The big, blue car. It was sitting right across the street. And that man was in it.

Jake Halloran saw the little girl come out of the house and tiptoe across to the garage. He thought it was the same little girl he saw out on the road earlier. He wondered if she was Delaney's kid. He wondered if there were any others. He guessed that was Delaney's wife in the garage with him. He wished the little girl would go back into the house. He lit a cigarette and blew smoke rings, one inside the other, a series of small rings racing through a larger ring.

Eddie watched the smoke rings. She giggled. She watched the man put his cigarette out on the little mirror that stuck out by the window. She watched him wipe his forehead and hands with a handkerchief. She watched the man take a rifle from the back seat of the car and point it at her. She ran toward the house. But she stopped just outside the back door. She had to look back. She watched the man shoot the rifle, time after time after time, into the garage . . . until there was a great explosion. She watched the man put the rifle back down on the seat. She watched him drive away in the big, blue car. She watched the blazing fire.

4.   Caroline

In the spring of 1939, Tom Pendergast went to prison for income tax evasion.

In the spring of 1939, Jake Halloran drove his big, blue car from Beech Grove, California, to Yuma, Arizona, and checked into the Oasis Motel. When he got into the room, he bolted the door, closed the drapes and turned the radio to full volume. He removed a bottle of bourbon from his suitcase and downed it. He took a piece of Oasis Motel stationery from the desk drawer and wrote a letter to the Kansas City Star. He addressed the envelope, sealed it, and propped it up on the desk. He took his rifle out of his suitcase, reassembled it, put the muzzle into his mouth, and pulled the trigger.

The Kansas City Star reported in the morning edition they had just learned from the Yuma Police that fugitive Jake Halloran had committed suicide in that Arizona town. They reported that Halloran had been wanted by the Kansas City Police for questioning in the Pendergast case. They reported that Halloran had left a suicide note in which he confessed to the murder of his longtime friend, Matthew Delaney. They reported that Delaney had also been sought for questioning because of his former association with Pendergast and because of a packet of records, dating as far back as 1915, which had been found in Delaney's Bar in Kansas City during a raid by police last year. The Star reported that Halloran's note had not given a motive for the murder, not did it implicate

Pendergast in any way. Halloran had no known survivors, the paper reported.

In the spring of 1939, Esther came to Beech Grove. Sante Fe brought her west and dropped her off in Riverside. Greyhound brought her south and dropped her off at the Beech Grove turnoff. Her feet brought her the five miles from the highway and dropped her off in a rocking chair on Leonard's front porch.

"Hi," Eddie said, looking up from her storybook.

"Hello chile. You mus' be Miss Caroline," Esther said between puffs.

"I'm Eddie. Caroline's my sister."

"O my."

"I run fast."

"I bet you do, honey."

"You're old, huh?"

"I guess I am."

"How old?"

"Le'me see . . . seventy . . . nine."

"That's old."

"Very," Esther said, slipping off her shoes and rubbing her feet.

"Daddy's over at the hotel," Eddie said.

"Honey, tha' man ain' . . ." Esther stopped abruptly.

"I know he isn't my real Daddy, if that's what you were going to say. I saw my real Daddy blown up. Mama, too. Uncle Leonard's my new Daddy. Aunt Amelia's my new Mama. But she's not here either."

Esther couldn't speak. Eddie picked up her storybook and opened it.

"Do you know how to read?"

"Yes'm, I do," Esther replied with a touch of forgivable pride.

"What's this word?" Eddie asked, climbing up on Esther's lap and pointing to the page.

"Well, Eddie, less'n they changed things since yo' real daddy showed me how ta read, that word is tingle."

"What's tingle?"

"Tingle is what you get when you walks inta yo' room in the dark and scares yo'self when you catches y'own reflection in the mirra'."

"Oh! I did that once."

"An' it's when you tries on a new dress, too."

"I don't like dresses," Eddie told her.

"You don'?"

"Nope. I like baseball caps, though. Is that the same thing?"

"Well, I don't know. I guess it coul' be."

There was a moment of silence, then Esther started to chuckle, then laugh. Eddie got the giggles, then the hiccups.

That's the way Caroline found them when she charged out the front door, slamming it behind her.

"What is going on out here?" Caroline demanded.

"Hic," Eddie said, giggling.

"Hello, Miss Caroline," Esther beamed.

"Who are you?"

"Why, honey! It's me, Esther!"

"I don't know you."

"Maybe you was too small when you lef'. I useta take care of you. Took care of yo' daddy and his brother, too."

"My father is dead."

"O honey, I know."

"There's no one home right now. You shouldn't be here."

"But I've come ta stay," Esther said.

"Here?"

"Yes'm."

"Wait'll Amelia hears this," Caroline said as she raced down the porch steps and off toward the hotel.

"Dumb . . . hic . . . isn't she?" Eddie said.

"Tha's not a nice wor' ta use on yo' sister, Miss Eddie."

"She is."

"Still's not nice."

"Okay."

A moment of silence.

"Persnickety! Tha's the word you wan'!" Esther blurted out, then let loose with the biggest laugh Eddie had ever heard in her life.

"Persnickety! That's wonderful! Persnickety Carolinickety!" cried Eddie, trying out her own version of the belly laugh she'd just learned. She kissed Esther on the cheek, then got the hiccups again.

The chair was rocking furiously. Eddie threw her arms around Esther's neck, still giggling, still hiccuping. Every time it seemed that they were about to stop laughing, Eddie yelled "Persnickety!" and they'd start all over again. And the chair would start up again.

That's the way Leonard and Amelia found them when they rushed home from the hotel.

"Esther!" Leonard shouted, leaping up the porch steps.

"O Mattie!" cried Esther.

"Who's Mattie?" Eddie wondered aloud.

"An' Miss Amelia! I am jus' so happy ta see y'all."

There were no Olympic Games in 1944. A leap year. The world was at war again. Roosevelt was elected to a fourth term as President. Truman was Vice President. Sartre wrote "No Exit." Williams wrote "The Glass Menagerie." Prokofiev's "War and Peace" opera played Moscow. "Rum and Coca-Cola" and "Sentimental Journey" were the popular songs. "Lifeboat" and "Going My Way" were popular films. The cost of living rose almost thirty percent. The G.I. Bill of Rights provided benefits for veterans. The Normandy Invasion, D-Day, set the mood for the last year of WWII on June 6, 1944.

Little Don Russell went to war in 1944. Caroline gave him a going away party at the hotel.

"Esther, why are these cakes sitting out here on the dining room table?" Caroline asked as she stomped into the kitchen.

"They are there, Miss Caroline, because I put them there," Esther replied calmly and with deliberation, giving much thought to the new California accent Eddie was patiently teaching her.

"I expressly told you they were to be taken over to the hotel, Esther. They are for *Donald's* party!"

"An' I 'spressly ain' a-goin' to the hotel jus' now, honey. So iffen you want'em there now, you hasta take'm yo'self. Or ast *Donald* ta do it."

"Esther!"

"Miss Caroline!"

Miss Caroline stomped out the back door. Esther returned to her dirty dishes with a grin that did not make her feel guilty. She heard Miss Caroline tiptoe in the front door, take the two cakes from the dining room table, and tiptoe back out with them.

Eddie passed her sister on the front porch. They did not speak.

"What was that all about?" Eddie asked when she got into the kitchen.

"Miss Caroline was playin', play*ing*, at being Mistress of the House again," Esther laughed.

"You'd think she'd learn after a while," Eddie said, taking two cookies from the jar and then straddling a kitchen chair backwards.

"Can't you sit like a lady?"

"No. What time's the whing-ding?"

"The what?"

"Whing-ding. You know, Little Don's party."

"Oh. Two."

"You goin'?" Eddie asked.

"Go*ing*," Esther corrected.

"Are you?"

"Yes. Are you?"

"No, I ain' goin'," Eddie said.

"Eddie, you stop that. And you should go."

"He's dumb."

"He is not."

"Well, she's dumb."

"And you should stop using that word, young lady."

"Persnickety!" Eddie shouted, then laughed.

Esther looked around first to make sure no one could her them, then she laughed.

"Now, you go get ready for the whing-ding," she told Eddie.

"I ain' goin'!"

"Really, Eddie, you can speak better than that," Amelia said, entering from the dining room. "And where is it that you are not going?"

"Oh mama," Eddie said and ran out of the room.

"Eddie! You come back here!" Amelia cried.

"No use, ma'am. You know how she's been lately," said Esther.

"Oh yes, I know. Those are the first two words she's said to me in a week. She talks to you, Esther. What is wrong with her?"

"She doesn't talk about that, even to me."

"Perhaps if you asked her outright?"

"I don't know."

"Will you try?"

"Yes'm, I'll try."

"Thank you, Esther. I'm at my wits' end."

"Mother!" Caroline shouted from the dining room.

"There's the other one. Give me strength," Amelia sighed, and went to see what Caroline wanted.

Esther finished the dishes and went to look for Eddie. She found her sitting at the edge of the creek, throwing rocks into the water.

"You make an old woman climb down this hill to talk to you. Could've broke my neck," Esther said, lowering herself onto a rock next to Eddie.

"It's not as though I asked you to come," Eddie said.

"Honey, what is the matter with you these days?"

"Nothin'."

"You are sullen and moody all the time. Cranky most of the time. You don't talk to people, 'cept me. And then you won't tell what's wrong."

"There's nothin' wrong, damnit!"

"You listen to me, daughter. First, you don't talk like that to me. Second, you can't go on like this. You're almost twelve now, and you . . ."

"Exactly!"

"What?"

"Twelve!"

"Twelve what?" Esther asked. "What's that supposed to mean?"

"Nothin'."

"Tell me."

"It means I'm gonna die! That's what it means!" Eddie cried out.

"Lordy child, what made you think that?"

"Caroline told me."

"Oh she did, did she."

"Yes. And I almost remember the doctor saying it myself. 'She'll be lucky if she lives to be twelve,' he said. 'It affects the heart,' he said."

"Oh, Eddie, you haven't had any problems with that all these years. They said you'd have problems first if anything was really wrong. And that doctor last year up in Riverside, he said you was sounding 'real good' to him. Your heart is fine, honey, but you're going to fret yourself to death. And as a certain little girl I know would say, 'That's dumb.' Now, I'd give you a big hug, but I don't think these old bones will let me bend over that far."

Eddie raised herself into Esther's arms.

On June 21, 1944, Eddie turned twelve without a mishap. Esther made a chocolate cake with fudge icing for the party. Eddie invited Carl and the chef's son, Hugh, and the barber's daughter, Gloria. She even invited her sister, but Caroline graciously declined, saying she was too old for children's parties and that she had to get Donald's sweater finished. That was fine with Eddie; she only invited Caroline to the party because Esther told her she had to. They played tag and hide-and-seek outside, then came inside for quieter games. They even played spin-the-bottle. Kissing didn't seem quite as yechy as they once thought. Although Carl, at ten, still wasn't so sure about it.

On June 21, 1944, while Carl was at Eddie's party, his parents got the telegram from the War Deprtment. The War Department said they wanted to inform the Russells that their brave son, Donald, had given his life for his country. They said the Russells could be proud that their son had died in action. They said that Little Don was one of the heroes at Normandy on D-Day.

Gandhi was assassinated in 1948. A leap year. Chiang Kai-shek was reelected President of China. Harry S. Truman was (re)elected President of the United States. Swing and bebop danced. Existentialism was. Cole Porter's "Kiss Me, Kate" opened in New York. David Lean made "Oliver Twist." D.W. Griffith died. Prince Charles was born. The LP record was invented. The Olympics resumed after a hiatus for the war. Kinsey published his "Sexual Behavior in the Human Male." America sang "Buttons and Bows" and "All I Want for Christmas Is My Two Front Teeth."

The old bus coughed and sputtered as it jerked its way from the highway to the Beech Grove Hot Springs Hotel. The banner on the side of the bus said "King Kole and His Krazy Kats." King Kole was a Glenn Miller dropout whose real name was Homer Alsop, according to one of the Kool Kats. The Kool Kats were Homer's wife, Ellie, and her two cousins, Gert and Sally. Homer was on a self-proclaimed mission to help the West make the transfer from swing to bebop, then to the new "cool jazz." Gert said she didn't think the West was ready. King and the Kats played the out-of-the-way places, the dives and wherever their bus broke down. On Saturday, July 3, 1948, their bus broke down just outside Beech Grove.

Leonard was already in his cups—as they said in those days, or gassed as King Kole said—when the Kool Kats' bus chugged up to the hotel. Leonard hired the Kats to play for the big Independence Day Dance he just decided to have on Sunday night.

Grampa Leonard was gassed most of the time in those days. The hotel was enjoying a post-war revival, so there was plenty of money coming in. Leonard had hired another six or seven employes, leaving him with very little to do, except drink. A dozen or so new families had settled into Beech Grove by '48, and once all the existing houses were taken, Leonard allowed people to build new ones on the other side of the creek, as long as they kept them far apart and stayed within the general style of the rest of the village. By '48, Beech Grove had its own gas pump, a general store with its own pharmacy, a little school house with its own real school teacher. There was also a part-time doctor. The hotel chef opened a snack bar for those who didn't want to eat in the restaurant and let his son, Hugh, run it. And in 1948, Beech Grove got a one-lane bowling alley, which was the result of one of Leonard's drunken binges and which cut off the veranda that used to run all the way around the hotel. On July

4, 1948, Beech Grove had a big Independence Day Dance, featuring a ragtag combo called "King Kole and His Krazy Kats."

Since Leonard was unwittingly paying the Kats twice their usual gig fee, they offered to play for the Sunday Service at no charge.

Amelia had started the Sunday Service during the war. Initially, it was just Amelia, Ginny Russell and Lydia Vance, Hugh's mom. Within six months, they had all the kids involved; by the end of the year, most of the town was in attendance every Sunday morning. Many had been hesitant because it wasn't a real Church service, while others stayed away because they thought it might be. The early meetings were Bible readings, then poetry became an acceptable alternative. Then music, quiet music until Grampa Leonard booked "King Kole and His Kool Kats" to play at the Sunday Service.

Amelia was not pleased. Gram's idea of music for Sunday Service—her idea of music, period—was a little Brahms played quietly on the piano or, perhaps, the children singing a hymn. Amelia was the choir director, and her choir opened and closed the meeting every Sunday. There were twelve members of Amelia's choir, thirteen if you counted my mother. Amelia said Eddie sang like a sick frog, but she looked so nice up there with the other children that she wouldn't think of not having Eddie in the choir. All the kids in Beech Grove had to be in the choir, but Eddie was the only one who wasn't allowed to sing. The choir thought the Kats were the best thing that ever happened to Sunday Service, the best thing that ever happened to Beech Grove. It was usually so boring.

That night the kids actually danced to that strange music, that bebop, that cool jazz. Even the little ones. But Homer Alsop wasn't stupid; he threw in a couple of swing numbers here and there to keep the old people happy. The rest of the time, the old people just drank and shook their heads.

Eddie and Hugh were sweet on each other that summer. They were sixteen. They thought they were probably in love. Poor Carl and Gloria, fourteen and fifteen respectively, got stuck with each other as there was no one else their age in the village at that time. The next batch of kids down the ladder were five or six years younger, *children*, they said.

Caroline wasn't at the dance. Aunt Caroline was at home in her room, taking phenobarbital—goofballs—one every hour until she passed out. For years, it had been chloral hydrate—mickey finns—starting the day after that telegram from the War Department came, saying how proud they could all be that Little Don had died in action. Aunt Caroline couldn't make herself feel "proud." The doctor gave her chloral hydrate. After a couple of years, he changed her to goofballs, thinking she might have become addicted to the mickeys. So Caroline wasn't at the big Independence Day Dance, featuring the Kool Kats.

Mom and "Uncle" Hugh danced every number that night, and went for a long walk afterwards. They talked about the stars and the moon. They talked about Beech Grove. They talked about Hugh's plans to become a chef like his father. They talked about Eddie's plans to see the world, or maybe go to college and become a teacher, or maybe to fall in love and get married and have children. They sat by the creek, his arm around her shoulders, and threw rocks into the water.

Eddie could hear the shouting long before they got to the house; then she gave Hugh a little peck on the cheek and sent him home. She walked quietly up onto the porch and sat in the old wooden swing. She didn't want to hear the fight, but she couldn't force herself to leave.

Leonard was drunk again. He'd been drunk all evening and, according to Amelia, had made a fool of himself at the dance.

"It was bad enough you had that awful band here once," Amelia shouted, "but I cannot believe you actually invited them to come back next year!"

"The kids liked them."

"The children are not the only ones who had to listen to that noise!"

"You coulda left, Amelia. No one was holding you."

"You would've liked that, wouldn't you? You would've liked me to leave, so you could throw yourself at that . . . at that floozy!"

"Floozy?"

"The fat one with the saxophone!"

"Clarinet. And Gert wasn't fat."

"*Gert* was obese, you bastard! And if you weren't blind drunk, you'd know it!"

"Amelia, such language."

"Don't get cute, Leonard. I'm sick and tired of your lechery—your fornication—and I'm warning you right now, if you ever . . ."

"You don't warn me, bitch!"

"Shut up! shut up! shut up!! You've got to stop this! I can't stand it anymore! I saw you with her!"

"Who?!"

Amelia had tensed every muscle in her body, pulling herself erect, with her arms rigid and shaking. Suddenly, the tension disappeared. She slumped into a chair, drained.

"With Caroline," she whispered.

"I . . ."

"Don't you deny it," she said calmly. "I saw you there. I walked into that room and I saw you, slavering on that poor, half-conscious girl. I saw you with your head down betwe . . . down there. I saw you, damn you, I saw you. What has happened to you that you could do such a thing? Poor Caroline. God knows she's just a walking zombie, she didn't even know you were there."

"Amelia, honey, I'm . . . please . . . ?

"Oh, I don't suppose that was the first time you used her body like that. You've always been somewhat of a pervert, haven't you?"

"Really, dear."

"Oh, I know about Jake, too. I know you and Jake Halloran were . . . I know he came to Beech Grove that day . . . in the big, blue car Eddie tried to tell us about. I know you saw him that day. I know you talked to him. What did you talk to your old boyfriend about? What would Jake Halloran and Matthew Delaney have to say to each other after all those years? Good times, maybe? Maybe not. Maybe they talked about murder. Maybe they talked about twins, and how no one would know which twin had been killed. Just have to make sure no one saw that ear, Mark's funny ear. No problem it turned out—no one saw anything. Did you stop to consider that my sister might be with Mark when it happened? Tell me, dear, what did you and Jake talk about that day?"

Eddie didn't wait for his reply, if he had one. She walked slowly down the porch steps and around to the back of the house. She opened the back door quietly and sneaked through the kitchen to Esther's room. She knocked very softly on Esther's door. The door opened immediately, as though Esther had been expecting the knock. Esther looked through her own tears at the tears streaming down Eddie's face. Esther closed the door and led Eddie to the edge of the bed and sat her down. Esther sat next to my mother and cradled her in her arms. Esther sang a lullaby she remembered from her childhood in Missouri—a lullaby about pretty little fireflies you could hold in your hand.

Eisenhower became President in 1953. Elizabeth II was crowned Queen of England. Khrushchev took power in the U.S.S.R.

Dag Hammarskjöld became the first Secretary-General of the United Nations. Eugene O'Neill and Dylan Thomas died. Sergei Prokofiev died. The Piltdown Man was revealed as a hoax. Kinsey published his "Sexual Behavior in the Human Female." Robert Anderson wrote "Tea and Sympathy." Arthur Miller wrote "The Crucible." Cigarette smoking was first mentioned as a cause of lung cancer. America sang "Ebb Tide" and "Doggie in the Window." The war in Korea was coming to a close in 1953.

Somewhere in their late teens, Beech Grove's inseparable foursome changed partners. Carl and Gloria never did get romantically involved, but everyone was sure Hugh and Eddie would wind up married. Then, overnight it seemed to everybody, Hugh and Gloria started dating and Eddie stopped thinking of Carl as a little brother.

Hugh and Gloria got married first, with Eddie and Carl standing up for them. Then, six months later, the day before Carl went into the Navy, they switched places at the altar and Mom and Dad said their vows.

Carl said he wouldn't mind if they sent him over to Korea, since Truman had had the good sense to get rid of MacArthur. Carl was scheduled to go to Korea, but he got the measles and his ship left without him. Where it left him was in Long Beach, California.

Dad had easy duty with weekends off, so Mom, Hugh and Gloria used to drive to Long Beach every weekend and the three of them would terrorize the Nu-Pike Amusement Park. When Mom tells the story, their little holidays were all shopping in the odd little shops, playing games for Kewpie Dolls and romantic walks along the famous Rainbow Pier, the wonderful old arc of a boardwalk which used to run out over the water around the Municipal Auditorium. When Dad tells the story, out of Mom's hearing, those were weekends of roller coaster riding, drinking and screwing. Until the night they went on The Rotor.

I rode The Rotor a few times shortly before they tore down the Nu-Pike. The Rotor was a padded, giant coffee can. You walked into it through a little door at the bottom of the cylinder, then everybody stood along the wall facing the middle. Once you were all in position, the little door would close and the cylinder began to turn slowly. There would be a few squeals and groans as the speed picked up and centrifugal force flattened you against the wall. The groans and squeals increased with the speed. The screams reached hysteria when the bottom dropped out. And there was no warning either— the floor simply fell about five feet all at once, leaving you pasted to the padded wall. The female screams remained throughout the ride, but the male screams quickly changed to laughter, then to teasing. I once saw a woman, a very fat woman, slide an inch at a time all the way down to the floor five feet below, screaming hysterically for them to stop the ride and fighting furiously with her dress to keep it from coming up over her head. They did not stop the ride and her dress did come up over her head.

Carl and Hugh had been trying for months to get Eddie and Gloria to go on The Rotor. One Saturday night, a pitcher of frozen peach daiquiris got Gloria in the mood. Eddie was dragged along, protesting. She protested when the little door closed, protested when the thing started to turn, protested when the floor dropped. She screamed something about it might hurt the baby! Now, they never stopped that ride for hysterical sliding fat ladies and they never stopped that ride for people who threatened to vomit, or actually did, but when Carl shouted, "You stop this goddamn ride!" they stopped that ride. That was always the way with Dad: he was a quiet, easygoing man, but when he felt strongly about something he spoke up and you knew he meant it. They stopped that ride.

Aunt Caroline kicked her drug habit to help Eddie out during what was supposed to be a difficult pregnancy, but wasn't. The doctor was afraid Eddie would put a strain on her heart, but she didn't. Eddie had to find things for her sister to do because she didn't really need her help. She did, however, want Caroline to stay off the drugs, so she found things for Caroline to do. But Caroline caught on to Mom's little game and started popping a few now and then. When it turned out there was only one of me, instead of two, Aunt Caroline went back to her pills full time.

I was supposed to be twins and would be too much for Eddie to handle alone and she would need Caroline's help. But I wasn't. Apparently, I had been echoing in there because the doctor told Mom and Dad there were two heartbeats. Therefore, I would be twins. When I came out alone, they went in to get the other one out, but there was nobody in there. They even searched me, for extraneous growths that might have once been a sibling. I was clean. But since I came out alone, I got both of the names they had picked out for the twins. Matthew and Mark. If I had been born a girl, I would be Sarah and Virginia. That was in 1955.

"Rock Around the Clock" put rock and roll on the popular charts in 1955. Diamonds were aritficially manufactured for the first time. Alexander Fleming, Thomas Mann, James Agee and Charlie "Bird" Parker died. Prokofiev's opera, "Fiery Angel," debuted in Venice. Cole Porter's "Silk Stockings" opened in New York. So did "Damn Yankees." Nabokov wrote "Lolita." Inge wrote "Bus Stop." Nuclear power was first used in the United States. Albert Einstein died in 1955.

5. Learning The Secrets

The biggest part of growing up isn't attaining either your height or your pubic hairs. It's not losing your virginity. It's not finally being old enough to drive a car, or die for your country or drink booze in a public place.

The biggest part of growing up is learning all the secrets. And it's not just the revelations themselves, it's where they come from and how you react to them.

Take the secret of self-importance, for example. When Earth learned it wasn't the center of the universe, it was shocked and resentful—many refused to believe it. When isolationist America learned it wasn't the center of the universe, it was shocked and resentful—many refused to believe it. When a human being learns it isn't the center of the universe, it is shocked and resentful—many refuse to believe it.

Gods are probably the greatest secret. It's all tied in with the death secret, the eternity secret, and it allows for the greatest use of imagination. No one can spoil that secret for you because by the time you find out whether you're right or wrong, it doesn't matter anymore.

Sex is a great secret. It, also, allows for a good deal of imagination. It lasts a lifetime, from the first time your little hands find their way to your lap until . . . whenever. It's another one of the secrets that cause a lot of shock and resentment—many refuse to believe it.

But, overall, it seems that human beings take the big secrets for granted—the balance of nature, the cosmos, the human body, nuclear anihilation—preferring to devote most of their concern and energy to the little secrets, the personal secrets, the family secrets.

John F. Kennedy was inaugurated in 1961. It was the year of the Bay of Pigs and the Freedom Riders. The Berlin Wall was built. "Catch-22." "Stranger in a Strange Land." "The Carpetbaggers." Hammarskjöld, Hemingway, Hammett, Kaufman, Thurber, Jung, Saarinen, DeForest, Beecham, Cobb, Trujillo, Rayburn, Grandma Moses, Gary Cooper and the Orient Express died in 1961.

BABY CAROLINE. Mom and I lived with Big Don and Ginny, Dad's parents, until he got out of the Navy. I remember potted plants everywhere. I remember heavy quilts on the bed. And flannel sheets in the winter. I remember making rugs out of rags. I remember snuff. And coffee cans for spit next to the two living room rockers. I remember Gramma Ginny combing out her long, gray hair and then braiding it up on top of her head. I remember Big Don letting me help him build a cedar chest. I wasn't very good with my hands, and I remember Big Don telling me that Carl wasn't very good either when he first started, but that he had stayed with it and got to be even better than his dad. I remember getting spanked when I crawled into that cedar chest and closed the lid. I told Big Don I wanted to see what it was like to be dead. He told me I'd know soon enough. I remember the smell inside that cedar chest.

Carl got out of the Navy when I was four, and we moved into our own house, one that someone else had moved out of. Those people went back to the city. It was a small, wood frame, two bedroom place and Carl started adding on the day we moved in. A den with a fireplace was his first add-on. He had to do most of the work on weekends, though, because Big Don had retired and Carl inherited all the carpentry work in town.

Aunt Caroline lived just up the road, in the house where Grampa Leonard's twin brother and his wife used to live. Aunt Caroline never came out of that house. And I never saw anyone go in. Mom had told me that Uncle Hugh took her groceries all the time. I asked Dad why Aunt Caroline stayed in her house all the time. I was six and I was helping Dad build the new fireplace in the new den.

"You know your mother's going to have a baby, don't you?" he asked me.

"I guess so."

"No guess about it. She is."

"Okay."

"And when the baby comes, it will be your little brother or little sister. Right?"

"I guess so."

"Right?"

"Right."

"You've seen how Mama's gotten bigger in front?"

"How could you miss it?"

"Yes," Dad said. "Well, do you remember when you were three and your mama looked like that?"

"No."

"Well, she did. And she had a baby. Just like she had you. And like she's going to have your little brother or sister."

"Where is it?"

"It was a little girl. And she . . . passed away. She died."

"Oh."

"We named her Caroline, after your aunt. And we all called her Baby Caroline."

"Is she still dead?"

"I'm afraid so, son. When we die, we stay dead."

"Was she sick?"

"No, she . . ."

"Did she die in a war?"

"She was just a baby!"

"You told me people die in wars and . . ."

"Matt, just be quiet a second and I'll tell you."

"Okay."

"Baby Caroline died of something they call crib death. It means that a baby just stops breathing, and they don't know exactly why."

"You still didn't tell me why Aunt Caroline won't come out of her house," I insisted.

"Your aunt was very upset by the baby's death. She was taking care of Baby Caroline when it happened, and she—or we think that she—blamed herself."

"Did she kill it?"

"No!"

"Am I gonna get the crib death?"

"I think you're safe."

"Will the new baby get it?"

"No!"

In October of 1961, the new baby arrived. I asked if they were going to call him Luke and John, since I was Matthew and Mark. They didn't answer me, but they did tell me I had to stay Matthew and Mark. At first, Mom wanted to name him Dag, after some United Nations man, but Dad didn't particularly like the name. I settled it when I told them I thought Dog was a great name for a little brother. They decided on Donald Edward. And they called him Donny. He didn't get the crib death.

Richard M. Nixon was elected in 1968. Martin Luther King, Jr. was assassinated. Robert F. Kennedy was assassinated. Riots and police brutality marked the Democratic convention in Chicago. Helen

Keller died. Jackie Married Ari. It was the year for "Hair" and "The Boys in the Band," "Myra Breckenridge" and "Airport," "Funny Girl" and "2001: A Space Odyssey." Mexico hosted the Olympic Games in 1968.

CHOCOLATE CAKE. When Donny was six, so I must've been twelve, he woke up one night screaming bloody murder and pushing his fists into his stomach. I jumped out of bed and turned on the lights, and I was just about to run after Mom and Dad, when it dawned on me that it may have been my fault that he was sick.

Earlier that night, we had been chasing each other all around the bedroom—over and under the twin beds, in and out of the closet. The radio was blaring in the den, so Mom and Dad didn't hear all the noise we were making. The radio was always blaring in the den because Dad's ears got hurt in the war. Anyway, Donny and I were running around like half-naked savages, grabbing and tickling, giggling and howling, being kids. I caught him under my bed and tickled him until he lost control, then pulled off his underpants. He started to cry, so I let him pull mine off. I got stiff immediately and Donny thought that was just about the greatest thing he'd ever seen. He was all over me, grabbing me and pulling on it. He even put his mouth on it, but I made him stop; I knew that had to be wrong. But I did let him beat me off until I felt the tingle. Then we put our underpants back on and went to bed. He was still pounding away over there when I fell asleep.

It was probably about three o'clock in the morning when he started screaming and, while I was standing there afraid to go get anybody, Mom and Dad ran into the room. I tried to confess. Only with Donny's screaming and Mom and Dad's arguing about what could be wrong and what they should do, I was ignored. But I persisted and finally was told it was something he ate and that, unless I made him swallow something, it wasn't my fault. And since I hadn't made him swallow anything, I shut up.

Dad went to get Doctor Weston, leaving Mom and me to keep an eye on Donny. Mom started crying, so I did too. She put her arm around me and we sat on my bed, watching my baby brother scream.

"I wish Esther was here," Mom said. "She'd know what to do."

"Who's Esther?" I asked.

"Oh, she was this wonderful woman who used to live with us and take care of us."

"What happened to her?"

"She died."

"How?"

"She was sick for a long time, honey. It was a disease they call diabetes. She was very old, almost ninety, when she got it and they couldn't help her. Her feet and legs swelled up so big she couldn't walk, so she had to stay in bed all the time. We had to feed her and bathe her, and help her go to the bathroom, for almost two years."

"Did she get the crib death?"

"No, she . . . how do you know about crib death?"

"Daddy told me."

"No, Esther didn't get crib death, honey. She was suffering so much that she wanted to die. She just didn't want to hurt anymore. So, finally . . . she wasn't supposed to eat sugar or sweet things because of her diabetes. The doctor said it might even kill her. So, finally . . . she begged so hard . . . and someone gave her a great big piece of cake. She ate it. And died. Just like the doctor said she might."

Mom got very quiet.

"Who gave her the cake?" I asked.

"I . . . did."

"Oh."

My family's a bunch of murderers, I thought. First Aunt Caroline, now Mom.

"The funny thing, though, Mattie . . ."

"Don't call me Mattie!"

"Okay, Matthew. The funny thing was that the only cake we had in the house that night was chocolate. And Esther just hated chocolate cake."

Dad came back with Doc Weston. Donny just had a bellyache.

Four students were killed by the National Guard at Kent State in 1970. Gold fell below $35 an ounce. There were over 230 million TV sets in the world. There were over 205 million people in the United States. John Dos Passos, Erle Stanley Gardner, John O'Hara and Gypsy Rose Lee died. "True Grit" and "Woodstock" were popular films in 1970.

LESBIAN. I got my so-called "only one spanking" when I was fifteen. Carl had always said that we would each get only one spanking and that it'd be a good one. I thought that was terrific because I had already had mine years before from Big Don, for crawling into the cedar chest.

"The one you got from your grandpa doesn't count," Dad said.

"You mean everybody gets a whack at me?" I shouted. I wasn't a rebellious teenager, but the image of the whole town of Beech Grove lining up to give me my "only one spanking" had startled me. So I shouted at my father.

"Don't you yell at me, Matt, or I'll make an exception in your case," he said. "My father was responsible for you then. And if he thought you deserved a whipping, then you did. But I'm responsible for you now and you deserve it now. So you're gonna get it. Understand?"

"No!"

I got my so-called "only one spanking" for telling Donny everything. After being told not to tell Donny because he was still to young. I told Donny about Mom and Dad's orgies with Uncle Hugh and Aunt Gloria in Long Beach before I was born. I told him about Aunt Caroline and Baby Caroline. I told him about Mom and that woman, Esther, with the chocolate cake. I told him Aunt Gloria was a lesbian.

Donny was nine and probably still too young.

"What's a lesbian?" he asked me.

"A female homosexual," I told him.

"What's a . . . ?"

"Anybody that fucks with anybody the same sex."

"Am I a lesbian?" he asked.

"No, you're a homo."

Donny told Dad that I said Aunt Caroline killed our sister, that Mom had killed the maid, that Aunt Gloria fucks somebody of the same sex, and that I called him a homo. So I got my "only one spanking"—whipped to within an inch of my life, it seemed to me. And I got told never to repeat those stories again. And never to call Donny a homo again.

But he was.

I guess I was as horny as any teenager, but Donny was a nymphomaniac at nine, if a little boy can be called that. I'd be reading at night and he'd want to read his book on my bed because he said the light was better. And he'd wind up between my legs, on top of the blanket, with his book on my stomach and his hands on my crotch, kneeding. Or he'd crawl into bed with me in the morning to cuddle and his foot would somehow find its way to my morning hard-on. One night I was babysitting him. I'd sent him to bed, then stretched out on the den floor to read when Donny came out of the bedroom, wearing one of my old T-shirts with nothing underneath, and stuck his ass right up in my face. He asked me to scratch his asshole for him. I whacked him a good one.

He must've beat off two or three times a day, and I don't think his hand left his pecker for a couple of years there. Mom caught him once. We had separate bedrooms by then. Carl had added on a new master bedroom with bath, so I got their old room and Donny stayed in the one we had been sharing. Eddie didn't actually catch Donny beating off. He'd fallen asleep the night before, spread out naked on top of the covers with dick in hand. He was still that way when Mom went in the next morning to get him up for breakfast. He didn't get his "only one spanking" for that. And I never told them about all the other stuff he did, so he didn't get it for that either.

I got mine for snitching on Aunt Gloria, plus all the other stuff I blabbed about.

The only reason I knew about Aunt Gloria was that I was listening when she and former Uncle Hugh had their big fight about it.

Hugh had taken over the restaurant at the hotel. Business had been very good for several years there in the mid-sixties and Leonard decided Beech Grove should have a better restaurant for the guests. Hugh had become the chef when his father retired, and he told Leonard he would be glad to make it into a better restaurant—if it was his. Leonard gave him the restaurant. He also gave Hugh the money to remodel. And he gave him some of the best old furniture from the hotel lobby, like the giant hutches that grace the back wall between the french doors.

The first thing Hugh bought was an espresso machine, one of those huge brass and copper ones with the eagle perched on the top. It sits behind the bar. It had never been used.

The second thing Hugh bought was a neon sign. A used neon sign. It said *Respighi's*.

So the new restaurant was called Respighi's. The only Italian food that has ever been served in Respighi's Restaurant is Hugh's spaghetti, which tastes suspiciously like Franco-American Spahetti-O's. The best thing Hugh cooks is hamburgers, probably because of his early training in the snack bar his father opened when Hugh was a teenager. Hugh's hamburgers are like what I call Bowling Alley Burgers. In Southern California, no one serves tastier or greasier burgers than bowling alley coffee shops. And Hugh's burgers rank up there with the best.

After school, I used to clean up the kitchen for Hugh, which was mostly just scraping grease off of everything. It wasn't hard work and I usually had plenty of time to sit around drinking Cokes, sneaking smokes outside the back door, and eavesdropping on Hugh's fights with Gloria. I usually got a big kick out of their fights, but I wasn't ready for this one.

She just came right out and told him that she was in love with a *woman*. And that she was going to leave *him* and live with *her*.

I didn't dare move a muscle or even take a breath for what seemed like ten minutes.

Hugh was as shocked as I was. Not only was she going to divorce Hugh, she was going to live in Beech Grove with her lover. He broke a dozen dishes before he started screaming. Then she screamed. He called her names. She called him names. They both got red in the face.

I ran. I told Donny. I got spanked.

Watergate was in 1973. "Deep Throat" was declared an obscene movie. Billy Jean King defeated Bobby Riggs. Vice President Agnew resigned and was replaced by Gerald Ford, who would become President the following year when Nixon resigned. It was the year of "The Changing Room" and the revival of "Irene," the year of "Gravity's Rainbow" and "Breakfast of Champions," the year of "Cabaret" and "The Godfather."

HOMOSEXUAL. There were only two of us in my high school graduation class, so the ceremony was very short. We invited the whole town to the Grad Night Party because we couldn't figure out how the two of us could be much of a party.

Before Josh and his family moved to Beech Grove, I had been the only member of the class of '73. There were no students in the two years behind me, and just two silly girls in the class three years behind. I pretty much had high school all to myself until Josh Bowen and his family moved to Beech Grove.

Josh's dad worked for a big insurance company back East, and when the company transferred him to San Diego, he decided he wanted to live in some out-of-the-way place. Beech Grove was definitely out of the way. He said he'd had enough of the city for awhile. He was our first commuter.

Josh and I hit it off immediately, being the only two seventeen-year-olds around, so my senior year was considerably less boring and lonely.

Josh had a dark complexion, large brown eyes and wavy, almost curly, brown hair. He was tall and muscular even as a teenager, a natural athlete and extremely competitive. He always had an excess of energy to burn off, racing everywhere he went, always beating me. We couldn't get near the swimming pool without doing race laps. We raced to school in the morning, raced home every afternoon. If Mom sent us to the store for something, we raced to and from.

He was like a colt being set free in the wilderness, but he seemed to view it more as being a stallion being put out to pasture in his prime. Beech Grove was too quiet, too slow, too confining for a boy who used to wander the streets of Baltimore, its neighboring cities and countryside. I'd watch the steam build up in him and I'd force myself to give more to our games. I'd try harder at our one-on-one basketball fiascos, usually getting knocked on my ass, but satisfied that I had made him play harder. I'd push my body to its limits in our races, knowing he'd have to run faster, knowing he had to win. I'd collect old bleach bottles and on Saturdays we'd bike over to the dump, where he'd bust them on the rocks and old car parts, laughing as the shattered pieces of brown glass flew in all directions. His week-long frown would fade even with the first broken bottle and would totally disappear after three or four rounds of exploding glass.

Some, but not all, of my desire to help Josh release his pent-up emotions was selfish. I knew that if he didn't get rid of his steam elsewhere, he'd take it on me in our sparring and wrestling bouts, which I always lost anyway, but hopefully with a minimum of pain. If he'd ever lost his temper during one of those bouts, I would've been one dead sparring partner. As it was, his temper went into the bleach bottles and our endless races.

Josh tolerated my lack of athletic prowess, partly because I was the only in in Beech Grove who would even try to compete with him, and because we were friends. And because I was no threat to him, just as he was no threat to me in academics. Josh hated to study. He didn't mind school particularly. In fact, he thought it was fun, in a social sense; he just had no use for books. So, just as he tolerated and helped me in our physical relationship, I tolerated and helped him in our intellectual relationship.

Then, the summer after graduation, his dad's company reversed themselves and told the Bowens they had to return to Baltimore. None of them wanted to go, but Josh simply refused. He and I had both been accepted at the University of California in Riverside—he in physical education and therapy, me in journalism—and there didn't seem to be much point in Josh going all the way to Baltimore and then back out here in the fall, so he stayed with us for the summer. We put the other twin bed back into my room and gave Josh's double bed to Donny.

It was the summer of the first Beech Grove Art Festival, held in conjunction with our annual Founder's Day Program—and Eddie's birthday—June 21.

Grampa Leonard was concerned about the sagging tourist trade and thought some kind of annual event would lure them back out to the middle of nowhere. Besides, he was bored. He'd given up drinking when Baby Caroline died. Amelia had given him up years before and moved into the guest bedroom at the other end of the hall. So Leonard sponsored an Art Festival. He invited artists from all over Southern California. He didn't get any famous artists, but he did get a few good ones and a lot of mediocre ones. Plus there were two artists, a retired bus driver and his wife, already living in Beech Grove who entered their works in the first festival.

Leonard took out small ads in the newspapers' Sunday supplements and got a pretty fair turnout, most notably two seventeen-year-old girls from San Diego. I think their names were Suzie and Linda, or Melinda. The festival ran the whole weekend, and they showed up on Saturday afternoon in Suzie's old VW van.

The sun was barely over the hill when the four of us hit the back of that van with a couple of secreted six-packs and what seemed to me like a lifetime of unrequited lust. Clothing flew in every directions. Steam fogged up the windows. Hands groped for new sensations.

I was with Suzie and Josh was with Linda, or Melinda. We were sprawled out side by side on the carpet in the back of the van. Suzie and I were trying to swallow each others' tongues, and from the sounds I heard behind me, Josh and his girl were doing the same. I could feel Josh's naked ass pressed against mine, sticking with our sweat. And he kept pressing against me, pushing me harder into the soft flesh lying in front of me. My dick slid between Suzie's legs. She bit my tongue. Then she screamed and shoved me into Josh and whatsername and the three of us wound up on the other side of the van. In the pandemonium of screaming, flailing arms and flying clothes which followed, Josh and I somehow wound up outside the van bare-ass naked with only a portion of our clothes at our feet. The van took off, never to be seen in Beech Grove again. We walked home, Josh in his cutoffs, torn shirt and shoes with no sox, me in shorts, no shirt and sox with no shoes.

We cursed those little prick-teasers all the way back to the house, and half-way through the night. I couldn't get to sleep. My nuts were swollen from the little workup we'd had earlier and I just tossed and turned. Josh did, too. Then he was sitting on the edge of my bed, looking into my eyes and grinning. He pulled the sheet down to my knees; I kicked it the rest of the way off. He wrapped his fingers around my cock, just barely making contact as he slid his hand back and forth. The sensation was unbelievable. I reached over to do the same light touch for him, but he squeezed my hand for a tighter grip. I could sense him tightening all his muscles—all except the one hand. It was over incredibly quick. Nothing was said. He wiped us both off with his torn shirt and then went back to his bed. I pulled the sheet up to my waist and went to sleep.

We were abruptly awakened the next morning by Eddie stomping around the house, slamming doors, throwing things and cursing at the top of her lungs. She was specifically cursing the Superintendent of County Schools for being narrow minded, uptight, bigoted and generally dumb for firing Jack Gresham, Beech Grove's secondary level teacher and school principal.

When Beech Grove finally opened a real school, back in Mom and Dad's teen years, the county sent a widow by the name of Mrs. Blankenship. She remained our sole teacher for almost twenty-five years. Then, when she retired, the county hired her daughter, Miss Blankenship. When we got over forty students in town, they sent Jack to take over the upper grades, leaving Miss Blankenship for the lower grades. Jack's an excellent teacher, and a likable person, a great incentive to the students to pass sixth grade so they can get out of Miss

Blankenship's class into his. Miss Blankenship is not a particularly likable person.

Jack did a lot to improve education in Beech Grove. He had always made sure the school had the latest and best textbooks. He even conned a complete science lab out of one of the other county schools. He had yet to confess how he pulled it off, revealing only that it was a bet of some kind. He has always pushed students to work up to their capabilities, giving up many of his nights and weekends for personal tutoring.

Jack was fired for taking part in a Gay Pride March in Hollywood. More accurately, he was fired for getting his picture in the newspapers marching for gay pride.

"I didn't even know he was gay," I said to everyone's astonishment. Apparently I was the only one who didn't know.

"I worry about you sometimes," Josh said.

"Did you think he and Dennis were just room-mates . . . at their age?" twelve-year-old Donny said. Even he knew.

Carl made some crack about sending his older son off to college with a lot of book knowledge and very little common sense. Eddie just shook her head, muttered something which I missed, cursed the Superintendent again, then called Hugh. Hugh has just gotten off the phone with Leonard. Leonard had just gotten off the phone with the Superintendent. They wouldn't budge.

We had a town meeting at noon. Jack got so embarrassed by the testimonials to his character that he had to leave the meeting. The vote was unanimous: Jack would stay, whatever it took. They drafted a letter to the county, telling them that the town of Beech Grove no longer required their educational services, that they were, as of the fall of '73, enrolling all their children in the New Beech Grove Private School. Said school would be under the direction of the new headmaster, Jack

Gresham, and his able assistant, Miss Eudora Blankenship. Our lawyers would be contacting them, we said in the letter. "Our lawyers" was a euphemism for Dennis' younger brother, who was studying law at UC San Diego. But that worked out well. The brother got his entire class working on our case and we ended up with a fully accredited, fully legal private school, with a fully certificated Jack Gresham as headmaster.

Josh, Donny and I went swimming after the meeting. But not at the hot springs. We had our own private pool up in the hills where the creek came out of the rocks. The spa pools were too hot for summer. Besides, we had to wear swim trunks at the hot springs.

Donny was the first in, as usual. Seeing him naked always made me wonder how a twelve-year-old could have a better build than his eighteen-year-old brother. Donny got his body from Mom's side of the family—stocky, muscular. He got the dark hair and the blue eyes, too. He was really a good-looking kid.

I got everything from Dad's side—sandy hair, lanky body, skinny legs and hazel eyes. And the promise of a beer belly to go with middle age.

Josh and I smoked a cigarette, then joined Donny in the water. Donny started playing grab-ass the minute we got in the pool. That was always Donny's favorite game and he always grabbed more than a little ass. In the scramble, Donny got tossed against the rocks we had used to fortify the natural dam. He said he wasn't hurt, so we resumed the game. Donny flinched the next time one of us fell against him and I made him get out of the water. There was blood running down his legs. He'd gashed the side of his dick on one of the rocks and all that exercise was causing the blood to pump out in dollops. We tied a sock around the wound, got dressed and carried him to the doctor. It took seven stitches and a lot of screaming to put Donny back together again.

Josh and I took Donny home and then went back up to the swimming hole.

"You knew Jack was gay, huh?" I asked him.

"Sure. I don't know how you didn't," he said.

"Do you think Donny's gay?"

"He's still pretty young."

"Yeah, but he acts like he's going to be, doesn't he?"

"I guess. If he is, he is."

"Yeah," I sighed.

"Don't sound so dejected. It's not the end of the world. It's not so bad, really."

"He's not your brother."

"I was thinking a little closer to home, actually."

"What?"

"I was talking about me."

"You?"

I think I backed away. I know my mouth was open.

"Me," he said, grinning. He was enjoying my discomfort. "What do you think that was all about in your bed last night?"

"Frustration. Like me."

"Frustration, yes . . . but not like you, I'm afraid."

"I, uh, don't know what to say."

"Then don't."

He dove to the bottom of the pool.

I got out of the water, put on my shorts, and lit a cigarette.

We still had a good time that summer. We didn't touch as much as we had before. The wrestling and grab-ass games stopped. I excluded Donny more and more as the weeks went by. I knew he was hurt, but I felt strange when I was with the two of them. I don't think it was a conscious effort to keep them apart—although it may have been—I just felt too uncomfortable with them.

The last week of summer, the week before Josh and I left

for college, I couldn't stand that hurt puppy look on Donny's face all the time, so I let him tag along all week. We got along fine, the three of us, and nothing happened. Until the night before we left.

Josh and I were packing. He went out to the garage for something, when Donny came into the room and asked me if I'd sleep in his room that night so he could be with Josh.

"Hell no!" I shouted at him.

"Jealous?"

I lost control and started slapping him across the face with both hands. He was screaming and crying and begging me to stop, but I couldn't. I just kept slapping him.

Josh came up behind me, grabbed me by the arms and threw me against the closet door. He hit me in the stomach and then slammed me up against the door again. I slumped to the floor.

Josh took a handkerchief from his suitcase and handed it to Donny, then put his arm around Donny's shoulders and they stood there, staring at me.

"I'm sorry, Donny," I said.

"If you're not in love with him, I don't know why you have to be so possessive," he cried and ran out of the room.

Josh picked me up off the floor and deposited me on my bed without saying a word. He finished packing and went to bed.

I didn't finish packing. I didn't even bother to take my suitcase off the bed. I didn't sleep.

Jimmy Carter was elected in 1976. Smokey the Bear died. Howard Hughes died. J. Paul Getty died. "One Flew Over the Cuckoo's Nest" swept the Oscars. Agatha Christie died. The United States celebrated a birthday. The Raid on Entebbe was in 1976.

MURDER. There were no bodies, that we knew of, buried

in Beech Grove. If the earlier inhabitants had ever buried anyone there, we didn't find them—and no one had been buried there since Leonard found Beech Grove in 1932. The two graves for Matthew and Mark Delaney were empty. Mark Delaney (aka Richard Henderson) and his wife, Sarah, burned up with the garage. Little Don Russell's body never found its way back from Normandy. Baby Caroline was buried in a kids' cemetery in the nearest real town, Escondido. She was buried in a tiny little cedar chest Carl had made to give her on her first birthday, which never came. Esther was shipped to Kansas City. When Matthew Delaney (aka Leonard Briggs) died, he was cremated in Escondido and then his ashes were scattered over his twin brother's ashes, where the garage used to be, at the house where Aunt Caroline lived in seclusion.

I was in my senior year in college. Josh and I had remained friends, though our separate studies and my job kept us from seeing much of each other. Leonard paid for my school fees and books, but I had to work to pay my room and board. The job kept me from going home, too. Christmases were the only trips I made to Beech Grove those four years. I wrote to them a lot, especially Donny. He wrote once, not saying much, and I finally gave up on him. Eddie kept me up to date on everything that was happening back home—Dad's hearing getting worse, his refusing to wear a hearing aid, Donny's bad grades—and she was the one who called me when Grampa Leonard died. I went home for the service.

Leonard's ashes were in a cardboard box. We each took a handful and threw them out on the ground, around the ruins of the old garage. Aunt Caroline watched from her bedroom window.

The first I heard anything about the really big Delaney family secret was when I was twelve and Donny was six. Somebody slipped and said something about Eddie's father and Leonard doing something. They said it as though the two were not the same person.

"But I thought Grampa Leonard was your father?"

So I got a story about Leonard having a twin brother and that the twin brother was actually Mom's father, but he and Mom's real mother were killed in a car accident, so Grampa Leonard and Gram Amelia just sort of adopted Mom and Aunt Caroline.

Donny pouted for a week; he thought they had played some kind of a joke on him. I just wanted to know if I was still supposed to call Leonard and Amelia, Grampa and Gram. I didn't even know those other people. I also wanted to know why, if Mom's father was Mark and her uncle was Matthew, why I wasn't named Mark Matthew. Mom told me not to be ridiculous.

A few years later, I got to asking questions about that garage that had burned to the ground at Aunt Caroline's house. I got a story about gangsters in Missouri who hated Grampa Leonard enough to murder him, but who had killed the twin brother by mistake. I thought it was a rotten deal, but it didn't really upset me. Donny was angry at such injustice and he was a holy terror for weeks.

Because of his reaction to the previous versions of the big secret, I decided not to tell him about the final version, the supposed truth, I got at the funeral—the story about a man named Jake, his friend Matthew, and murder.

Leonard swore to Eddie, just before he finally succumbed to the massive stroke he'd suffered, that he did not know Jake was going to kill Mark in his place.

Eddie still had her doubts and so she talked it out with me as we walked down to the creek after the service. She was clutching a piece of wood against her chest, and when we sat down by the water, I asked her to show it to me. It had a verse branded into to:

> Give me but one yellow rose . . .
>   it will be our life's bouquet.

> Give me but one yellow rose . . .
> for it is our love today.

She said her father had given it to her mother on the day they were killed. She said it was the only thing that didn't burn in the fire. She said she had kept it under her mattress all these years and that she had clutched it to her chest the same way on the day Leonard had spoken a few words over the ashes of her parents and the garage.

Eddie said she had shown the piece of wood with the verse on it to Carl that day, while Leonard was saying his few words. Carl was five. Eddie was seven. She said Carl read the words on the shingle, asking her about one of the words, then handed it back to her. He told her to wait right there for him and he ran off down the street. Ten minutes later, Carl came back, out of breath and bleeding from a dozen scratches along his forearms. He was holding a yellow rose behind his back. He handed it to her and then kissed her on the cheek.

6. Queenie

There are no beech trees in Beech Grove.

When Professor Alexander Dhunwhit of the UCR Department of Agriculture saw the little ad I placed in the campus paper for the Third Annual Beech Grove Art Festival, he drove all the way down to Beech Grove to study the beech trees . . . because there shouldn't have been any beech trees there. He traipsed through the foothills for hours before running into my mother down by the creek. Eddie proudly told him that her son was a student at UCR, that he should look me up when he got back to Riverside, that I was the scholarly one in the village, and that I might be able to shed some light on the subject. I couldn't, but he could.

"Dhhewnit," he said, between puffs on his cherry scented pipe. "It's not Duhoonwhit, nor Donut. Dhhewnit."

"Yes, sir," I said. I hadn't even tried to say his name, addressing him only as Professor, but apparently he felt it necessary to perform his name ritual.

"Young man," Professor Alexander Dhunwhit said, "don't you think it's a bit presumptuous of your little village to call itself Beech Grove when, in fact, you have no beech trees?"

"It was already named when my grandfather . . ."

"The beech family of trees, *Fagus* of the family *Fagaceae*, is native to the northeastern portion of the United States. These trees require cold, damp weather, loam soil, north-facing slopes. Good heavens, man, even in the foothills there, you're a desert. Surely you don't . . ."

"But I . . ."

"Surely you wouldn't expect a tree of this variety to survive there?"

"I don't expect anything," I pleaded.

"But you did, didn't you? I found traces out there of poor, decaying beeches, someone tried to grow beech trees there forty or fifty years ago, but they only lived three or four years. Didn't they?"

"I'm only twenty years old, sir."

"People should research these things better, before they go off planting trees where they can't survive," the Professor concluded, then walked out.

There are no beech trees in Beech Grove.

"That's stupid," my wife, Elizabeth said when we moved to Beech Grove.

It was to be the subject of our first big fight, our first annual big fight.

It is often said that we remember the good things from our past, that we protect our fragile psyches by forgetting the painful things. I think that applies to those times or situations which one has escaped. If you're still caught up in something, you can easily remember the bad.

What stands out in my mind about our first seven years of marriage are the annual arguments. Not unlike Carl's idea of "only one spanking," Elizabeth and I developed the idea of "only one fight"—one really big brouhaha, once a year—and for some reason, always in June. Maybe it's because that's when we held our first annual. Maybe it's because Mom's birthday is in June. Or maybe because the festival is in June. Anyway, our annual big fight is always in June.

Our first one was about the lack of beech trees in Beech Grove.

Elizabeth and I were married during our senior year at

UCR. We were married at the Chapel of the White Bells in Las Vegas, Nevada, and we have yet to be forgiven by either of our families. We'd only known each other for a couple of months; in fact, we met the week I got back to school from Leonard's ash-scattering. I had been assigned to do a piece for the paper on the college's string quartet, in which Elizabeth was the viola.

Elizabeth was, is, clean—freshly scrubbed, pink cheeked, makeup free, Southern California clean. She has shiny, sandy brown hair which she usually wears in a ponytail or a single, large braid. She does things to her hair, alternately, with vinegar or lemon juice. She also puts raw egg white on her face and lets it dry to a slick, pulling finish. She bathes even though we have a shower. She bathes in herbs and other fragrant things. She does yoga exercises. And she meditates.

We fell in love. And we got married, initially with the idea that she would continue her music studies and that I would go to work for the Riverside Press.

Then, Hugh got the bright idea, and talked the rest of the town into it, that Beech Grove should have its own little newspaper, that the town should subsidize the aforementioned paper if necessary, and that Matthew Russell, me, should be the editor. Well, who the hell wants to be a gofer on a large paper when you could be the editor of your own paper?

Elizabeth "Queenie" Russell, née Mann, didn't know what she was getting into by marrying a boy from a village of only 162 adults and 47 children, and then moving there with him. I didn't tell her, either. I probably even lied to her.

I took a crash course in printing from a friend who owned a shop, then bought a truckload of equipment with the town's money. And then moved home with my new wife.

There are no beech trees in Beech Grove.

"That's stupid," Elizabeth said.

"They died," I defended.

"I didn't mean it's stupid that there are no beech trees, that's to be expected out here. I meant that it's stupid to call the place Beech Grove, given the fact that there aren't any.

"Bullshit, Queenie, you're just . . ."

"Don't call me Queenie!"

"All right. Bullshit, *Elizabeth*, you're just criticizing because you didn't want to move to my home town."

"But I did move here, didn't it?"

"Yeah. And look at you: you've been pouting since we got here."

"It's only been three days!"

"Three days is a long time not to go to someone's house."

"Whose house?"

"My mother's!" I shouted.

"I have been unpacking."

"For three days?"

"Yes, for three days! You cart me off without any notice whatsoever, and . . ."

"A week's notice."

". . . with no notice, so I had to just throw everything together. You move me into a house that hadn't been cleaned in ten years. You run off to your print shop and . . ."

"It happens to be the town newspaper!"

"It also happens to be the town print shop. You happen to be the town printer."

"And editor!"

"And I happen to be left alone to do all the cleaning, all the arranging, all the unpacking, all the—I don't have time to run over for coffee and idle chitchat with your mother or anybody else!"

"Why don't you ask Eddie to help you?"

"I'm sure *Eddie* has enough to do without my asking her to do *our* housework for us. What with her reading group, her Volunteer Fire Department, her parents group at the school, her . . . her *tending bar* . . . her . . ."

"Why'd you say it like that?"

"What?"

"*Tending bar*."

"I didn't say it like anything. It was just part of the goddamn list!"

It went downhill from there. We started name-calling and accusing, and wound up not speaking for two days.

The first week, Elizabeth wouldn't go to the Sunday Service, saying she still had too much to do. She didn't meet us at Mom and Dad's for dinner either. Eddie told me to stop worrying about it, and to stop nagging Elizabeth about it.

The following week, Eddie sent a note to Elizabeth, telling her that she was going to read something on the coming Sunday she thought Elizabeth would really enjoy. If Elizabeth had the time, Eddie said in the note, "I would especially like you to hear it."

What Eddie read to us on Sunday morning, including Elizabeth, was an excerpt from an interview with Pablo Casals in which he talked about an artist's commitment to the community, as well as to Art. Eddie concluded her presentation by saying how fortunate Beech Grove was to have an accomplished musician living among us and perhaps, after Elizabeth got settled in, she'd be able to find the time to play for us.

We all, including Elizabeth, took the long way home— over the hill and through the woods—to Mom and Dad's house, where we had coffee and cookies, followed by beer with pretzels, then feasted on fried chicken, mashed potatoes with gravy, green beens, corn, assorted pickles and olives, homemade dinner rolls, two kinds of pie, and then coffee on the veranda. Elizabeth helped Eddie with the dishes and they talked about Pablo Casals, while Carl, Donny and I carried out our ritual on the porch.

It was, unfortunately, not the total breakthrough I had hoped for. Sunday Service and dinner at Mom's remained

Elizabeth's only involvement that year. And no amount of encouragement could get her to play her viola for the town. She wouldn't even play for me. She played in the den, alone, while I was at work. She seemed to resent everything and everybody. She finally even stopped playing for herself in the den. She stopped working on the quartet pieces she had been composing for years. She became my devoted wife, my completely dependent wife.

Carl's father, Big Don, died of a heart attack that winter. Dad took it very hard: He stopped wearing his hearing aid altogether, rather than just turning it down or off; he gave in to his arthritis, after ignoring it all those years. Ginny took it even harder. She seemed to be eating, but she kept losing weight. In four months, she melted away, from the happy, round, soft, chubby gramma I used to cuddle into, to sad skin and bones. In six months, she joined Big Don at the Crestview Cemetery in Escondido. Their urns shared a nook in the Crestview Columbarium. Elizabeth thought it was beautiful, and somehow romantic, that a person could pine away for a lost love. I thought it was a waste of a human being. I thought, and said so, that when a person ceases to be an individual, there is nothing there for someone else to love.

I told Elizabeth that it was boredom that was causing her to be too dependent on me, that I didn't need a big dinner every night of the week, that I didn't want my lunch brought to me at work every day, that it wasn't necessary to iron my T-shirts, and that I couldn't stand her following me around everywhere like a goddamn lost puppy dog! It was our second annual big fight, which ended much like the first: name-calling, accusation, and then two or three days of silence.

But that time, the days of silence were productive. Elizabeth took up painting. She had dabbled, as they say of amateur artists, in college and was almost as good as most of the local artists and better than some, so it wasn't too difficult to encourage her once she actually sat down with paints and easel.

Elizabeth devoted herself to her painting. The only big meal I got was on Sundays at Mom's. I got to eat Hugh's hamburgers for lunch every day. And I wore wrinkled T-shirts. We started getting along a lot better. Elizabeth even helped out with the Art Festival that next spring and she sold her first painting, the one called "Red Ball Under a Beech Tree." We made love twice that night. *Ars longa, vita brevis*, I always say.

And that pretty much became our established routine. I put out my little eight-page "Clarion" every week, doing odd printing jobs from time to time. Elizabeth painted and worked on the festival. And we had our annual fights.

One year was supposedly about Art, but was really about the damn cat she had adopted and had allowed to use my closet to have her kittens in.

"We are all one," she said.

"What?"

"We are all one," said Elizabeth again.

"I know that!" said I, shouting. "But what the hell does that have to do with letting the fucking cat whelp in amongst my shoes?!"

"Dogs whelp," she said.

"Foal then!"

"Horses."

"What then?"

"I don't know."

"I thought you were the goddamn expert!"

"What difference does it make?" she asked.

"You started it," I said.

"All I said was 'We are all one,'" she said.

"Okay, okay, he said, calmly, trying to restore logic and order to their conversation. Would you care to expand on that theme, relating it—directly, if possible—to our discussion of the littering process in my clothing storage room?"

"Cute, Mattie. Very cute."

"Thank you. Ready when you are."

"Given that God, or the Absolute, if you prefer, is everything and everything is God—you will give that?"

"Yes."

"And space is part of everything?"

"Okay."

"And we, meaning you and I, are part of that everything?"

"Go on."

"And cats and kittens and shoes and closets?"

"Elizabeth."

"And cats and kittens and shoes and closets?"

"Yes. Tentatively."

"No tentatively."

"I want to hear the punch line before I commit to anything."

"There's no punch line," Elizabeth said. "Just simply that if we're all here under the same auspices, then we all . . . then everything has the right to be what it is, and where it is."

"You're mixing Eastern mysticism with Western logic," I said.

"I am not. What if I am?"

"They're not compatible."

"They are."

"According to you, if a bear walked into this house right now, we'd have to let him move in with us."

"Him?"

"Her! It! Who cares?! Answer the question!"

"There are no bears around here to come walking or moving in."

"A bobcat then! You're being evasive!"

"And you're trying to sidetrack me! As usual!"

"I'm only repeating your logic!"

"We have the right to protect ourselves!"

"Not bad."

"Thanks."

"Okay then, I have the right to protect my closet from invading cats."

"You're impossible!"

"And they're going out!"

"You better not hurt those kittens!"

"I won't!"

"I hope she scratches you!"

She did.

Another year, the pretext for our fight was communism, but the focus seemed to be on Beech Grove's unique structure and the fact that newcomers couldn't vote for the first five years and, thus, weren't able to get their own pet projects adopted at the town meetings. Leonard had left his property, the town of Beech Grove, in trust to the established citizens, with restrictions on newcomers, which some newcomers resented. Elizabeth's biggest complaint was that a hundred hours a year of community service was one of the requirements for being an established citizen, and you have to put those hours in even during the probationary five years. She also bitched that the donation of a painting to be sold at the festival was worth only twenty credits. And that one could only satisfy half the required credits with donations. There was no way around it, she was going to have to go out and get involved in the community if she wanted to take part in the town meetings. That fight lasted at least three days, followed by the mandatory days of silence.

One of our biggies was about healthy eating habits, especially my lack of, but what it got down to was that she preferred bran muffins and I preferred blueberry. The actual screaming part came when I said something about health nuts being neurotically preoccupied with excretory elimination.

Year before last, the argument started over the cat's litter box, progressed to just which one of us it was who was taking the other for granted in bed, then wound up on my "Christmas Spirit" editorial, for which I was given the Southern California Press Association for Excellence in Journalism, in the small newspaper category.

"You were gloating," she had said.

"Gloating? It was a . . . it expressed the essence of human kindness. It was touching."

"A country boy goes off to college in the big city and holds an umbrella over some little old lady's head. Very touching. Who wouldn't?"

"A lot of people! That was the whole point of the goddamn editorial! A lot of people wouldn't!"

"Oh really, Mattie."

"Don't call me Mattie, Queenie!"

Then more name-calling, as usual. Then accusations. Then the silence.

Last year's fight was our best ever. It was about Josh— straight out, with no pretext. Josh had stayed up in Riverside after college. He was a therapist and exercise instructor at one of those health clubs. Then when Beech Grove's spa director retired after some forty-odd years, Hugh got the bright idea, and talked the rest of the town into it, that Josh should be our new spa director. He accepted.

Josh moved into the hotel, but spent most of his free time at our house. He played pool with Dad and me when Dad's spirits were high enough for him to ignore his arthritis. He helped me with the paper when things were slow at the spa.

Josh hadn't changed a lot since we were kids together, racing from one end of Beech Grove to the other. Physically, he was even more strikingly handsome and powerful. Emotionally, he was still tense, his temper always in the ready position, but usually under control. As an adult, I haven't been able to help him as much as I used to. I can't run, swim, spar, wrestle or play one-on-one the way I could as a teenager—and I wasn't all that hot back then. And bleach is now packaged in plastic bottles. Donny's a good competitor for Josh, as is Pat's son, J.D. They give Josh a good run, so he gets to let off his steam with them. And I get my rest.

Josh actually was happy to be back in Beech Grove, despite his years of dissatisfaction with our little town. He said he had missed the peace, even if the pace was too slow. He made friends, easily, with the newcomers who had moved to the village during his absence. He renewed relations with old friends. He put a great deal of effort into improving the spa facilities and services. To my mind, his best improvement was the addition of massages: Swedish for general relaxation and for toning the muscles; and Shiatsu for relief of illness-causing tension and fatigue. Besides, Josh was generous with his talents: He gave me massages when I allowed the tension to built up into neck and backaches.

"I wish you wouldn't let him do that," Elizabeth said.

"I don't let him do anything. I ask him to."

"You shouldn't ask him."

"You won't do it."

"You said I don't do it well."

"You don't."

"You shouldn't be naked with him."

"I wear a towel, for chrissake!"

"Lot of good that does."

"I don't even get a hard-on."

"It's still bound to be tempting for him."

"Thanks for the compliment, but I'm afraid what you mean is that it might be tempting for me."

"That isn't what I said."

"I know what you said, darling, but I learned a long time ago that what you say and what you mean are not always the same thing. I wish to God I hadn't told you about our little experience."

"Experien*ces*."

"If I hadn't told you, you wouldn't give a damn about the stupid massages."

"He's still a homosexual, whether you ever made it with him or not. And you shouldn't be lying on a table naked with his hands all over you."

"Shit! I told you there's nothing to be jealous about! He's a goddamn professional!"

"I'm not jealous! You just go ahead and get your massages. If you prefer his touch to mine, I guess there's nothing I can do about it!"

"I do not prefer his touch to yours! And it's not a touch! It's a push. It's a k-need! There's no fucking! There are no blowjobs! No mutual masturbation! No nothing!"

"No M & M's?" she started to howl.

(Elizabeth has always made sport of the fact that I used to call myself Matthew and Mark, and her first pet name for me, back in college, was M & M: he melts in your mouth, not in your hand. And, in another of my sharing moments, I had told her that we used to call mutual masturbation, M & M's. It became one of her all-time favorite private jokes.)

"No M & M's," I laughed.

"Melt in your mouth, not in your hand!" she added.

"Prove it!" I dared.

She did.

But then, I couldn't leave well enough alone.

"Could you lighten up your grip a little?" I asked.

"Whatayou mean, 'lighten up?'"

"You know, just barely touch it with your fingers."

"Oh, you mean the way Josh does it! Sure!"

She got a vice grip on my cock and yanked it down between my legs. I screamed. We didn't speak for at least a week on that one.

One thing about our big annual fights, though, is that when we finally get back together, we do that up big, too.

After the beech tree fight, we mauled each other under a sycamore up in the hills on the way back from the Sunday Service. We lagged behind the others as we all walked home that day, telling them that Elizabeth had broken her sandal. We were an hour late for dinner. It took me ten minutes to rip that strap off her sandal, and two dollars to get it fixed. But it was worth it.

After the bran versus blueberry fight, we made it on the kitchen floor, smeared head to toe in batter.

One time, we locked ourselves in the bedroom for three days and scared the hell out of everybody. Actually, Donny did the scaring by planting the idea in people's minds that maybe we had made a suicide pact. I made Donny repair the door they bashed in when they came to save us.

After the Josh fight, we used up every bottle of baby oil and skin lotion in the house during a marathon, mutual massage, which also included a half-bottle of poly-unsaturated, cholesterol-free, safflower oil. We also had to replace the mattress afterwards.

That was also the fight and making up session which inspired Elizabeth's contribution to the festival. In addition to the Founder's Day Program and Art Festival, Elizabeth thought we should have a Summer Solstice Music and Dance Celebration to boost the sagging attendance. The idea came to her during the safflower oil. The connection was beyond my comprehension, but she said it made perfect sense to her: something to do with lard and flutes.

Then she disappeared into her studio for what seemed like two days.

"Working on a new painting?" I asked when she finally emerged.

"Meditating," she said.

Elizabeth had been into meditation as long as I had known her, but that was the first time she'd ever done a marathon meditate.

"For two days?"

"I had a lot to accomplish and it wasn't two days. This solstice thing presents a lot of problems."

"So you were conjuring up solutions in meditation?"

"No. Results."

"This I gotta hear," I said.

"Not if you're going to take that attitude."

"I'm sorry. I didn't mean it that way. I am interested."

"I've been reading about creative visualization and how it can change so-called reality."

"So-called?"

"You know, the idea that material substance is only a shadow, that the physical world is dependent on our perception of it."

"Yeah, okay."

"Well, the idea is that objective reality is produced through imagination, that nothing in this world exists that did not first exist in imagination. Imagining creates reality."

"Certainly a bold thought."

"It's like nothing really being solid and colors being only the way light hits the eye . . . and relativity."

"Equally abstract, anyway."

"But you do admit reality is questionable."

"Yes."

"What you have to do, then, is imagine yourself already to be living in the reality you desire."

"Daydreaming."

"No, more concentrated. It has to be concentrated. It has to be stable. You have to believe you've already achieved the result you wanted, to live in it. Plus you must have the meditative contact with your inner self, *our* inner self. The Absolute. Imagination."

"That's why you locked yourself up then."

"Yes, to concentrate, meditate on the image. Now I have

to live as though the results were already true. I accept the fact that I already have everything I need for the Solstice Celebration. So I do have everything."

There wasn't enough money in the festival budget to buy the musical instruments and costumes Elizabeth wanted. There wasn't even enough money to buy the materials to make them, so Elizabeth got it into her head that Amelia should donate the money out of the nest egg Leonard had left her. Elizabeth, armed with her new faith, spent four days and nights in Amelia's living room, listening to fond memories and family stories. They were suddenly the best of friends. On the fourth day, Elizabeth emerged from Amelia's house with all the money she needed. Elizabeth called it the power of Human Imagination. I called it blackmail.

Elizabeth also got it into her head that little brother, Donny, should lead the opening dance ceremony—as Pan.

"He'll never do it," I told her.

"Why not?"

"Mainly because you're married to me and he hates my guts."

"Well, he doesn't hate my guts," Elizabeth said. "And I don't think he hates you either. Just last Sunday, he . . ."

"Donny tolerates us because he is under orders to, or else. Mom will not have her Sundays disrupted with petty squabbles. Haven't you noticed that Sundays are the only time he sees or talks to us?"

"That may be the only time he talks to you, dear. He talks to me all the time."

"When?" I asked.

"While you're at work, mostly."

"He comes here?"

"Yes. He's, uh, been helping me with . . . around the house."

"Doing what?"

"Oh, it's a surprise."

"What kind of surprise?"

"You'll see when it's . . . when I get . . . you'll see."

"Well, you'll be very lucky if he sticks it out. He never finishes anything he starts. He's worked for damn near everyone in this town, but never for more than two or three weeks. Years ago, he started working with Dad on those miniature cedar chests they sell at the festival, and he is yet to finish one on his own. All he wants is to have that goddamn noisy music blaring in his ears. And enough alcohol and probably dope, knowing him, to keep reality out of his life. He's useless, Queenie, and he won't do it for you!"

"You're ranting."

"He pisses me off!"

"On the other hand, Donny is a sensitive and introspective person. He has the most penetrating blue eyes I've ever seen. He is a terrific dancer. And he is a gorgeous hunk naked. He's perfect for Pan."

"How do you know what he looks like naked?"

"Well, in swim trunks, anyway."

"That's better. Is your Pan going to be naked?"

"Not entirely. I thought I'd glue hair on his legs."

"What about the part between the legs? Don't you think you'd better glue something there?"

"I'll think of something."

Donny refused when Elizabeth asked him to lead the dance, and she let it slide for awhile. Then they went swimming one afternoon up at the top of the creek and she came back with a star for her pageant. If I hadn't been absolutely positive Donny was gay, I would've accused her of doing something. At that, I'm not totally convinced she didn't.

They rehearsed, in private, at Amelia's. No one saw or heard anything until the opening day of the festival, the summer solstice.

Amelia made the Founder's Day speech, a yearly tribute

to Grampa Leonard and his great generosity. Then Eddie offered a few words about the quality of the art that year. Then Elizabeth took over.

We were on the big lawn that lies between the hotel entrance and the shops across the way. First, the children's choir danced out onto the grass, each in some sort of springlike costume, each with an authentic early musical instrument. They sang a medieval chant, then sat on the lawn in a large circle and began to play. The music was eerie. It had a "tribal" quality to it: ritual dances, songs to the gods. The kids seemed to be really getting into it, and they played very well, I thought.

The audience, which was of a fairly good size that year, didn't know what to think at first. There was a general restlessness, squirming, then the rhythmic patterns of the music began to cast their spell. It was time for Pan.

A flute called from behind the three oaks at the far end of the lawn. Donny leapt out from behind the trees. We all stared in fascination as he danced—no, ran—in leaping strides around the perimeter of the great lawn. He was incredible. There were two small horns jutting out of his tousled hair. His tanned body was gleaming with sweat. There was long, white and brown animal hair flowing down from his naked groin and ass, with shorter and darker hair continuing on down to his feet. And Elizabeth had done something to his eyes so that you could see the blue in them even when he was on the far side of the lawn. He leapt, skipped, cartwheeled and somersaulted as he weaved in and out of the seated musicians, serenading them with his panpipe. The finale came in the center of the musicians circle. Donny let the panpipe hang from the leather thong around his neck, and he began to spin, first with his arms outstretched, then raising them slowly and gracefully over his head, still turning a dizzying speed. The musicians, the children, jumped to their feet. They played louder and faster. Donny began a steady, low moan which increased both in volume and pitch with each successive spin. The kids blew harder, hit their drums harder, and began to scream with Donny. The audience was stomping and clapping to the repetitive beat of the primitive drums.

Suddenly, Donny stopped dead still. The music stopped simultaneously. The clapping stopped. Donny stood there for a moment, his eyes cast skyward. Sweat was streaming down his body, matting the hair on his loins. He jumped straight up in the air, let out a frightening scream at the top of his lungs, and then fell to the ground. The kids piled on him, screaming, with arms and legs flailing. I started to run out there to rescue him, but Elizabeth grabbed my arm.

The frenzy stopped as abruptly as it had begun. The children got to their feet and made a circle around Donny. The circle opened and Donny strutted out to greet his audience, his arms stretched high and wide to the gods, his body covered in hundreds of flower petals.

The crowd applauded wildly, whistling and yelling bravos! to Donny. Dozens of them ran out onto the lawn to congratulate the performers.

My adrenaline was pumping like mad, a real high. I kissed Elizabeth, then Amelia, and ran into the crowd to find Donny.

He was down on his hands and knees being kissed by a little girl who wanted one of his little flowers. When she turned away, I reached under Donny's arms from the back and pulled him to his feet. I turned him around. He looked a bit confused by the ear-to-ear smile I was wearing, but he did return the smile. I threw my arms around him, kissed him on the mouth, then just held on.

"I love you!" I shouted, as my excitement, my strange high, reached still another peak.

"I don't know what you're on," Donny said, "but I like it."

I kissed him again.

7. The Sunday Night Regulars

I think one of the reasons Eddie reacted so strongly to Donny's announcement was that it came exactly one week after the fight at the bar, which Dennis has since dubbed as The Queer Night Riot.

It had been a Sunday in early May like all our Sundays: the morning meeting, followed by overindulgence at Mom's and the usual arguments, then off to the bar at five. The difference that day was that when Carl, Eddie and I arrived at the hotel, there were several four wheel drive vehicles sitting in the parking lot, those pickup and jeep type trucks that have flags and spotlights and deep tread tires, and that stand about three feet off the ground. They weren't an unusual sight in Beech Grove on weekends, but they were always gone by late Sunday afternoon.

The three of us stopped at the same time, halfway across the big lawn, each of us with the same thought: In three hours, The Sunday Night Regulars would descend upon Resphigi's, exhibiting a lifestyle that could in no way be considered compatible with the straight and narrow attitudes of the types who normally accompany those 4x4's. I was already trying to remember which of the cue sticks was the heaviest. I wondered if that look on Carl's face meant he was thinking similarly. Eddie was expressionless, staring at the three oaks at the far end of the lawn. Then she pulled herself erect and marched off, without speaking, across the lawn, up the steps and into the bar. Dad and I followed.

Eddie had predicted something like this would happen when Hugh decided to make Sunday a special night for the gay and lesbian customers. Hugh had argued that they were in there every Sunday night anyway, that everyone else in town had a special night for half priced drinks, so why shouldn't they have one? Eddie argued that making it special would make it stand out and that making it stand out would make it trouble. Hugh's three quarter interest in the business outvoted Eddie's one quarter and The Regulars took claim to Sunday nights. Hugh also insisted that they be able to do all the things that the straights were allowed to do on the other nights. And that included dancing, holding hands, hugging, kissing and even that discreet kind of petting one sees in bars, if one looks. Hugh reminded Eddie that Saturday nights, aka Music Nights, at Respighi's included all of these things and more, and that they were not going to discriminate. Hugh said Mom ought to be grateful it was only one night a week.

Hugh had three votes to Mom's one.

That was last November.

That was when Dennis named it Queer Night at Respighi's.

That was when Eddie "eighty-sixed" Donny.

Eddie was already behind the bar when Carl and I walked in. Gordy, the day bartender, was sitting at the far end of the bar finishing his cash count and beginning his first drink. There was a young couple next to him, sipping cocktails and gazing longingly into each other's eyes. And, standing around the pool table, were eight men. They were sunburned and covered with dust from the hills. They wore shorts or cutoffs and colorful T-shirts with beer ads or sexual boasts printed on the back. They all had baseball-type caps with plastic, adjustable straps in the back.

Carl and I played gin rummy since we couldn't get to the

pool table. Those guys downed at least four, if not five, beers in the first hour we were there. At one point, Eddie tried to get them out of there by telling them that she ran out of Coors, which she hadn't, but they said they'd drink "that light shit" and increased their consumption. Eddie cautioned them about having to drive so far to get home, but they ignored her.

As Dad and I finished our umpteenth game of gin, Dennis walked in. It was only twenty till eight. I jumped out of my chair and ran to the door to bring him over to our table. I plopped him down next to Carl and went up to the bar to get his drink. Dennis was already boozed up, and when he saw the bunch back at the pool table, he got a strange gleam in his eye, an omen of things to come, I thought.

Dennis has never been my favorite of The Regulars. He's always mouthing off about something and strangers don't seem to care much for his outspoken nature. He had been an advertising executive in New York before he and Jack got together. Somewhere along the line, he had been transferred to the West Coast and then was fired a few years later for drinking too much. He must have had some money in reserve because he never went back to work. He took up painting when he and Jack moved to Beech Grove and that's what he's been doing since—that and drinking. And mouthing off.

Carl quickly got him into a conversation about his days on Madison Avenue—Dennis' favorite subject to bitch about—hoping to keep his attention from the men at the pool table.

Rae and Gloria arrived a little early, too, and joined us at our table. They looked especially nice that evening. They had spent the afternoon trying out new hair styles on each other. Aunt Gloria's gray was gone, having been replaced by a strawberry blond tint, and her shoulder length flip had become a shag. Rae's hair was brilliantined and masculine-short. I recognized it as being the way she wore it in the only old movies of hers I'd ever seen: A B-grade imitation of "The

Blue Angel" in which Rae played an Austrian chanteuse. Gloria was in a pastel green dress. Rae had on slacks, a sport coat and tie. They made a very handsome couple.

I expected a reaction from our visitors, but none came. On the other hand, Rae and Gloria were acutely aware of the alien presence at the back of the room. The usually chatty Gloria shut up completely; the usually quiet Rae tugged at her clothes and talked on about nothing.

Hugh must have noticed that the 4x4's were still in the parking lot, too, because he kept coming in from the dining room to check on things that didn't need checking on. Donny was helping Hugh in the restaurant that night, standing in for an indisposed waiter, and he tried to follow Hugh into the bar on a couple of those in and out trips, but Eddie ushered him back out immediately. Josh followed Hugh one of the times, and he was allowed to stay. He took one look at the pool table and started weighing cue sticks in his mind. He stopped at the bar on his way to our table and got beers for himself, Dad and me. He also brought three shots of whisky. I don't know if they were just "for show" or because he thought we needed the fortification. Probably both.

Jack, Gwen and Pat danced in from the veranda, singing "What I Did For Love," but came to an abrupt halt, midstep and midchorus, when they spotted the Coors crowd. Jack escorted the two women to the table next to ours and went up to the bar for their drinks. Pat filled me in on the dozen or two things that had gone wrong at the Clarion Friday afternoon (I had played hooky to go down to Escondido to have three cavities filled) and she was about to tell me her son, J.D.'s latest misadventure, when I noticed that Gwen was clinching her fists. Pat tried to calm her, but Gwen wasn't to be calmed: one of the guys at the pool table was staring at her.

He smiled at her. She growled under her breath. He started to walk toward us, but one of his buddies caught him by the elbow. That same buddy got the check from Eddie and start collecting money. Pat talked Gwen into switching chairs with her, so that Gwen would be facing away from the pool table. Carl was keeping Dennis entrenched in Madison Avenue.

I was almost beginning to believe we were going to make it through the evening, when Terry entered. His hair was bleached out even more than usual and he was poured into his jeans. His tank top said "Daddy's Boy." He made his usual move to the pinball machine to pose. Kurt came in almost immediately and began his game of sliding across the room for the score. Both were oblivious to their audience.

"Will you look at this," said the man who had been staring at Gwen.

"Leave 'em alone," his friend said. "We're paid up. Let's get out of here."

"What? And leave Pretty Boy without a good-bye kiss? Never."

"C'mon, Blake!"

"Not till I get my kiss! Maybe a little more. Whataya say, sweetheart?" Blake said to Terry, who had frozen in his pose position.

Kurt moved toward Terry, but Blake cut him off.

"Stay out of it, old man! Pretty Boy don't want an old fart like you. Not when there's young meat around, like me. Right, Pretty Boy?"

The man's friends began to move slowly toward us. We all stood. Pat pulled Gwen back against one of the video games. Rae and Gloria moved to the bar.

Dennis picked up a chair. "Hey motherfucker! Why don't you just get your ass back out to your dune buggy and . . ."

"What's this? Another fruit? Hey guys, this place is crawling with faggots! Shit, we can have a dance. One of you dikes go play some music."

"I'll play music," Gwen shouted, "on your fucking head!"

Dennis raised the chair over his head. "You assholes come out here every week and tear up the hills with your fucking trucks and the law says we can't stop you! But we can, and will, stop you from fucking with our people!"

He got a few cheers for his speech. Unfortunately, those cheers encouraged him to raise the chair even higher, too high and too far back over his head. He fell over backwards, smashing a table full of drinks and banging his head on one of the other chairs.

The man called Blake grabbed Terry, and when Kurt tried to intervene, Blake knocked him to the floor. Josh and I went for cue sticks.

"Goddamn pansies think they can fight with a real man!" Blake said as he put his arms around Terry.

Terry began to cry.

"Oh, don't cry, Pretty. I'm not gonna hurt you. I'll be gentle. I promise."

Josh whacked the handle of the cue stick on top of one of the tables. It sounded like a gun shot.

"Let me tell you about the pansies in Beech Grove, mister!" Josh screamed. "We don't like you out of town perverts coming here and fucking with our boyfriends! So, if you want to get out of here in one piece, I suggest you do like the man said and scoot on out to your dune buggy!"

Terry bit his captor on the hand, then spun around and kneed him in the balls. Kurt pulled him away before Blake could recover and hit back. Donny came flying in from the restaurant, primed for the fight. He was followed closely by Hugh with meat cleaver in hand. Eddie took it away from him before he could hurt anyone. She also sent Donny back to the restaurant. She also called the sheriff's office.

"You and me, Mister Blake! Okay?" Josh said.

"You got it, fairy!"

"Not in here you don't!" Eddie shouted from behind the bar.

"Shall we?" Josh asked, indicating the front door.

Blake followed Josh out of the door, down the steps and out onto the great lawn. We all followed.

I never cared for boxing, but it's tame compared to watching two men slug it out bare fisted. I felt every blow in the pit of my stomach, and I hurt as much for Blake as I did for Josh. We supposedly had followed them out to the lawn to cheer them on, but we all just stood there in a state of mild trauma, including those we had considered as our enemies, unable to encourage our two warriors as their knuckles hit bone and tore flesh. There was a unanimous sigh of relief when the patrol car sped up the driveway.

Deputy Sheriff Michael Pilsudski, the official arm of the law for our little corner of the county, was the real hero to us that night—he stopped the fight before either of them got seriously hurt. And he sent the strangers on their way, with a polite, but firm, request not to return.

Hugh bought a round of drinks and we toasted Josh for his bravery in the face of danger, for his valiant defense of friends and community, for becoming the ninth and newest member of The Sunday Night Regulars.

I helped Josh up to his room, out of his clothes and onto his bed.

"Gimme a rubdown, Matt?"

"Sure."

While I was in the bathroom, he slipped out of his shorts. He was lying there naked, on his back, grinning at me when I came back with the oil.

"Is that sore, too?" I asked.

"No, just wanted to be comfortable," he said, still smiling.

"Roll over!"

"Anything you say."

"Ha ha."

I splashed the cold oil on his bruised back and sides.

"Shit!" he screamed.

"I thought that's what you wanted."

"Ha ha."

I rubbed oil into his back and shoulder muscles. He moaned.

"Why didn't you tell me you were planning your 'coming out' party tonight, Josh. I would've sent flowers or something."

"I didn't exactly plan it."

"You sure did it up big, though. A real whing-ding."

"Glad you enjoyed it. You know me, only the best."

"Yeah, I know."

"Remember the one I gave at school?"

"One what?"

"Party. The one with ten kegs, where that girl ran naked out into the street, right in front of the cops. Then afterwards, you and I . . ."

"I remember."

"Stay tonight? For old time's sake?"

"I can't."

"Yeah."

"You okay?"

"I'm fine."

"Sure?"

"Yeah. Really. Thanks for helping me. Thanks for . . . being a friend."

"Never doubt it, Josh. Never doubt it."

"Can I at least get a hug out of you?"

"Uh huh."

He rolled onto his back and propped himself up on his elbows. I leaned over him and tried to put my arms around him, but every time I touched him or either of us tried to move, he jerked with pain. We gave up.

"I owe you one," I said.

"I'll remember that. You'd better wash that grease off

before you go home. Elizabeth will think you've been messing around."

"Don't be ridiculous," I said, then went into the bathroom and washed the oil off my hands and arms.

It was closing time when I got back to the bar and I started to help Dad clean up, but Eddie asked me to go see if Donny was all right. She said he seemed stranger than usual when she threw him out of the bar earlier.

He was sitting on the front porch when I got to the house.

"Hey Donny."

"What are you doing here?"

"I love you, too."

"Sure."

"Just out for some air," I said.

"Bullshit," Donny said.

"Okay, I came to see if you were okay. Mom said you were acting strange . . . er."

"She would."

"Are you?"

"Strange? Yes."

"See? She was right."

"As always."

"Mom's are supposed to be right."

"Did you want something else?"

I sat next to him on the old porch swing and put my hand on top of his. He pulled away.

"Yeah. I'd like to know what the fuck is going on in that head of yours," I sounded meaner than I felt.

"Nothing, according to most people."

"Something."

"What do you care?"

"You're my brother."

"Big fucking deal."

"Donny, I do care about you."

"Since when?"

"Always."

"Always, Matt?"

Silence.

"Did you know Josh was going to tell everybody tonight?" Donny asked.

"You heard?"

"Yeah, I heard."

"I didn't know he was going to do it."

"Are you mad at him, Matt?"

"No. Why should I be?"

"For telling."

"Why should that bother me?"

"I don't know. I thought . . . I thought maybe it'd embarrass you or something. I don't know."

"No. I'm not embarrassed. Or mad. What Josh does is his business. He's my friend whatever he does."

"Do you love him?"

"Yes."

"Are you lovers?"

"No."

Silence.

"Would you be mad at me if I told everybody I'm gay?"

"Uh . . . I . . . guess not. Or I'd try not to be, anyway. Are you planning to do that, Donny?"

"Maybe. I'm really tired of pretending."

"Yeah. When?"

"Next Sunday."

"Next Sunday?"

"Yeah."

"Mother's Day? You're gonna do something like that on Mother's Day?"

"Why not?"

"Because it's Mother's Day! Why not Tuesday or Thursday, or even Saturday?"

"I want to do it at the bar. On Queer Night."

"Okay, then wait another week. Don't do it on Mother's Day. Please!"

"See how totally different we are, Matt. The way I see it, Mother's Day is the only day for something like this."

I left him sitting there on the porch, rocking back and forth in the swing, smirking as he went over and over his plans for Mother's Day. I told myself he would chicken out before the week was over.

It was almost two when I got home. Elizabeth was in bed, reading.

"Well, good morning!" Elizabeth said.

"Hi," I said.

"You look strange."

"Good. Then it matches the way I feel."

"Have you been a bad boy?" she asked.

"No. As a matter of fact, I've been an exceptionally good boy. I stood up for my friends against a gang of drunk and fairly large hoodlums. I helped our champion bind his wounds. And I did my duty to my family. A very good boy!"

"Well, that calls for something special. Did you bring your cue stick lance home? We could break a bottle of champagne over it."

"How'd you . . . ?"

"How did I know? Let's see. Ah yes. Eddie called. Aunt Gloria called. Jack called. Oh, and Gwen and Pat had to come here to pick up J.D. because he was here this evening—also being a good boy. Where was I? Oh yes. Well, I had to tell those people that I hadn't heard about the fight. And that the reason I hadn't heard about the fight was because you weren't home. And that I didn't know where you were. Or what time you'd be home."

"I'm sorry."

"Where the hell were you?"

"First, putting Josh to bed. Alone! Then I talked to

Donny because Mom was worried about him. He says he's going to pull a Josh next Sunday. Did they tell you what Josh did tonight, besides the fight?"

"Yes. And that part I'm happy about."

"You are?"

"Very. Why pretend?"

"Hm."

"What?"

"That's what Donny said tonight."

"He's right."

"I hope so. One thing, it's going to be one hell of a Mother's Day at Respighi's. Wanta come?"

"I'll pass."

"You sure?"

"I'm sure."

"You'll be missing a humdinger."

"I'll read about it in the Clarion."

"Front page."

"With banner headlines."

"Wanta rubdown?"

"Sure."

It didn't make headlines in the Clarion, but Donny kept his word and made his announcement as planned. It definitely was one hell of a Mother's Day at Respighi's.

Donny said the last thing he heard before he finally fell asleep that night was sort of a thud—whack—tinkle—crash.

Thud. Heavy piece of pottery hitting wood. The only thing made out of clay in the den was an ashtray—an ashtray Donny made for Mom in his seventh grade Arts and Crafts class. The wood, he guessed, was the mantel over the fireplace.

Whack. Pottery against glass, he thought. The glass in a picture frame.

Tinkle. The glass falling to the tile hearth.

Crash. Ashtray to hearth.

There were three photographs on the mantelpiece at that time. One was of the four of us taken at the zoo. The second was a picture of Eddie's father and his twin brother taken the year Eddie was born. The third was a copy of an old photograph of their father, Eddie's grandfather, Dick Delaney, taken with Buffalo Bill and Annie Oakely on the night that the twins, Matthew and Mark, were born.

8.   The Cinderella Music Box

When Esther died, when Esther ate the chocolate cake and then died, she left Eddie her one and only valuable possession. It was a music box. The box itself was made out of cherry wood. It was hand carved with minute designs, almost like an etching. The bottom pedestal was round and slightly separated from the upper pedestal, which was round at the bottom, but then became a hexagon at the top. Six triangular petals, came up from that forming a point at the very top. As the upper pedestal turned, the six petals would open to reveal a dancing, porcelain Cinderella. The insides of the petals were inset with mirrors which reflected light onto the figurine. Cinderella was bending slightly forward with her arms draped in front of her. Her hands were turned inward almost touching and her head was tilted to the side, looking at the glass slippers lying at the edge of the pedestal. The tune was the theme from Prokofiev's "Cinderella" ballet.

Eddie said she went to sleep to that tune every night for a month after Esther died. It made her dance in her dreams, she said. When Carl was in the Navy, when Eddie was running off to Long Beach every weekend, he got her a deluxe Hi-Fi set, complete with phonograph, and a recording of Prokofiev's "Cinderella." It was one of those new long-playing records. Eddie wore it out in less than a month, so Carl bought her three more copies of it.

Over the next few years—my early childhood—Eddie

expanded her record collection, but only with compositions
by Prokofiev: operas, ballets, symphonies and a boxed set of
the piano concertos, a collector's edition. That's the only
music I remember hearing as a child in that house. I enjoyed
it, I guess, but music wasn't very important to me in those
days and I tuned it out most of the time. Carl went to his
workshop when he didn't want to hear it and in later years
turned off his hearing aid. Mom's music was never a problem,
until Donny, as a teenager, discovered rock and roll.

We had a fairly decent stereo by that time and Donny
found that he could get one of the rock stations from San
Diego on the FM. Mom went into shock. She had no idea that
music had deteriorated so much since her youth, the days of
King Kole and His Krazy Kats. She tried to ban the playing of
rock and roll in the house, but Carl took Donny's side and the
battle was on. It wasn't that Carl liked rock music—he turned
his hearing aid off for that, too—he just wanted to be fair to
everyone. So, under the new rules Carl instituted, Donny and
Mom were supposed to take turns on the stereo, but whenever
one of them would leave the room for a minute, the other
would run over and change the music. That quickly became
unbearable, so Carl bought Donny his own stereo, to be
played only in his room. And "keep the damned door shut!"
Then we had Prokofiev blaring in the den and The Rolling
Stones blaring from Donny's room. I used to have to take my
homework over to Josh's to do it. And when college came
along, which everyone else said was noisy, it was like moving
into a soundproof room for me.

It became a part of their daily lives, cranking up the
volume to drown the other one out. I was astounded when I
returned to Beech Grove with Elizabeth and they were still
doing it. We had our own house, so I didn't have to listen to
the battle of the bands anymore, but I did have to listen to
them bitch about each other's music. I immediately bought
Donny the Sony Walkman with the earphones so he could

encase his head and scramble his brains with the latest and loudest heavy metal rock and roll, without disturbing Mom or either of them bitching to me.

I gave it to him on his sixteenth birthday.

"No cassettes?" he asked.

"Greedy. They're in the other box. And Elizabeth picked them out, so don't blame me if you don't like them."

He grabbed the cassettes and started off toward his room.

"Aren't you going to thank me . . . us?" I asked him.

"You didn't buy this for me. You bought it to make Mom happy. I'm sure she'll be thankful enough for the both of us." And he went to his room.

"That ungrateful little fu . . . !" I started to say, but was cut off by Eddie.

"Thank you, Matt," she said. "The perfect gift."

Donny and I didn't have another civil conversation from that day until last year's festival when he danced the Solstice Celebration as Pan and I ran out onto the lawn to hug and kiss him.

Donny had been only half right about the thud-whack-tinkle-crash he heard that night from the den, the night he made his announcement. Mother's Day night. It was the ashtray that he'd made for Eddie back in the seventh grade. It was not, however, one of the photographs she broke when she threw the ashtray. It was the Cinderella music box.

I went over there the next morning before going to work. I walked in the kitchen door and got blasted with the climax of Prokofiev's "Cinderella." There was no one in the kitchen. There were no dirty dishes in the sink. I poured myself a cup of coffee and went into the living room. The music coming up from the adjoining, sunken den was deafening. I stepped down into the den and lowered the volume, which had been cranked up to maximum.

That's when I saw that the music box was lying shattered on the hearth. Cinderella was in at least a dozen pieces. The wooden petals from the cone had all flown off their hinges, their mirrors cracked, and were scattered about the room. The bottom pedestal had rolled under a side table and the top pedestal was belly-up on the tile with its toothy mechanism exposed and its coil sprung.

"Leave that music alone!" I heard my mother scream from the master bedroom, on her way out to the den. "Oh, it's you," she said.

"Hi," I said.

"Shouldn't you be at the Clarion?"

"We ran out of coffee at home," I lied, "and I thought I'd stop by for a cup with you."

"Elizabeth bought a three-pound can on Friday," Eddie said.

"Well, Mom, how are you this morning? Where is everybody?"

"Your father is in his workshop as always."

"And . . . ?"

"And you should be at work."

"Mother, this is stupid!" I shouted. "Donny has every right to . . ."

"I don't want to talk about that! Or him!"

"He's your son!"

"I said . . . !"

"Okay, have it your way. Just tell me why you broke the music box."

"I didn't do it on purpose, you idiot! I was aiming for the photograph!" she said and left the room.

She didn't say which photograph she wanted to hit. And I didn't have the nerve to ask. I went to work.

Elizabeth was the only one of us Eddie talked to that whole week. Elizabeth said there were no dirty dishes in the sink because Eddie was refusing to cook. Dad made the coffee as usual when he got up and then he and Donny went out to the workshop for the rest of the day. They were making miniature cedar chests to sell at the upcoming festival and Donny was getting quite skillful at it, Elizabeth said.

It was a strange week. The two women spent day and night together, ignoring the rest of us completely. I finally got tired of cooking for myself and invited Carl and Donny over to eat with me. Donny thought my cooking was mediocre, or crappy as he called it, until I reminded him that they had had nothing but peanut butter sandwiches until I started feeding them. We didn't find out until Sunday what Elizabeth and Eddie had been up to.

Sunday began as usual with muffins—blueberry because it was my week to make the muffins—and coffee on the front porch. About two sips into the first cup of coffee, Donny appeared at the bottom of the porch steps with suitcase in hand.

"Good morning," I said.

"Maybe for you," he said.

"Want a muffin?" Elizabeth asked.

"Which week is it?" Donny hedged.

"It's blueberry! Jesus!" Elizabeth said.

"Okay." He came up the steps, put his suitcase by the front door and sat next to me on the rattan sofa.

"Coffee?"

"Sure."

"Are you going someplace?" I asked, indicating the luggage.

"I was . . . uh . . . hoping to . . . uh . . . come here."

"Here. Meaning?"

"Your house."

"Oh," Elizabeth and I said.

"I guess I could . . ." Donny began.

"You and Mom have it out?" I asked.

"No. She won't even speak to me so that we can fight it out. She just ignores me, like I'm not even there! She finally cooked a meal last night and she wouldn't let me have any of it!"

"You're exaggerating," I said.

"I am not! And she threw out the leftovers!"

"Elizabeth, you've been with her all week. Is he exaggerating?"

"I don't think so. She still won't say his name."

"Please let me stay with you. She's making me crazy!" Donny said.

"We'll have to have a conference," I said.

"You want me to get lost for a while?"

"No, we can go inside. Have some more to eat."

"Matt, if the purpose of this conference is to convince me Donny should stay here, we can skip it. Of course he can stay with us."

"Sure?"

"Yes."

"Okay kid, you got a new home. Temporarily."

"Thanks Matt. Thanks Elizabeth."

"If you want to go to the meeting with us this morning, I'll sit with you," I offered.

"I don't think I can take it today. You guys go without me."

"Okay. C'mon Queenie, we're late. Donny, will you clean this up?"

"Gotta do something to pay my rent. Right?"

"Right."

We left Donny with one blueberry muffin in his mouth and another poised in his hand. I had meant for him to clean up the dishes, not the muffins.

It was a beautiful, sunny morning, so the Sunday Service was held on the great lawn. Amelia's choir was singing "Amazing Grace" as we arrived. J.D. waved to us from the back row of the choir and got a scolding glare from Amelia. After the song, Hugh read the weekly announcements, mostly to do with the festival which was only a month away. He said there had been an offer from some early music society to play for the Solstice Celebration this year. There was polite applause. Elizabeth said we were declining the offer because the children did such a good job last year. There was generous applause. Gloria read an epic poem which I missed because my mind was straying. The sun was bright and there was a warm breeze wafting across the lawn. I stretched out on my back and gazed up at the top branches of the three oaks at the far end of the lawn. I looked for animal shapes, an old childhood game. My attention was brought back to the podium, however, when I heard Eddie's voice.

I sat up too quickly and got a head rush. It took me a second or two to focus, then I found myself looking at my mother as though it were the first time I'd ever seen her. Her hair was much grayer than I had realized. Her face was older, wrinkled. She had heavy neck lines and jowls were beginning to appear on the sides of her mouth. Her skin was tanned, which made her blue eyes stand out. For some reason she was wearing a blue smock.

"Why is she wearing a smock?" I whispered to Elizabeth.

"You'll see."

Eddie was reading from Gibran's *The Prophet*, one of the parts about children. I tried not to listen because I knew what it was leading to: our semi-annual lecture on why Elizabeth and I should have children . . . immediately. It started as soon as we got to Mom and Dad's house.

"Did you enjoy the piece I read this morning?" Eddie asked innocently.

"Very pretty, Mom," I said.

"Gibran's always been one of my favorites," Elizabeth said.

"He's so inspirational," Eddie continued. "Especially the things he says about children. Don't you think?"

"Is there any more coffee?" I asked.

"I'll get you some, dear," Elizabeth said.

"That's all right. I can get it."

I practically ran to the kitchen. I had to regroup my thoughts. I wanted to immediately counterattack with something about Donny—if she thought kids were such a great idea—but I knew I'd be cutting my own throat if I even mentioned his name. I was going to have to find some other diversion or Elizabeth and I were going to get three or four hours of haranguing about not giving Eddie some grandchildren. Carl saved the day.

"Psst," he called from outside the kitchen door.

"What?"

"Come out here. There's something you should see." I followed him around the back of the house to the window of my former bedroom, which had become Eddie's all-purpose room. Carl pointed through the window.

There was a partially painted canvas sitting on an easel in the middle of the room. The painting was of a music box. The box had six sides and the petals were open, but there was no Cinderella in the middle.

"Did Mom paint that?" I asked.

"Yeah. That's what she and Elizabeth have been doing all week. They even tried to glue the old box back together for a model, but it ain't so hot."

I looked at the table on the far side of the room. The broken music box was sitting on a velvet drape in the middle of the table. It was a mess. Only three of the six sides were up in their usual position and all the mirrors were cracked. The glass slippers were gone. And poor little Cinderella's head, half of her gown and one of her arms were missing.

I rushed back into the house, pretending not to hear Carl's pleas behind me.

"Mother!" I yelled as I ran into the living room, startling both of them.

"What?"

"I saw it!"

"Saw what?"

"He saw your painting," Elizabeth guessed.

"I like it," I said. "Are you going to do the Cinderella in the middle or something else?"

"I'm not sure," Eddie said. "I'm not even sure I'll finish it."

"You gotta finish it. How long you been working on it? I didn't even know you could paint."

Elizabeth gave me a "you're babbling" look, but I didn't care.

"Elizabeth's been helping me," Mom said.

"I like your smock, too," I said.

Elizabeth just shook her head.

"Elizabeth gave me several," Eddie said.

We kept up that mindless chatter all the way through the meal, mostly because of my efforts to avoid the subject of children. Elizabeth was no help at all, or very little. I was beginning to suspect that she secretly wanted the discussion to take place. During dessert, I brought up the other subject we were supposed to be avoiding.

"Donny seemed pretty upset this morning," I said.

Eddie slammed her knife and fork on the plate. Then silence. Elizabeth looked at me. I looked at Carl. He looked at Eddie. We all looked at Eddie. She got up, took her plate and dumped the whole thing—plate, silverware, napkin and pie—into the garbage can.

"Don't you want to know how your son is?" I shouted at her. "If you're going to throw your children out into the street, the least you could do is care what happens to them!"

Eddie went to the bedroom. Carl and Elizabeth just stared at me.

"Matt, your mother didn't . . ." Carl began.

"I know, Dad. I know she didn't throw him out. But she

drove him out. And I can't stand this idiotic game we're playing!"

"Time," he said.

"Yeah, time. And meantime we all go bananas!"

Eddie came out of the bedroom in a red smock, got her purse from the table by the front door, and went out.

"Where's she going?" I asked. "It's too early for her to be going to the bar."

"Probably wants to be alone is all," Carl said.

"C'mon, let's clean up the dishes before we go down there."

"You're going to the bar tonight?" Elizabeth asked.

"Of course I'm going. I always go."

"But . . . oh shit, I give up," she said and started carrying dishes to the sink.

Carl and I walked Elizabeth back to our house and went in to talk to Donny. He wasn't there. In a way, I hoped he'd show up at Respighi's that night, but I wasn't so sure I was up to that either.

Donny wasn't at the bar. Josh had loaned him his old motorcycle that afternoon and Donny had taken off into the hills.

The evening went as usual: The Regulars played bridge, argued, danced and drank; Dad, Josh and I played pool and drank. Every time one of us heard a noise outside, we'd all look to the door, expecting Donny to come walking in. But he didn't. At eleven, Eddie told Carl and me not to wait around for cleanup, so we walked home without her.

"You know, Matt," Carl said, "your mother isn't just thinking of herself when she tries to get you two to have kids. It appears that Donny's not going to be raising a family, and that makes you the end of the line. The end of the Russells."

"Didn't Big Don have any brothers?"

"Just sisters. You're the last."

"I don't know if keeping a family name going is enough justification for bringing kids into the world."

"I didn't mean you should do it just for that. Jesus, boy, don't you want a family?"

"We aren't sure."

"We? I asked you."

"I don't know yet."

"Elizabeth's not getting any younger."

"She's only twenty-eight! I really wish you wouldn't do this. It's hard enough dealing with Mom on the subject."

"All right. No more. Just wanted you to know how I felt."

He patted me on the back, then took off for home. Elizabeth was waiting up for me.

"Donny back yet?" I asked.

"No. Wasn't he at the bar?"

"He borrowed Josh's bike this afternoon. I thought he'd be back by now."

"Don't worry. He knows how to handle it. How did you and Eddie get along tonight?"

"Not one word."

"Are you surprised? You did get a little heavy over dessert."

"Well shit, it's not as though he committed murder!"

"A year ago, you weren't singing his praises either, if you'll recall."

"So he grew up. Or I grew up. She's a mother, for chrissake! She's not supposed to act like this!"

"Because she's a mother?"

"Yes!"

"You're amazing!"

"What?"

"Matt, she's also a human being. A person, just like every other person. With emotions. With needs. Anger. Fear. A person, darling . . . like you."

"But . . ."

"No buts. She's angry. She's frightened. She's hurt. And you don't help things by attacking her like that."

"I didn't att . . . I guess I did."

"Give her time."

"Time."

"I'm going to bed. You coming?"

"I think I'll wait for Donny."

Time. Time is what I need right now, I thought. The people in my life aren't acting normal. And I don't seem prepared to handle it. Donny's behavior was no big surprise, it just made me uneasy, as always. But Mom! Mom was being vindictive and I didn't want to believe she was capable of such things. I knew Elizabeth had an ulterior motive for pointing out to me that Mom was just being human. It was Elizabeth's contention that I had always compared her to Eddie, and Elizabeth was thinking that the comparison would be easier to live with after I saw that Eddie wasn't perfect. I wouldn't admit to Elizabeth that I had ever made such a comparison, but I decided that night that she was right.

I fell asleep on the couch sometime after two. Donny wasn't home yet.

9.   Brothers

There are no television sets in Beech Grove. We're too far out in the middle of nowhere, and blocked by mountains in every direction, to use conventional antennae. A few years ago, someone tried to sell us on a community antenna, which would have been placed on the highest hill and then cabled to each home, but the supporters couldn't get enough votes at the town meeting to pay for it. Same thing for the satellite system someone tried to sell us the year before last.

Actually, there is one TV set in Beech Grove. Rae and Gloria have a video cassette machine so Rae can show her old movies. About once a month, they throw a party and play more recent movies they get from some video club.

Never having been exposed to television as a child, it didn't bother me that we didn't have one. What disappointed me was that all the great shows had disappeared from radio by the time I was old enough to listen to them, shows that I wouldn't even have known existed except for the fact that every night after dinner, Carl would go sit by the radio and run the dial back and forth from one end to the other, complaining that all the great shows were gone. So, he'd tell me about them in great detail: Who the characters were and all the things that had happened to them over the years. Then last year, I got a catalog in the mail from a new company up in L.A. that was selling cassettes of old radio shows. I ordered a dozen on the first round and have been buying three or four a month since. When the new ones come in the mail, Carl and I hole up in his den with beer and popcorn and play them each twice. Fibber McGee & Molly, the Shadow, Grand Central Station, Superman, Lum 'n Abner, Burns and Allen, Jack Benny, Fred Allen, Lux Radio Theater, on and on; instant nostalgia, even if you weren't there at the time.

One of the problems I've found with not having a television is that when you can't sleep at night, you can't bury yourself in the late, late movies—something I learned to do in college when I did have a TV. So, when I can't sleep, I listen to old radio programs. But unlike TV, radio doesn't require you to be anchored in one spot, which allows you to run around and putter. When I can't sleep at night, I clean the house or rearrange the pictures on the walls or wash windows.

The cat usually helps me. The same cat Elizabeth adopted and then allowed to use my closet for littering her kittens. Her name was Panther Piss: black as a panther, full of piss and vinegar. I wanted to keep one of the cute little boy kittens and give all the others away, including their mother, Panther Piss. Elizabeth insisted we keep P.P. and give away the kittens. I insisted we have P.P. spayed, which Elizabeth said she would take care of. After the second litter, I took the cat to the vet myself. She didn't speak to me for months. The cat that is. Elizabeth's silent treatment only lasted a few days. When Panther Piss finally forgave me, we became the best of friends. And she used to help me clean house or rearrange pictures or wash windows when I couldn't sleep at night.

I awoke with a start at about three from my back-breaking nap on the couch. Donny still wasn't home, so I washed the windows in the living room. I was just starting on the kitchen, when I saw Donny coming up the driveway. He was pushing the motorcycle.

"Do you know it's four o'clock in the morning?" I said when he came in the back door.

"I know it's a quarter till," he said.

"Real smart. Where the hell have you been?"

"I ran out of gas."

"Couldn't you have called?"

"They don't have phones up in the hills," he said.

"What were you doing up in the hills in the middle of the night anyway?"

"I was riding the bike. Until I ran out of gas."

"You should've known better than to try to go that far, that long, on a tank of gas. You . . ." I stopped.

"Yes mother," he said.

"Yeah, I heard that, too. Sorry."

"I'm used to it. Kind of miss it lately."

I laughed. He looked like he was about to fall down. His clothes were torn and covered with dirt and grease. I pulled out one of the kitchen chairs from under the table and shoved it behind him. He plopped into it.

"What happened to your clothes?" I asked.

"The fucking bike fell over on me. You know that curve just beyond the pond where the road slopes the wrong way? I slipped on some loose gravel and down we went, me on the bottom."

"Shit. Are you hurt?"

"I don't think so."

"Did you accomplish anything on your ride?"

"I did. Until I had to push the sonofabitch all the way home!"

"Like what?"

"I lost it. My . . . uh . . . I can't think."

"Yeah. Let's get some sleep. We can talk tonight. Okay?"

"Sure."

I think Donny and I talked more that week than we had in our entire lives together. In the mornings, I went to work at the paper and Donny made miniature cedar chests with Carl, carefully avoiding going near the house and Mom. Josh was having a slow week, leading into the Memorial Day weekend, so the three of us played hooky in the afternoons to go hiking or motorcycle riding in the hills and to renew acquaintance with our private pool at the top of the creek.

Elizabeth and I barely saw each other all week. She was working on two paintings for the festival, neither of which I was allowed to see, and she had started rehearsals with the musicians and dancers for the Solstice Celebration.

I went over to Mom and Dad's house a couple of times. Carl was still spending most of his time out in the workshop, counting on "time" to smooth everything out. Eddie wouldn't talk to me about Donny, and I wouldn't *not* talk about Donny, so our conversations that week were tense and extremely brief. She had stopped work on her painting; the music box still had no Cinderella.

In the evenings that week, Elizabeth would come home from rehearsal and go straight into her art studio—formerly known as my den—to paint. Josh, Donny and I sat around the living room, ate junk food, drank beer and shot the bull. Josh left early most nights because his mornings began at six. Donny and I tried to get to know one another.

I don't know how it's possible to grow up in the same house with someone and not know anything about him, but I had somehow done just that. Everything I thought I knew about Donny was merely assumption on my part. And most of that was based on the assumption that he was like me. It never occurred to me that his life was not the same as mine.

Even the one thing I was certain about, his overactive sex drive, turned out not to be the way I had perceived it. Donny was a very horny twelve when I went away to college, sixteen when I returned. I assumed he went through the usual experimentation with other boys. I assumed that he then had gone on to girls, with all the frustrations that entails, losing his virginity to some hot-pantsed, out of town visitor to the festival. I assumed that he then, by some process I wouldn't be able to understand, had decided he was gay. And the rest was the history we were living at that moment, I assumed. What I learned in talking to Donny those nights, was that he hadn't had any sex life at all.

"You've got to be kidding," was my response.

"Nope," he said.

"No one?"

"No one."

"That's not normal," I blurted out, again showing my incredible sensitivity.

"Believe me, I know," he said quietly.

"I didn't mean that, Donny. What, uh, I mean . . . you used to be all over me. I assumed that you . . ."

"You left."

"What does . . . I'm your brother, for chrissake!"

"So I've been told a thousand times."

"What does that mean?"

"It means that's all I've heard as long as I can remember. Your brother does this, your brother does that. Your brother doesn't do this, your brother doesn't do that."

"Who?"

"Eddie!"

"Mom's never been like that."

"To you maybe. But then you didn't have the perfect older brother."

"I don't believe you."

"Suit yourself."

"I didn't mean that either. I don't know what to think. She was never anything but understanding with me. Dad, too."

"They were understanding with you because you never did anything wrong."

"That's not exactly true."

"Not to hear her tell it."

"Not Carl?"

"Shit, I don't ever remember him even getting involved

in any of it. He was always out in his workshop—or 'turned off.'"

"Well, he had to get involved when you got your spanking."

"Jesus, where were you? Oh yeah, you always had your nose in some book. Dad never spanked me. Mom did."

"Really?"

"Really. And plenty of times, too."

"But Carl said only one."

"Carl didn't know anything about it. I asked for it most of the time, I guess, but sometimes it was just little stuff, like tearing my clothes after school or forgetting to bring my lunch pail home."

"Did she hit you hard?"

"Just once," Donny said, then got a strange look on his face, a painful look. "Third grade. Miss Blankenship kept the whole class after school one day and I had to piss so bad I thought I was gonna explode. I raised my hand once, but she waved that ruler of hers at me and I put my hand down in a hurry. I knew I wouldn't be able to hold it for the whole hour she was keeping us, but I didn't want to get swatted with the ruler or take home the note I knew she'd send to Mom if I disobeyed. So I sat there fidgeting and crossing and uncrossing my legs until I couldn't hold it any longer. At first, I couldn't believe it was really happening. I was pissing my pants! My lap and the insides of my legs got hot and then I could feel the piss running into my shoes. And I could hear it hitting the floor when it ran off the edge of the seat. I wanted to scream, I wanted to cry. I just froze. And I blushed hotter than I thought my face could get. I sat there shaking. The piss was starting to get cold. I was waiting for the whole world to cave in on me. I knew what was coming. I knew Miss Blankenship was going to scream at me in front of the other kids. I knew the kids were going to laugh and call me names. I wished I was dead right then, Matt. I really wanted to die, so I wouldn't have to go through what they were going to do to me. Suddenly, Miss Blankenship stood up at her desk. I could hear my heart pounding out loud. She dismissed the class. I couldn't believe it! It had only been about a half an hour. I fumbled with the papers and books on my desk so I could be the last one out of the room. At least if she caught me, it wouldn't be in front of the entire class. She got up from her desk and said something about having to run an errand and she asked me if I'd mind cleaning the blackboards for her while she was gone. She told me there was a box of old rags in the closet I could use."

"You think she knew?"

"She knew."

"I didn't think the old bitch could be that . . . understanding."

"And I never thought of her as an old bitch."

"Is that why Mom spanked you? For wetting your pants?"

"Yeah. And while I was still in my wet pants. With a belt."

"Ouch. What'd she say?"

"Jesus, Matt, I really don't remember."

"Yeah, I guess not. I don't know what to say, Donny. I guess I was . . . I'm sorry."

I don't know if I was expecting some kind of forgiveness from him or what, but I felt disappointed when he got up from the couch, without saying a word, and went to bed. I sat there by myself for almost an hour trying to figure out why I thought he should forgive me and wondering how two boys could grow up in the same family and have such different lives.

Panther Piss jumped into my lap with a meow and a purr. I threw her off and went to bed.

The Memorial Day weekend was a disaster. Elizabeth had her music and dance to rehearse and her paintings to paint, so I didn't see her all weekend. We were supposed to have Saturday night together, but on Friday night, Amelia climbed up on a stepladder to change a light bulb and fell off, breaking her leg. Doc Weston and Carl took Amelia to a hospital in Riverside. Elizabeth took over the choir, which had to practice on Saturday night, so they would sound beautiful on Sunday morning. The Beech Grove Hot Springs Hotel was jammed with tense guests from the city who all wanted hot baths and massages, so Josh had to work double shifts all weekend. He hired Donny to clean out the rooms, keep up with towels and so on. Eddie and I weren't speaking. Carl had to keep Eddie company. I was all alone.

On Saturday, I worked on the special edition of The Clarion we would be putting out for the festival, but half of the stuff I needed hadn't come in yet, so I gave up and went home. I made a peanut butter and banana sandwich and listened to my cassette of Orson Welles' infamous Mercury Theater presentation of H.G. Welles' "The War of the Worlds."

On Sunday, Elizabeth had to leave early to work with the choir before the service, which meant we didn't have our muffins and coffee on the front porch. I borrowed Josh's motorcycle and went riding up in the hills. I just wasn't in the mood for inspirational readings at Sunday Service. It was the first time I'd gone riding alone. Usually I rode behind Josh or borrowed a bike from someone in town and we'd take off racing over those narrow, bumpy dirt roads, shouting at each other over the horrible racket of the engines and generally acting like adolescents. You don't see much or do much thinking when you go riding up in the hills like that. I could see why Donny liked to go up there alone. I found myself looking at things I'd never noticed before. There were trees that I didn't know we had. I wondered if one of them could be a beech tree. That'd frost old Professor Dhunwhit, I thought. I really got into that ride, stopping a few times to climb a boulder or a low tree, just to sit and look around. I went as far back into the hills as the fire roads would let me, and before I knew it, it was getting dark. I headed back toward the village, but the damn bike conked out on me less than halfway back. I was out of gas! I had to push the sonofabitch all the way home. And there was no one there to yell at me for being so stupid. I took a shower and went to bed hungry, wondering if it meant anything that this was the first Sunday I'd ever spent in Beech Grove without having dinner at Mom's house.

On Monday, Elizabeth had gone off somewhere before I even woke up. I made blueberry muffins and coffee for myself. I sat on the front porch by myself. I ate all the muffins and drank all the coffee by myself. I also washed the dishes by myself. Then I walked over to Mom and Dad's house, not remembering until I was all the way up the steps that they had gone to Riverside to bring Amelia home from the hospital. I went to the hotel to see what Josh and Donny were up to. Generally, they were up to their ears in fat women and hairy old men and, at that particular moment, mud.

The mud pond is secluded at the far southwest corner of the hotel property, behind a row of olive trees. It's a bowl-shaped pool, concrete lined, with about a foot of clay mud at the bottom and a foot of water on top of that.

When I arrived, one of Josh's assistants said he and Donny were at the mud pond, so I wandered on back there. The path to the pond was roped off, a little sign indicated that it was temporariy unavailable to guests. I stepped over the rope and followed the path through the row of olive trees to the pond.

Josh was giving Donny a lesson in the therapeutic attributes of mud. At least that's what Josh said he was doing. To all appearances, it seemed he was ritualistically making love to Donny's body. As I arrived pondside, Josh was standing behind and slightly off to the side of Donny, with one hand on Donny's hip and the other on his belly. Josh was rubbing mud into Donny's belly button, paying inordinate attention, I thought, to the narrow row of hair running down from Donny's navel into his swim trunks.

I cleared my throat. They both flinched.

"Oh, and be sure to warn them not to wear light-colored bathings suits," Josh said. "Hi Matt, whatcha doin'?"

"Interrupting, apparently," I said.

"No problem. Why don't you join us?"

"Yeah," Donny said. "Josh's showing me the best way to use the mud."

"So I see."

"You coming in or what?" Josh asked as his hand slid down Donny's lower belly and came to rest on the elastic of Donny's trunks.

"No thanks," I said. "I've got work to do."

"Sorry you can't join us," Josh said.

"Sure you are. Just remember that anyone can step over that little rope you have out there, just like I did."

"I'll remember."

"Seeya Matt," Donny said, then noticed that I was staring at his growing erection. He sat down in the mud.

"Don't wash it off yet, Donny," Josh said. "You're supposed to lie out in the sun and let the mud dry first."

"Bye," I said. And left.

I went home. I poured myself a beer in a chilled mug, then stretched out on the couch to listen to a radio dramatization of Jack London's *The Call of the Wild*. Panther Piss crawled up onto my stomach and we both fell asleep.

When I woke, around eight that evening, Elizabeth was standing at the end of the couch with one of her many large handbags draped from her shoulder.

"You finally getting home?" I asked, not awake.

"I've been home for hours, painting. I'm just on my way out again. I left you some soup on the kitchen table. I'll be late. Don't wait up for me.

She left. I dragged myself off the couch and went into the kitchen. Donny came in the back door just as I sat down to the soup. Good, I thought, now I'll have someone to talk to.

"You just getting off?" I asked him.

"Yeah. Goddamn, what a weekend! Those people are crazy! The guests, I mean. They want everything done for them, and they want it now. Jesus! I'm really beat. Josh says I can help out every weekend, if I want. Hell, it pays more than those stupid little cedar chests. Besides, I can be with Josh more that way. He's . . ."

"You can be what?"

". . . really terrific! No wonder you guys stayed friends all these years. I bet you used to make it with him, didn't you?"

"No!"

"I wouldn't blame you. That guy sure knows his way around a bed."

"He knows what?"

"He says he used to mess around a lot in college, but . . ."

"Where were you last night, anyway?"

". . . that he's looking for something on a more permanent basis now. He asked . . ."

"Oh he is, is he?"

". . . me to move in with him at the hotel and I think I should. You . . ."

"He what?"

". . . and Elizabeth can have the house to yourselves again now. Bet that's a relief, huh? I'm gonna get my stuff together and go on over there tonight. I'll see you tomorrow. Or sometime during the week, probably. Bye."

"Bye."

I ran through a myriad of unfamiliar emotions sitting there over that bowl of coagulating tomato soup. Unfamiliar in connection with my little brother and my best friend, anyway.

The first was repulsion. As much as I tried to avoid it, I kept getting an image of Josh and Donny fucking, and it made me feel slightly ill. For some reason, though, my imagination wouldn't identify who was fucking whom, but it was definitely the two of them locked in sweaty, anal intercourse. I tried to dispel my feelings of disgust by remembering that I'd had sexual experiences with both of them, but it didn't work. My times with each of them had been in youthful exuberance, adolescent horniness, those days of perpetual hard-ons and sexual confusion. There had been no romance, no thoughts of love, no real desperation, no reality.

I felt guilt, which I was unable to explain to my complete satisfaction. Guilt perhaps because I thought, as a supposed open-minded individual, I shouldn't have been turned off by their relationship. I thought I had accepted the gay couples I knew, but apparently I had not been deeply enough involved with any of them to evoke such an emotional response in me. Guilt, perhaps, because I wondered if I had somehow failed Donny as a brother.

The reaction that blew me away, the one I tried to suppress immediately, the feeling I fought but ultimately couldn't deny—was jealousy. And that scared me. Did I secretly want to be lovers with one of them? I thought not. How could their relationship threaten me? Why was I not elated by the promise of their finding love in each other? It was a loss; something was lost to me. I loved them both. Wouldn't their love for one another lessen their love for me? Nonsense, I told myself. But, if not, why this incredible sense of loneliness?

I felt Elizabeth's hands slide over my shoulders and down my chest to my belly, then return to the shoulders with her fingernails barely gliding over the surface of the skin. I felt her lips against the side of my neck, behind my ear. I felt her teeth biting gently at my earlobe. I felt her soft breathing in my ear, the wetness of her tongue, blocking out the sounds of my mind.

I felt the cool sheets along my back and on the backs of my legs, her smooth caress over my chest and belly, her light touch on my cock. I felt her warm body under mine. I felt the softness of her breasts with my cheek and with my lips. I felt the strength of her back as I reached around her and held the world in my arms. I felt her hot moisture engulf me.

I felt the gentle purring of a cat against the inside of my leg. I felt the softness of its pure black hair, the warmth of its sleek sides. I felt a gentle caress as its tail moved across the back of my leg, and as it touched Elizabeth's thigh.

I felt my eardrum cave in as Elizabeth screamed! Then as the cat screamed! I felt the cat's claws dig into my scrotum. I felt my cock shrivel to nothingness as the cat struggled in vain to free herself from my stretching, bleeding flesh. I felt excruciating pain as I reached down and slowly removed the claws, one by one.

I felt the sweetness of revenge as I picked up that fucking cat and threw her against the wall on the other side of the room.

10.   Diary of A Honeymoon

Friday, June 1. 10 p.m.   Elizabeth was cloistered in the den/art studio and I was buried in Oscar Wilde's "The Ballad of Reading Goal", when Josh and Donny burst in, shouting and jumping up and down like a couple of hyped up bubble gummers.

"Matt! Elizabeth!" Donny shouted from the entry hall.

"I'm right here, Donny," I said.

"Hi!" he said. "Where's Elizabeth?"

"Here," Elizabeth said, squeezing out through the half open door from her studio, ever-protective of her secret paintings.

"I . . . we . . . you . . ." Donny stammered.

Josh put a hand on Donny's shoulder and squeezed, but it didn't calm him. Josh had to tell the story.

"This old friend of mine from college, Gary—I think you met him once, Matt—anyway, he was one of that mob of guests we had at the hotel last weekend; didn't know I was working there or anything, just showed up and we gave him the royal treatment. I made sure he didn't get charged for anything. So, he just called and he's giving us—he's the assistant manager or something at the Hyatt Regency in Long Beach—he's giving us a suite tomorrow night. Free! It's honeymoon time!"

"That's great," I said—meaning it, but embarrassed by his honeymoon remark.

"You're going with us!" Donny said.

"Won't that be a little crowded?" Elizabeth asked.

"There's two bedrooms in the suite," Josh replied.

"Oh," I said.

"I don't . . ." Elizabeth began.

"You guys gotta go," Josh interrupted. "You never got a honeymoon. I know it's only two days and one night, but it's first class all the way!"

"We . . ." I began.

"Wasn't your dad in the navy there?" Josh interrupted.

"Yeah. And I used to go to the Pike a lot with this girl I worked with on the school paper."

"Who?" Elizabeth asked.

"Josh, I think that's when you and Gary were living together," I said.

"Living together?" Donny asked.

"Too bad they tore the Pike down. Ever go on the Rotor?" I hurried on, wishing I hadn't mentioned that girl or Gary.

"No," Josh said, also hurrying along. "Come on, go with us. There's lots of things to do there. The Queen Mary. The Spruce Goose. The Beach."

"Yeah, okay," I said. "What time do you want to leave?"

"Daybreak!" Donny said.

"We'll pick you up around seven," Josh said. "I'm borrowing one of the hotel station wagons."

"Better get packin'," Donny added. "Us too! Come on, Josh!"

Donny took Josh by the hand and led him out.

"See you in the morning!" I shouted after them.

"You might," Elizabeth said. "I won't."

"What?"

"I can't just run off on a moment's notice. I've got too much to do."

"It can wait two days."

"It cannot."

"I'll help you."

"Help me what?"

"Whatever."

"Well, I'm not about to let you touch one of my paintings."

"Touch? See!"

"So I guess you could work with J.D. on his fingering," she said.

"Fingering?" I said.

"Flute."

"Oh. Don't you have something else?"

"Melissa's bowing?"

"Try again."

"Choreography?"

"Skipped that class, too."

"You don't do much, do you?"

"Tell you what. Next week, I'll do all the work around here: washing, ironing, cooking, cleaning. You name it, I'll do it?"

"Anything?"

"Anything!" I said, already beginning to wonder if I had been set up.

"I would like to go, it sounds like fun," she said. "You'll do everything?"

"For a week," I said.

"Okay. Let's pack."

Elizabeth had been delighted when Josh and Donny got together. At first, I thought it was primarily because Donny had moved out of our house, but gradually she convinced me she was genuinely happy for them.

Eddie, on the other hand, was not delighted. She was still immovable on the subject, deaf to any sentence which included Donny's name. I didn't call her to tell her we were going away for the weekend. I couldn't have explained it without mentioning Josh and Donny, so she wouldn't have listened anyway.

Saturday, June 2. 9 a.m.   The Pike was gone. The beautiful old Municipal Auditorium was gone. Rainbow Pier was gone. Even the physical layout of the shoreline had been changed. An elevated, cement and brick promenade runs all the way from the downtown area out to the Hyatt hotel, then over the new Shoreline Drive highway to the new marina and shopping village. Next to the hotel is the new entertainment complex with a large theater, a small theater, a sports arena and a convention center. On the other side of the marina, across a waterway and on a small peninsula, are the Queen Mary, the Spruce Goose and another small shopping village.

We had a VIP suite on the seventeenth floor. Gary took us up himself after a tour of the meeting, lounging, sunning, swimming, drinking and eating facilities on the first three floors. (With Donny watching his every move, by the way.) It was first class all right. The parlor room, as Gary called it, was very large and very lush, with a wall of windows overlooking the entire harbor and the sea beyond. Everything was dark, seemingly hand carved woods. There was a dining table for six with matching étagère and a large wet bar. The sitting area had a wood framed sofa with dark green cushions and matching chairs. The black topped coffee table and side tables matched the dining table. There was a stereo with both cassette player and turntable. And, of course, a television set. Gary left, apologizing for not being able to pick up our food and drink tabs as well, which Josh assured him was no problem. Josh and Donny paid for everything else that weekend. Between them, they had made over four hundred dollars in tips over Memorial Day.

"Four hundred?" I gasped.

"Four hundred twenty-seven dollars and fifty cents," Josh said.

"You must be really good," Elizabeth said.

"He is," Donny said, which caused an abrupt halt to the conversation.

We each grabbed a suitcase and headed toward a bedroom, one at each end of the parlor. Josh and I both started toward one, Elizabeth and Donny toward the other. We all giggled, nervously, then changed partners and went off to our respective bedrooms to unpack. Supposedly by chance, Elizabeth and I got the room with the two double beds, while Josh and Donny got the room with the king.

"Let's go to the beach!" Josh shouted from their bedroom.

"Okay!" Elizabeth shouted from our bedroom and then started to undress.

"Whata you mean, 'okay?'" I asked in a whisper. "I want to eat first."

"You don't have to whisper," she said. "And we can get sandwiches and drinks to go. Get dressed. Undressed. Oh! First, go get my little bag out on the bar. I can't go out there like this." "This" meaning bra and skirt.

I went out into the center room. Josh and Donny were standing in the doorway to their room, kissing. I rushed back into our room and closed the door.

"Where's the bag?"

"They're kissing!" I shouted in a whisper.

"So what? I need the bag."

"I guess it'll have to wait."

"You're an idiot!" she announced, then opened the door and went out there in bra and skirt.

"I guess you two will have to close your door when you kiss," she told Josh and Donny. "It embarrasses Matt."

"Elizabeth!" I called from the bedroom.

"See?" she said and then came back and stood in our doorway.

"What are you doing?" I asked.

"Come here."

"Huh?"

"Come here."

"Why?"

"Just come over here a second. Will you please?"

I walked slowly over to her. She grabbed me by the neck with both hands and locked us into a kiss. Josh and Donny applauded from their doorway. I broke loose from her, after some struggle, and slammed the door!

Saturday. Noon.   I took the time to unpack everything and carefully put things away—and got accused of pouting—so we didn't leave for the beach till almost noon. We stopped at the village bakery and got two croissant sandwiches each, bottled juices and a dozen muffins, half bran and half blueberry. The beach didn't start until the far end of the marina, so we got to see how the other half, the yacht half, lives as we walked the half mile or so to the sand.

Right where the boat slips stop and the beach begins, they had a large, fenced area set off, which was filled with sailboats of every description, including wind-surfers and catamarans. A man leaning on the fence told us the sailors were competing for places on the U.S. Olympic team. I wanted to find a place on the sand near there so we could watch them when they went out for the afternoon, but Josh insisted we go farther down the beach—where it wasn't so crowded, he said.

We walked at least another half mile, passing any number of clean, uncrowded places, and Josh just kept pushing on.

"See? It's closer to the bathrooms and the lifeguard," Josh said when he finally tossed his towel on the sand.

"Yeah, I guess so," I said, unconvinced.

Donny was smirking as we laid out the blankets, towels, oils, lotions, drinks and food. I had ripped the cellophane off and had almost devoured my first sandwich before I took a good look around us. In the first place, it was even more crowded than the place back by the sailboats. But the outstanding feature of that little stretch of beach was that the men were with other men and the women were with other women.

"I think we're on a gay beach," I whispered.

"No shit, Sherlock," said Donny.

"This boy is quick," said Josh.

"Darling, you amaze me at times," said Elizabeth.

That's when I noticed that Josh and Donny were practically on top of each other at the other end of our blanket. Elizabeth took my hand when she saw that I was staring at them.

"It's like any other part of the beach, Matt," she said. "Couples lying out on the sand, holding hands, a little kiss now and then."

"Was the conspiracy necessary? You could've simply told me you wanted to go to a gay beach."

"And you wouldn't have gone," Josh said.

"I might have," I said.

"Bull," Donny said.

"Be brave, dear," Elizabeth said. "I'll protect you."

"I'm not worried about that."

"Then what are you worrying about?"

"Nothing."

I got out another sandwich and ate it, watching some kids playing in the water back up the beach a few yards. Josh and Elizabeth decided to go for a swim. When they left, Donny moved over closer to me.

"Matt?"

"What?"

"Don't be mad."

"I'm not," I lied.

"I remember reading an editorial you wrote about prejudice."

"You read one of my editorials? I didn't know you could even read."

"I don't read very well, Matt. It never came easy for me the way it did for you. I have to stop all the time and figure out the hard words, so . . ."

"Shit, Donny, I didn't mean to . . ."

"But, when there's something I really want to read, I take the time to work it out. I always like your editorials, so I take the time to read them."

"I remember that one on prejudice. And I am being very prejudicial. And an asshole. I'm sorry. Hey, let's go swimming!"

When we got into the surf, Elizabeth pulled me off to the side, out of Donny's hearing. Josh was way out by the buoy.

"I told you we shouldn't have come on this trip," she said.

"But not because of them and my attitude. You said it was because you had too much to do."

"At the time, I thought that was the reason."

"So?"

"Well, just because I thought it was the reason doesn't mean that it was."

"I can't argue with your superior logic."

When we got back up on the sand, Elizabeth covered my backside with lotion and I stretched out on my stomach, hoping to fall asleep. Elizabeth grabbed her pad and went off to sketch the lifeguard. Josh and Donny took turns oiling one another down, then lay on the blanket facing each other.

"Water wasn't as cold as I thought it'd be," Josh said.

"Yeah," Donny said.

"You going to work with me next weekend?"

"I'd like to."

"I was thinking about putting you on the whirlpools this time. You know, helping people in and out, making sure they don't stay in too long."

"Okay."

"It's not as menial as the cleanup job."

"I don't care about that. I'll do anything."

"Think you'd like to do this sort of thing for a living?" Josh asked Donny.

"I don't know. I guess so."

"Don't you think it's time you started thinking about what you're going to do with your life?"

"Not particularly."

"Shit, Donny, you can't just bum around forever."

"I wasn't planning to."

"What about your dad's business? Ever thought about going in with him?"

"He wants me to. I think it's boring, day after day out in the workshop, doing the same thing week after week."

"Maybe, but there's the odd jobs around town."

"For people who want you to do next-to-impossible stuff, for next-to-nothing money. I like what you do better."

"Why don't you let me train you then?"

"What would I have to do?" Donny asked.

"Whatever it takes! Damnit, Donny, don't be so lazy!"

"Hey! I didn't mean it that way. I was just curious."

"Sorry. Uh, well, you'd do just about everything around there. Except physical therapy and massages; you have to be licensed for that. Later, I could send you to school, if you're still interested."

"You'd do that for me?"

"Yeah, sure."

"Thanks."

"You're welcome."

"I wish we were back in the room right now."

"Me too. That's okay, we'll have *all* night."

"I know, but now would be so nice. I'm ready."

"So I see," Josh said.

"What if I put the towel over you?"

I choked. They both laughed. Donny rolled onto his stomach, reached over and patted me on the back of the head.

"Sorry, Matt," he said.

Saturday. 6 p.m.   We stayed on the beach until five o'clock, getting sunburned, sandscraped and waterlogged. Josh invited half the people on the beach to come to Beech Grove to see Donny dance as Pan in the Summer Solstice Celebration, "directed by my friend, Elizabeth," I heard him tell someone, "the pretty one over there next to the nervous straight guy in the blue trunks."

We got back to the Olympic competition area just in time to see them coming in, about forty of them sailing in a line around the end of the jetty and up onto the beach. We applauded them.

"Beautiful," I sighed.

"They sure are," said Elizabeth, ogling a muscular young man who had begun to peel off his wet suit.

"Hm," agreed Donny and Josh.

"Can we go back to the hotel now?" I asked.

There was complimentary champagne awaiting us in our suite, plus a full bar setup. We showered, dressed, killed the champagne and started on the cocktails.

Josh mixed the drinks; he seemed to be enjoying his role as our host. As soon as we each had a drink in hand, he raised his glass:

"To the honeymoon," he toasted.

"And the honeymoon night!" Donny added.

I hesitated. Elizabeth elbowed me. We all drank to the honeymoon.

"Matt, will you relax," Josh said. "We're not going to get it on out here in the *parlor*."

"Can we talk about something else?"

"No. We're here to have a good time, which we are going

to have, with you or without you. But it would be a hell of lot more fun if you weren't so uptight."

"I'm very sorry if I'm spoiling your honeymoon."

"You're not spoiling anyone's honeymoon. We'd just like to have you with us. We like you."

"Thanks."

"Elizabeth?" Josh pleaded.

"I don't know what to do with him either."

"Okay, okay," I said. "You made your point. I will stop being uptight as of right now. Hold hands, if you want. Kiss all you like. You can fuck on the dining room table for all I care. In fact, I'll sell tickets. And popcorn."

Josh grabbed Donny and laid him back on the dining table, burying his head between Donny's shoulder and neck, one leg up over Donny's hip.

"I didn't mean it!" I screamed.

"Just kidding," Josh said, collecting our glasses for another round of drinks.

"Where do we want to eat tonight?" I asked.

"Here," Josh said.

"The restaurant did look nice," I said.

"No, here in the room," he said. "I ordered our dinner sent up."

"I was hoping we'd go out," I said. What I was hoping was that we'd have dinner in a public, straight place so Josh and Donny couldn't have their hands all over each other during dinner.

Three waiters brought our banquet in and set it up. One stayed behind to serve. The gay one. He flirted with Donny all through dinner. And Donny ate it up. I wondered if Josh and/or Gary had arranged that, too. Dinner was prime ribs of beef with all the trimmings, topped off with fresh, organically-grown, huge strawberries in some kind of liqueur, and further topped with a bottle of Remy Martin cognac. We all got blitzed, including the waiter, whom Josh threw out the door because he went from cruising Donny to touching Donny.

Saturday. 10 p.m.   I was ready for bed at ten o'clock, but the Three Musketeers wanted to go downstairs to one of the bars. I told them they could go without me.

"Are you gonna start that shit again?" Josh asked.

"I'm not starting any shit. I'm tired. I want to go to sleep."

"We don't want to go without you," Donny said.

"Come on, Matt," Elizabeth said. "It's a short weekend. You can sleep when we get home."

"Let him stay up here and pout," Josh said.

"I'm not pouting!"

"So go with us. They've got a band in that lobby bar. Or, if you prefer something less strenuous, there's a piano bar in the restaurant cocktail area."

"It's late."

"It's not late."

"We won't touch each other!" Donnie blurted out.

They all laughed. I laughed.

"Okay," I said.

"Good!" Josh said. "Who shall we be?"

"Whata you mean, 'Who shall we be?' "

"When you're out of town drinking, you gotta pretend to be something. You know, you make an entrance with a flurry, arguing or talking loudly about the movie you just directed or the dinner you had with the Reagans, anything to shake up the place."

"I hardly think that's necessary."

"I could be a renowned artist," Elizabeth offered.

"No good," Josh said. "Most people in bars wouldn't know an artist if it bit 'em."

"Thanks a lot."

"You know what I mean."

"I don't see why we . . ." I tried.

"How about a visiting French delegation to the, uh, to the Olympics?" Josh suggested.

"Matt wouldn't get away with it. His French accent is terrible," Elizabeth said.

"Thanks, sharee."

"It's true."

"I don't even have a French accent to be terrible with," Donny said.

"Okay, not French. But what? C'mon guys."

"Why don't we do the movie thing, like you said in the first place?" Donny asked.

"Yeah!" Elizabeth said. "People are always impressed by Hollywood magic. You be the director, Josh, and I'll be the star . . . let."

"All right!" Josh said. "Donny, you're a, uh, producer!"

"He's too young," I said.

"Okay, *old man*, you be the producer," Donny said.

"I didn't mean . . ."

"I know. You were right. I am too young. I can be . . ."

"My lover!" Josh interrupted. "Hollywood people always have . . ."

"Forget it!" I said. "He can be your directorial assistant. No lovers!"

"Thought that'd get you interested. Okay, let's hit it!"

We entered the bar with the required flurry—and were completely ignored. Apparently those people were used to Hollywood magic. Or we weren't very convincing. I suspect the latter.

So we quietly took a table and ordered drinks. We sat through over an hour of Cole Porter songs from the pianist/singer, who was on the verge of being good, meaning that he sounded not-so-good with the first drink, better with the second drink, and good after three drinks.

Donny kept his promise and didn't touch Josh the whole

time we were in there. The fact that I sat between them may have had something to do with his behaving himself.

When the entertainer started to repeat his repertoire, I insisted we leave. Even with that much liquor in my system, I knew I wouldn't be able to sit through another time of his serenading Donny with his version of "Anything Goes."

Saturday. Midnight. We were exhausted from the long day, the hot sun, the fresh air, the food and the booze, so it was off to our respective bedrooms when we got back up to the suite.

"Damn! My shoulders are on fire!" I screamed as I fell onto the bed.

"I'll put some lotion on you. Get undressed. Oh! First, go out and get the rest of the cognac. We can have a nightcap while I rub you down."

"You know what happened the last time you sent me out there."

"I heard their door close. You're safe."

As I tiptoed out to the bar, I heard shouting from Josh and Donny's room. I grabbed the Remy and two glasses and was heading back to our room when I heard one of them use my name. I sneaked closer to their door.

". . . for his benefit," I heard Donny say.

"That's bullshit!" Josh shouted.

"I wasn't coming on to him, he was coming on to me!"

"And you let him!"

"What was I supposed to do? Slap him or something?"

"No. Just not smile so much at him. He thought you were interested."

"Maybe I was," Donny said.

"Well, he can have you."

"Josh, please don't say that. I'm sorry. I didn't know what I was supposed to do. I've never had a waiter flirt with me before. I didn't mean to hurt you."

"It's okay, baby."

"Please don't be mad at me, Josh. I can't take it. Please."

I turned away from the door, and unfortunately clinked the glasses against the bottle.

"Good night, Matt!" Josh shouted from the other side of the door.

I ran back to Elizabeth.

"Where have you been?" she asked.

"Getting the cognac."

"What took you so long?"

"I couldn't find the glasses."

"You were listening."

"What listening?"

"You were! You were eavesdropping on them."

"Only for a minute."

"Anything juicy?"

"No. They were having a fight."

"Oh, that's too bad. I wanted this weekend to be special for them. But, I guess everyone fights."

"I think they're making up."

"Good."

"They were fighting about the waiter."

"Brazen little hussy, wasn't he?"

"All because we stayed *in* for dinner."

"Matt, don't."

"I told you we should've gone out for dinner."

"But not because you were afraid they might have a fight. It was because you were afraid they might neck."

"At the time, I thought that was the reason."

"So?"

"Well, just because I thought it was the reason doesn't mean that it was."

"Kiss me," she said.

We shared the cognac. We shared the lotion. We shared one of the double beds.

Sunday, June 3. 11:30 a.m.   Josh and Donny were the first up that morning. They were sitting on the sofa, dressed only in towels and with wet hair, when I staggered, bleary-eyed and hungover, out into the parlor. They both smiled at me. I ran back into the bedroom to get Elizabeth. I didn't want to be alone with them in a half-awake state.

A complimentary continental breakfast was delivered to the suite: a quart of orange juice, fresh melon, a dozen danish with various fillings, and two pots of coffee. We all commented on how strange it was that we were all so hungry after that big dinner we'd eaten the night before. Those comments were followed by cheap honeymoon humor, then forced giggles and faked embarrassment. Theirs was faked; mine was genuine.

Elizabeth ruffled up the covers and pillows on the unused double bed in our room. We dressed and all went out for a day of sightseeing.

The Queen Mary was everything I imagined it to be. It's the kind of splendor what can make you doubt your non-materialistic principles. Elizabeth said it didn't make her question her philosophy, but that one little ocean cruise on a luxury liner—sometime—would not be so bad. If I should just happen to decide to take her on one. Maybe in August or September?

The Spruce Goose was more than I could ever imagine. It's in a dome that looks like it could cover a small city, and they've got the entrance laid out so that you don't see anything until you're all the way inside the dome. You walk down a corridor and then when you come around the corner, the gigantic Flying Boat is right there. And there. And there. And there. Eight engines. An eight-story tail. A hundred yard wingspan! That's three hundred feet, a football field. Oh, and there's a gift shop in which you can buy anything you could ever want with Spruce Goose stamped on it. Everything except the Howard Hughes' hats; they didn't say Spruce Goose.

We did a little looking around in the shopping village by the entrance to the ship, but Elizabeth had seen some shops in the other shopping village by the marina and the hotel that she just had to go into. So we went back across the waterway to the shopping area they called Shoreline Village.

The first thing we just had to do was ride the antique carousel, a genuine 1904 Charles Looff masterpeice, the little blurb said. It was, too. They had done a magnificent job restoring the animals—using the master's techniques, real animal hair and all, the little blurb said. Elizabeth ran to the black horse she just had to ride on. I walked calmly to the black one next to her. Josh and Donny rode the goats behind us. I knew they were probably holding hands back there, but I didn't turn around to verify it. Despite my reservations about riding a merry-go-round at my age, it was a lot of fun, and brought back some pleasant memories. Pleasant, that is, except for the tune that was playing on the calliope throughout the ride: "How Much Is That Doggie in the Window?" which I had always detested.

Then we went over to look at the Bounty, which was moored at the far side of the village. H.M.A.V. Bounty. His or Her Majesty's Armed Vessel. This was the reproduction they made for the newest version of the Bligh-Christian story, and it was in Long Beach for the upcoming Tall Ships Parade on the Fourth of July. It was a modern ship below deck, equipped with the latest scientific gear. But from the deck to the top of the tallest mast, it duplicated the original down to the last detail. For a buck, you could walk around topside. For free, you could stand on the dock and see the same thing. That's what we did.

After that, we hit the shops. The English shop, the art shop and the bake shop. The book shop, the nautical shop and the fish 'n' chips shop. The hammock, gift and chocolate shops. The hat, kite and ice cream shops. The sportswear, candle and candy shops. The pearl shop, the music box shop and the cookie shop. The yacht, movie memorabelia and pizza shops. The stuffed animal shop, the T-shirt shop and the popcorn shop.

I took my cheese-sprinkled popcorn, and my growing stomach ache, out to the boardwalk and fell onto a bench in the shade. A trio of youngish women in forties' attire was singing "Rum and Coca-Cola." Just the thought of a rum and Coke at that moment made me nauseous. Elizabeth looked a little green, too. They had followed me over into the shade. Josh sat next to me on the bench, Donny was watching the trio, and Elizabeth was standing in front of me, staring at me.

"Are you all right?" I asked her.

"No," she said.

"Want my seat?"

"No."

"Elizabeth!"

"Look!" she said, pointing behind me.

I dragged myself off the bench and turned around. The bench I had chosen as my refuge was in front of the music box shop, right in front of their display window. A display window we had not seen earlier from the inside of the shop.

Sitting in that display window was an old music box. It was made of cherry wood. It was hand carved with minute designs, almost like an etching. The bottom pedestal was round and slightly separated from the upper pedestal, which was round at the bottom, but then became a hexagon at the top. Six triangular petals came up from that forming a point at the very top. The clerk saw us looking at the music box and came over to turn it on. As the upper pedestal turned, the six petals opened to reveal a dancing, porcelain Cinderella. The insides of the petals were inset with mirrors which reflected light onto the figurine. Cinderella was bending slightly forward with her arms draped in front of her. Her hands were turned inward almost touching, and her head was tilted to the side, looking at the glass slippers lying at the edge of the pedestal. I pinned my ear to the window. The tune was the theme from Prokofiev's "Cinderella" ballet.

Sunday. 5 p.m.   Donny was funny about the music box. At first, he was excited. Then he started hedging. He said it was too expensive. I told him I was going to buy it whether or not he wanted to go in on it with me. Josh even told Donny he'd give him the money or loan it to him, if he wanted to chip in. I finally just charged it, telling Donny he could decide later what he wanted to do.

He carried the well-cushioned package back to the hotel room, wouldn't let us pack it in one of the suitcases, then sat with it on his lap the first half of the way back to Beech Grove. He and I were in the back seat, Elizabeth was up front with Josh, who drove. I don't remember what we had been talking about, something trivial, when suddenly Donny sat up straight and handed me the package. He leaned up against the back of the front seat, only inches from the back of Josh's head. I thought he was going to embarrass me again by kissing Josh on the neck, but he just put his forehead against the seat and lay there quietly for sometime. I watched his stomach moving in and out with each deep breath he took. Again suddenly, he jerked up straight and began asking Josh questions about Gary. How long were they together? Had he seen him between college and last weekend in Beech Grove? Who was on top?

Josh wouldn't answer, choosing to take the offensive instead.

"If you think for one minute," Josh shouted, "I'm gonna put up with your flirting every time we go out, you can think again!"

"Hey!" Don't give me orders, man! I've got enough mothers now!"

"I don't wanta be your goddamn mother, Donny! I wanta be your lover! And that means no fucking around!"

"What about you and Gary?!"

"That was years ago!"

"You were with him all last weekend at the hotel!"

"I was with you last weekend at the hotel, you little jerk!"

"One fucking night!"

"Will you stop it!" I shouted.

"You seemed to like it at the time!" Josh yelled.

"Yeah, well I faked it so I wouldn't hurt your feelings!" Donny said.

"I don't want to hear this!" I screamed.

"So don't listen, goddamnit!" Donny screamed back.

He hit Josh in the back of the head. I wished he'd hit me instead.

Josh slammed on the brakes and we skidded off the road onto the shoulder. Josh killed the motor and turned around in the seat, up on his knees. He reached over into the back seat and grabbed Donny by the shirt, lifting him off the seat.

"Look, you little fuck! Don't hit! Don't *ever* hit!"

Josh settled back behind the wheel, started the car and drove off. No one spoke the rest of the way home.

The honeymoon was over.

11.   The Arboretum

When Grampa Leonard put the town of Beech Grove in trust for its citizens, he stipulated that "should the voting members of the community decide by a two-thirds vote not to hold monthly meetings, they shall be required to establish an Executive Council of seven to act in their behalf." He went on to say that the Council should have regular monthly meetings and that any member of the board could call an emergency session. This way, the town as a whole only had to meet four times a year.

Since it was created in 1976, the Council has been made up of pretty much the same people, mostly because of the five year period newcomers had to wait before being eligible to vote or sit on the Council. Eddie was a board member a couple of times, Carl once. Carl hated it and used to turn off his hearing aid. Carl's dad, Big Don, was on it the first couple of years, until he died. The former hotel manager was on it, until he was fired last year for sneaking into the women's sauna and Josh replaced him, both at the hotel and on the Council.

The current Executive Council:

Amelia Briggs, charter member and widow of our esteemed founder and benefactor. Gram Amelia never served as chairperson, but she always wielded the power. The citizens of Beech Grove had always felt somewhat guilty about having been given everything on a silver platter—their homes, their town—and had always been in awe of the munificent Leonard. They accorded his widow the same fearful devotion, which she used to full advantage. No vote of the Council or the town-at-large had ever gone against Amelia's wishes.

Hugh Vance. Another charter member. Restaurateur and hometown boy, probably the most truly civic-minded of our civic leaders. Hugh had led the crusade to save our school and Jack's job. He had established the newspaper and my job. He has always fought for money to keep the resort facilities up-to-date in order to assure a steady flow of visitors—our bread and butter. Hugh had always been chairman of the Council, partly because he did such a good job and partly because no one else wanted it.

Bill Weston, M.D. Charter member and physician. Doc Weston brought most of us younger citizens into the world and has treated everyone in town at one time or another, usually at little or no fee. But he made up for that by squeezing money over the years out of the Council, or private donors, for upgrading the clinic, bringing specialists in when anybody contracted something odd, or for giving an occasional raise to his nurse, Gwen. When the issue was anything medical, Doc would stomp and holler till he turned red in the face, but on other matters, he sat docilely through the discussion, then voted with the majority, or with Amelia, whichever occurred first.

Jack Gresham. Teacher and principal. Jack let Miss Blankenship represent the educational interests on the board for the first couple of years, but finally unseated her when it became evident she didn't have the necessary strength to pry money out of the Council for the school. Jack is never unreasonable in his demands; he simply makes sure education gets its fair share.

Matthew Russell. Editor of the Beech Grove Clarion. But I'm not on the Council because of my position on the newspaper, as logical as that would be. I'm on the Council because Eddie got into an all-out war with Amelia over the question of cable television and then resigned in a huff when Amelia won. Eddie had been reading about all the educational programs for children being offered on Public TV and thought Beech Grove should get the cable for that purpose. But Amelia was adamantly opposed to letting the evil medium get a foothold in our, as yet, untainted village—Sesame Street or no Sesame Street! Mom refused "to serve even one more week on the board with that woman." Everyone thought there should be a Russell on the Council, and Carl wouldn't, so I got Eddie's seat.

Josh Bowen. The new general manager of the Beech Grove Hot Springs Hotel. Since the hotel is our livelihood, the town had said, it is imperative that the manager be on the Executive Council, whether he likes it or not. Josh did not like it. He wasn't quite ready, in his own mind, to take on the awesome responsibility of running the hotel, and he wasn't at all ready for the strains of sitting on the board with the likes of Amelia, Hugh and Jack. Josh listens to everything at the meetings, but never can make up his mind how to vote on anything. He usually watches me to see what I'm going to do. And he abstains till all the others have voted before he casts with the majority.

Randolph Kennedy. Charter and senior member of the Council, at age 82. Mr. Kennedy is Aunt Gloria's father. He used to be the barber at the hotel, until Gloria and Rae took it over. Mr. Kennedy has, somehow, gotten it into his head the last few years that he is Hugh's father instead of Gloria's. And he thinks that Hugh and Gloria are still married and living together. He often refers to his son, Hugh, and his daughter-in-law, Gloria. No one bothers to correct him anymore. He seldom expresses an opinion at the meetings and always votes with Amelia.

That's the current Executive Council of Beech Grove: Amelia, Hugh, Doc, Jack, me, Josh and Mr. Kennedy.

The Monday after our trip to Long Beach, Hugh called an emergency session for eight o'clock in the bar. Monday night is Family Night at Respighi's, so the bar is closed.

At a quarter after, six of us were seated at the oak tables awaiting Eddie and Amelia. Hugh was miffed because it had been Mom who asked him to call the session. They didn't arrive until eight-thirty, and Amelia was cursing under her breath as Eddie pushed her in from the veranda in a wheelchair. She was cursing because her leg wasn't healing properly and because sitting in that wheelchair caused the pain to shoot all the way up into her back and shoulders. She was cursing because the ramp Carl had built over her front steps was too steep and she always felt like she was going down a ski slope. She was cursing because she had hit her head on the car door when Eddie picked her up in one of the hotel station wagons. She was cursing because the only way to get into the hotel or restaurant in a wheelchair was to go all the way around to the back of the spa facilities and then weave in and around the Jacuzzis, the mud pond, the pools and the "massage parlor," as she called it, and then finally up the long ramp across the back of the hotel and up onto the veranda.

"This had better be good, Edwina," Amelia told her adopted daughter, "for you to drag me out of my sickbed."

"I didn't drag you out," Mom said. "You said there'd be hell to pay if we tried to hold a meeting without you."

"Never mind that," Amelia grumbled. "What is it that's so important?"

"The floor is yours," Hugh told Eddie.

"Okay. I've been doing some research, and it looks like the chances are very, very good that we could get a beech tree to grow here," Eddie began.

"A what?" Amelia shouted.

"A beech tree."

"That's an emergency?" Hugh asked.

"Not exactly, but it is timely," Eddie replied. "I've

located a tree we can have for nothing, but we have to take delivery on it soon or it's going to be destroyed. And it will take quite a bit of work to get the location prepared."

"And just where is this location?" Amelia asked.

"Where the garage burned."

"At Aunt Caroline's?" I asked.

"Did you ask Caroline about this?" Amelia asked.

"I don't need to ask her; it's not her property. Everything in town is *our* property. Remember?"

"She's right," Hugh said.

"How much is this little project going to cost us?" Amelia asked.

"Nothing. They'll even deliver it for nothing."

"How about the site preparation?" Doc asked.

"Volunteers," Jack answered. "The, uh, a bunch of us at Respighi's last night agreed to do the labor."

"Beech trees wouldn't grow here before," Amelia said. "What makes you think you can grow one now?"

"Whoever planted those beeches just plopped them in the ground and didn't work with them. What we'll do is bring in the right soil, control the moisture and keep it out of the hot sun until it has time to acclimate itself to its new home."

"How are you going to keep it out of the sun?" asked Hugh.

"With a canopy."

"A canopy?" I said. "Don't beech trees grow very tall?"

"We can string canvas between the two pines on either side and then move it up every year as the tree grows. After a few years, it shouldn't need it any more."

"Well, since it won't cost the town anything and all the work is voluntary, I say we do it," Hugh said. "Doc?"

"Aye."

"Josh?"

"I'd like to think about it a little longer."

"I thought you might. Matt?"

"Yes."

"Jack?"

"Yes."

"Amelia?"

"All right."

"Aye," said Mr. Kennedy.

"Yes," said Josh.

"Good! Beech Grove finally gets a beech tree! Eddie, we'll all be looking forward to the unveiling. Now, unless there's something else pending, let's . . ."

"There is one thing," Eddie interrupted. "I think we should dedicate our new, uh, arboretum to . . ."

Her pause was so long, it immediately drew our undivided attention.

". . . to Matthew and Mark Delaney," she said.

"Are you mad?" shouted Amelia.

"Who?" Josh asked.

"I'll tell you later," I whispered to him.

"It's no secret anymore," Eddie replied. "The mob's no longer after anyone. We should dedicate the tree to the two men who put our town together."

"This town was built on the name of Leonard I. Briggs!" Amelia said.

"Whose real name was Matthew Delaney. And he didn't do it alone. My father had a lot to do with it, and would've done a lot more if he had lived longer!"

"Now I remember," Josh said.

"Eddie, please," said Hugh.

"No," Mom said. "Beech Grove exists because of the Delaney brothers and I think we ought to honor their memory with this beech tree."

"I forbid it!" Amelia screamed. "If you must do this, dedicate it to Leonard Briggs and Richard Henderson."

"But that isn't who they were! This is a spiritual honor, not some legal document. They were brothers! They were twins! That means something and I don't think we can ignore that! Your own twin, my mother—doesn't that mean anything to you? Have you no emotions at all?"

The room was dead quiet. Amelia spoke softly and hesitantly.

"Yes, Sarah died that day. I loved her. I loved Mark as well. I even loved Leonard, most of the time. Was I supposed to stop living when they all died? We cope however we can, Eddie. I was Leonard's wife for forty-four years. Matthew was a very long time ago. I'm eighty-two years old now and . . ."

"You are not!" Mr. Kennedy interrupted. "I'm eighty-two and I know you're three or maybe four years younger than I am. I remember when you . . ."

"Shut up, Randolph!" Amelia said. "You're getting senile!"

"Amelia," Eddie said, "I'm sorry for what I said to you, but it doesn't change the way I feel about this dedication. Everyone in this town will still know you're the widow of our official founder."

"Eddie, this is wrong," Amelia said.

"You can always change your name back to Delaney. No one cares, Amelia," Eddie said. "I call for a vote."

"You can't. You're not on the Council," Hugh said.

"Then I call for a vote." I said.

"Do we dedicate the new beech tree to the memory of Matthew and Mark Delaney? Doc?"

"Yes."

"Josh?"

"Yes."

"Matt?"

"Yes."

"Jack."

"Yes."

"Amelia?"

"No!"

"Randolph?"

"Yes! Senile indeed."

"Six yes, one no—the motion carries. The meeting is adjourned. The drinks are on the house!" Hugh cried.

"Will someone please push me home?" Amelia said.

Eddie took her adoptive mother home.

I didn't see Donny until Tuesday night that week. When we got back from Long Beach on Sunday night, I had assumed Donny would stay at our house, but he went on up to the hotel with Josh. They patched up their quarrel and resumed their romance—until Tuesday.

I had worked our polling booth at the hotel that day and didn't get home till almost nine-thirty. Elizabeth was with a group of mothers trying to salvage last year's festival costumes for this year's larger children. I was waiting for the coffee to brew and raiding the refrigerator when Donny staggered in the back door.

"Oh, you're in fine shape," I said.

"Thanks. Howeryou?" he slurred.

"Aren't you in on the costume alterations tonight?"

"Mine's jus' hair. Remember?"

"Oh yeah."

"There's still enough to cover my dick. It hasn't grown any since las' year.

"Do you have to be so crude?"

"You don' wanna talk about my dick? Then fuckya!"

"Why are you drunk?"

"Why not?"

"You don't want to talk? Fine."

"I do."

"Then be nice."

"Okay."

He fell into one of the kitchen chairs. I poured us each a cup of coffee.

"Josh?" I guessed.

"Yep."

"What now?"

"He's mad 'cuz I was drinkin' today."

"Today? What time did you start?"

"I dunno. Ten or 'leven."

"This morning?"

"Well it ain' that . . . yet . . . tonight. Is it?"

"No."

"I din' think so."

"Why did you start drinking at ten this morning?"

"I dunno. Nervous."

"What are you nervous about?"

"I don' know. I was jus' shaking. So, I had a drink and it wen' away."

"That's not good."

"What? The shaking? Or the drinking?"

"Both."

"Yeah."

"Where'd you get the booze today? This town's supposed to be dry on election day, thanks to Grampa Leonard."

"Is it erection . . . ha, ha, ha . . . election day?"

"Yes. Didn't you vote?"

"I don' think so."

"Where'd you get the booze?"

"Dad's workship."

"He keeps liquor out there?"

"Jack Daniels even."

"Yeah?"

"Yeah. Always has. I used to fill it back up with water so he wouldn't know I drunk it, but I don't bother anymore."

"How long has this been going on?"

"Years. Eighth grade. I don't know."

"Jesus! And he never said anything?"

"Uh . . . 'don't drive!' "

"Very funny."

"True."

"That's all he said?"

"Uh. Yeah."

"Donny . . ."

"What?"

"I don't believe this."

"I'm not lyin'!"

"I don't mean that. I mean, I don't believe . . . I don't believe all this shit is going on."

"Me too!"

"Wasn't he there today?" I asked.

"Nope. Wasn't home. Wasn't there, I mean."

"So, what'd you do? Just get drunk and . . . ?"

"And had a fight with Josh. Yep."

I poured us more coffee and got down the large jar of cookies Elizabeth had brought home from Mom's the day before.

"What'd he say?" I asked.

"Who?"

"Josh."

"Oh. Uh, well, he said I shouldn't drink in the daytime and I go, 'What difference does it make if it's day or night?' And he goes, 'Cuz you haveta get stuff done in the daytime and then you relax and drink at night.' So, I says, 'What if you work at night? Then can you drink in the daylight?' And he started screaming at me. And I left."

"You're impossible," I said, but I couldn't keep from laughing as I said it.

"Josh said that, too, but he didn't laugh."

"That I believe."

"So, what do I do?"

"I don't know," I said. "Don't drink till dark, I guess!" We both broke up.

Donny got the giggles. Then the hiccups.

We split what was left of the previous night's lasagne and then Donny went back to the hotel to make up with Josh.

I went to the hotel twice on Wednesday to see Josh, but he was in a meeting the first time and off on some errand the second. I left a note for him to come by the house that night. Elizabeth was out, her note said, repairing easels. I threw together a meatloaf, hoping Josh would show up in time to help me eat it. If Elizabeth ate at all that week, she ate it elsewhere. I was just taking the loaf out of the oven when Josh arrived.

"Eat some meatloaf," I said.

"Is it the same shit you used to make?" he asked.

"No. It has 'improvements by Elizabeth!'"

"Then I'll have some. What's with it?"

"With it?"

"You know, like potatoes, beans, anything."

"This is all I made."

"Some cook."

"It has rice in it. Want some ketchup or mustard?"

"No thanks. Why'd you want to see me?"

"Just to talk."

"Okay."

"About Donny."

"Oh."

"Oh?"

"Face it, Matt, you little brother is weird."

"I know that, but I thought you were in love with him."

"Love? What's that?"

"You know—cohabitating, fighting, fucking."

"I think there's supposed to be more."

"Rumor."

"Huh?"

"Just a lot of rumors. No truth to 'em."

"Oh."

"Did Donny come back to your place last night?"

"Yeah. He said he talked to you."

"Why do you think he got drunk yesterday?"

"He's your brother!"

"He's your lover!"

"Maybe."

"You didn't make up last night?"

"Sort of. But I don't think Donny's ready for a relationship. He needs to get around some more first. He expects too much."

"Like what?"

"Like he wants me to pay attention to him every second. I just don't have the time—or the inclination, to be perfectly honest. I like working. I don't want to spend twenty-four hours a day with anyone."

"He'll get over that."

"Probably, but it's more than that. He needs to be exposed to more people, more gay men. I think the only reason he loves me, or thinks he loves me, is that I'm the only game in town."

"Meaning?"

"Count 'em, Matt. I'm the only single gay man in Beech Grove."

"Besides Donny. So maybe your theory is true in reverse as well."

"At least I've been around a little bit. Left a few broken hearts."

"You're too modest."

"But Donny thinks he has no other choice in life but to be with me. He thinks it's that or be alone."

"Are you sure you aren't letting your ego slip into your reasoning?"

"What?"

"You'd feel more loved if Donny had chosen you, rather than just taken the only available bachelor."

"You're crazy."

"Maybe. I think your point's vaild, Josh, but only from one direction. True, had Donny been given a choice, he might have picked someone else. But he also might have picked you. I think he would have. I think he does love you. He just has a lot to learn. You are his first. And not just his gay first. He's never gone through this with anyone, boy or girl. He doesn't understand the give and take part of it yet. Everything that isn't perfect, everything that doesn't live up to what he imagines love to be, is a rejection for him. Total rejection. Everything that comes out of your mouth that isn't affection, Donny takes to mean that you don't love him. And that it's over between you. If you do love him, and if you have incredible patience, he'll find out that relationships survive the daily stresses and the occasional arguments. If you don't love him, if you can't hack it, he'll just have to go on to someone else. Like we all have! He's just a few years late, that's all."

"Are you going to eat the rest of your meatloaf?" Josh asked me.

"I haven't had any yet," I said.

"My point, exactly."

"Oh," I said. "Been going on, have I?"

"I'm not giving up on him, Matt. But, he doesn't want me to correct him. He goes nuts every time I criticize him. That may ease up in time, but in the meantime, there's going to be an outburst whenever I say anything to him. I don't know what caused the drinking yesterday. We got along fine on Monday night. No fights, nothing. Shit, we must've fucked for three . . ."

"Josh! Skip the details. Please!"

"Prude."

"Possibly, but I still don't want to hear it. Where's Donny now?"

"Back at the hotel, I hope. I should get back. I told him I wouldn't be long. Thanks for the pep talk."

"Anytime."

He left. I threw the rest of the meatloaf in the trash.

Thursday night, Josh called me in a panic. He was just going into a meeting with the festival committee that would go on for at least two hours, and Donny had sent him a note saying he didn't think he could stand it anymore and that he was going away.

I got dressed and went looking for Donny. I didn't believe he'd really leave town, so I made the rounds of his favorite hiding places: the sports equipment shed at the school, the creek (but not the pond at the top because none of us ever went up there at night; too many wild animals!), and the mud baths at the spa. He wasn't at any of his usual places, but I spotted him on my way home from the hotel. At Aunt Caroline's.

He was standing in the middle of the foundation of the old garage that burned, the garage that was to become the new arboretum. The bright moon lit his features like a stage spotlight. I could see the curve of his brow, the cut of his cheekbones, the lines on his face. For the first time, he looked like a man to me, rather than a boy. But his stance was still that of a boy. I started to run to him, but something made me stop. Something about the way he stood, the way he was looking around his feet. It was as though he'd lost something there. Something very small. I don't know how long I watched him repeat the same sequence. He'd stand absolutely still for two or three minutes, gazing out at the trees at the back of the lot. Then he'd search the ground again, first from a standing position, then squatting. Eventually, he'd fall to his knees and put his hands up to his face. He'd shake his head and stand up again, walk a few steps and stare at the trees again.

When I heard him sob aloud, I walked slowly over to him and put my arm around his shoulders. I asked him if he wanted to come home with me, but he pulled me toward the hotel. I took him to Josh's room and put him to bed. When I pulled the blanket over him, he grabbed my hand. I sat on the edge of the bed, thinking he wanted to talk, but he just held onto my hand and said nothing. He nodded when I asked if he was going to be all right. He nodded when I told him I had to go. He nodded when I asked him if he was going to stay put, because I didn't want to have to go out looking for him again. He smiled when I kissed him on the forehead and wished him sweet dreams.

Josh talked Donny into working with him at the spa on Friday night. And by some miracle, Elizabeth was free. We hardly knew what to say to each other, it had been so long. We had an intimate dinner for two by candlelight. We danced to Guy Lombardo, a cassette of one of his New Year's Eve broadcasts. As we danced into the bedroom, I closed the door.

"Why are you closing the door?" she asked me.

"Need you ask?"

"It won't ever happen again."

"It better!"

"I mean the cat."

"I'm not taking any chances."

"I don't like the door closed," she said.

"Why not?"

"It's . . . it's confining."

"Pretend we have company sleeping in the other room."

"But we don't."

"Pretend."

"I don't want to."

"You just don't want to deny anything to that precious cat of yours. Go away, cat!" I shouted. Panther Piss was rubbing up against the other side of the door.

"You're being ridiculous."

"What I'm being, is sick and tired of having my life turned upside down by outside influences. And I'm not about to let a goddamn cat run my life for me!"

I grabbed my pillow and stomped over to the door. I opened it. The cat ran between my legs.

"Where are you going?" Elizabeth asked.

"To the guest room!"

"Isn't that letting the cat run your life?"

"Huh? Yeah, fuck her! Where are you, cat? Out! Now! Get out! Where the hell did you go?"

"Look under the bed."

"P.P., where are you? Kitty, kitty. Here kitty!"

Both Josh and Donny worked again on Saturday night, so we tried again. This time I locked the cat in the bathroom. And closed the bedroom door.

"Aren't you overdoing it?" Elizabeth asked.

"No!"

"For someone who wasn't going to let a cat run his life for him, you seem to be."

"Knock it off, okay? No more cats in the damn bedroom."

"She didn't even get up on the bed last night."

"I know. But just the thought of it spoils my uh, my mood."

"I remember."

"Ha, ha. It was your fault in the first place."

"My fault?"

"If you hadn't screamed that night, Panther Piss wouldn't have panicked and . . . done what she did."

"Oh brother."

"It's true. Do you want the light on or off tonight?"

"I don't care, Matt. Just come to bed."

There was a noise at the bedroom door.

"How could she have gotten out of the bathroom?"

I opened the door. Donny was lying on the floor, the back of his head pressed against the door frame, his knees pulled up to his chest.

"Oh fuck!" I said.

"Good night," Elizabeth said, as she pulled the covers over her head.

I carried Donny to the couch in the living room. He stared at me, his eyes blank.

"Are you on something?"

He shook his head.

"Are you drunk?"

He shook his head.

"You're going to have to talk to me, Donny. I can't do this alone."

"We had a fight," Donny said, very softly.

"I could've guessed that. What this time?"

He closed his eyes.

"I'm sorry I snapped at you, but you're driving me crazy. You're driving everybody crazy."

"I know."

"I'll stop, Okay? What you ought to know, what you have to know, Donny, is that I, *we* love you. And we want to help you. But we, *I* don't know what to do. Can't you tell me something?"

"I let a guy blow me today."

"Christ!"

"He was in one of the massage rooms when I went in to pick up towels and he asked me to help him get off the table. He said he was weak from the rubdown and when I did, his knees buckled and he . . . well, there he was . . . and I let him."

"I'm not saying you should've done it, but I don't think it's anything to get depressed about. The chances of your seeing him again are . . ."

"He invited me to his house."

"He did?"

"Yeah. In the Hollywood hills. He's a writer. He does plays. You shoulda seen him. He's a funny-looking guy with frizzy, reddish-blondish hair and, oh yeah, he wears round, tinted glasses, even in the sauna and pools. I guess he's forty, maybe less. His name's Benjamin."

"You got all that during a quickie in a massage room?"

"We went for coffee."

"You went for coffee?" I said, starting to laugh.

"What's wrong with that?"

"Nothing," I howled.

"Matt, don't laugh."

"I'm sorry. Donny, what were you thinking of? I thought you loved Josh."

"I do."

"Then don't fool around like that, especially at the hotel. You'll hurt him. You can't have it both ways, Donny. If you want your freedom, you have to . . ."

"He's really pissed."

"Josh?"

"Yeah."

"He caught you?"

"I told him."

"You told him?" I started laughing again. "You are unbelievable!"

"Why?"

"Well, I probably shouldn't advise you on the finer points of cheating, but honesty isn't always the best policy."

"I found that out."

"Donny, I think the problem may be that you don't have much experience with . . ."

"Much? I don't have any. Beating off may be fun, but it doesn't compare with . . ."

"I wasn't talking just about the sex."

"Don't you think it's important?"

"Sure, but . . ."

"I mean, it's not lonely. When you finally touch someone, it's so different than just doing it yourself. I used to think the only way to make it better was to find new ways to beat off, like when you'd leave your underpants . . ."

"Enough!"

"What's the matter?"

"I don't want to talk about your . . . your . . ."

"Jerking off?"

"I don't want to talk about any of the details of your sex life. I don't think that's the problem. What I want to talk about is why are you here, now, on my couch?"

"We had a fight. I told you."

"Elizabeth and I fight all the time and you don't find me on your couch."

"I'll go."

"No, dummy. You're welcome here, always. I just would prefer it under nicer circumstances. You're so unhappy all the time. Maybe you should get out of here altogether. Move to some place like L.A. where you could meet . . ."

"Why should I have to leave everybody just because I don't . . ." I could hear that tearful sound beginning to build in the back of his throat.

"You don't have to leave. But spend some time with the other gay people here in town. You can learn from them."

"They're all Mom's friends."

"They're your friends, too. And more than once, I've heard them take your side over hers."

"Really?"

"Yeah. But I'll tell you what you really have to work on, Donny. And that's this little habit you're getting into of running out on Josh every time you guys get into an argument."

"I . . ."

"If you're going to fight with Josh, fight with him. But finish it. Don't run away."

"I can't."

"You have to try. Bring him here with you, if you have to. Just get it in your mind that you have to let it go all the way to the end."

"That's what I'm afraid of. That it will end."

"If it does, it does. It's got to be better than what you're doing now. Doesn't it?"

"I don't know."

"Love and sex are a weird balance. It takes a long time for most people to get them figured out. Some never do."

"You mean like being gay?"

"For those who aren't sure, yes. Doubt's a real killer."

"I never doubted it."

"So I gather. But you did hold back."

"Who was I supposed to do it with? I mean everbody else can go on dates and run around holding hands and kissing in public—shit, even at the Sunday Service—but if you like guys, you don't just go up to some guy and ask him if he wants to go have a Coke with you and hold hands. Especially in a town where everybody knows you."

"I guess not. But we do have gays living openly here. And you won't find that in many towns our size. You could've talked about it with one of them, like Jack."

"Sure, you would've loved that. Me telling him I wanted to make it with my brother."

"That was a long time ago."

"Not that long," he said.

"But surely you were interested in other guys. I know you wanted Josh. Why didn't you . . ."

"I wanted to the night you guys left for college. Remember? You hit me."

"You were only twelve! I mean since he came back."

"In the first place, he never said he was gay and you didn't tell me, until that night he got into the fight. I almost said something to him a couple of times, but I chickened out. I just kept thinking about what he might do or say if I was wrong about him, what he might tell other people. And I kept hoping he would make the first move."

"I don't know why he didn't," I said. "Maybe he was afraid he'd sway you if you really hadn't made up your mind."

"Was Josh gay when he lived at our house?"

"Yes."

"Did you ever . . . ?" he started to ask.

"I don't think I should . . ."

"I don't mind. I always fantasized that you guys did it."

"Okay. We, uh, had sex. A couple of times. It wasn't love the way you think of it or the way Elizabeth and I have it, but I guess it was more than just physical. We do love each other, in a way; just not *in* love. I don't think Josh was ever in love with me, but I was afraid he was going to be, so I stopped it. I knew I wasn't gay, and that nothing could ever—that we could only be friends. What happened between us happened only because he was Josh. Now I love him the way I love you, little brother. And nothing would make me happier than if you two made a go of it. But if you don't, I will still love you both. Especially you, you little shit."

"Will you hold me?" Donny asked.

I put my arms around him and he began to cry. His whole body was shaking. He seemed to go the longest time without breathing, then he'd suck it all in at once, choking and jerking in spasms. I never saw so much water come out of someone's eyes; my shirt was soaked. I reached behind me to the library table in back of the couch and got a Kleenex. I wiped his nose, but he didn't even notice. He just kept sobbing. He seemed on the brink of hysteria and I didn't know if I should do anything or not, so I just held him tighter. Finally, the sobbing gave way to gentle crying and he started breathing normally again.

"That's so pretty," he said.

"What?"

"That light has long streams of color streaking out all around it, like one of those bible paintings."

He leaned forward to squint at the light, freeing my numb left arm. I stretched my legs out behind him and fell back, hitting my head on the arm of the sofa. Donny turned to me and rubbed my head, smiling. He curled up next to me, pulling my arm under his head and putting his arm across my chest. We fell asleep in each other's arms.

Something was pulling at my hair. I opened my eyes. Josh was standing over us, tapping me on the head.

"Good morning," Josh said.

"Uh," I said.

"You looked so cute together, I hated to wake you. But the muffins are done."

"Donny, you have company," I said.

"Huh?"

"Josh is here. He wants to take you home so I can get some sleep."

"No he doesn't," Josh said. "He wants to go out on the porch and eat blueberry muffins with you two cuddly guys."

"Blueberry?" I asked. "I thought it was bran week."

"It is. This is a special treat from Elizabeth and me. So get up!"

I staggered out to the veranda and was blinded by the sun. Elizabeth shoved sunglasses on my face and put a cup of coffee in my hand. I sat in the chair nearest the end of the porch, so the sun could bake my aching neck and shoulders. Josh and Donny sat together on the small rattan sofa and held hands. Elizabeth passed the muffins, and the four of us sat there all morning—peacefully and silently—munching and sipping.

I invited them to dinner on Monday night. I liked the feeling of us together: We made a good foursome. There was something kindred in our spirits. I especially liked that Donny didn't seem to get depressed or withdrawn when we were all together.

Elizabeth and I did our barbecued steak and lobster for them, and we were just sitting down to the table, when there came two terrible screeches from the driveway. I ran to the front door.

"It's Mother!" I cried. Eddie had just jumped out of the hotel station wagon and was running up the porch steps.

"Matt, I'm so sorry!"

"For what?"

"I ran over the cat!" Eddie said.

"Panther Piss!" Elizabeth screamed and ran out the door.

"Come in, Mom. What are you doing in the wagon, anyway? Why were you driving so fast?"

"I just got back from taking Amelia to the doctor in Riverside and I saw your old professor. Oh. I didn't know you had company."

"It's just . . ."

"I can come back later."

"They're not company, Mother! That one's your son. Remember? And that one's your new son-in-law!"

"Matt," Elizabeth scolded as she came back in.

"Where is she? Is she dead?"

"I'm so sorry," Eddie said.

"Yes, she's dead. I hope you're happy," Elizabeth said directly to me.

"Me?"

"You willed her to death."

"I what?"

"You wanted her out of the way, you said. You didn't want her interfering in your life anymore, you said. Now she's out of your way for good. So you should be happy."

"You're nuts."

"I shouldn't have been going so fast," Eddie said. "I was so excited over the beech tree and . . ."

"Mother?" Donny said.

". . . that your professor is going to help with the arboretum and . . ."

"Eddie," Josh said.

". . . supervise the whole . . ."

"Mother!" I shouted. "Someone is speaking to you!"

"What shall I do with her?" Elizabeth mumbled.

"Who?"

"Panther Piss, damnit! She's lying out there in the driveway! Dead!"

"I don't know. Can't we handle that later?"

"No!"

"Mom!" Donny screamed. "You can't do this to me anymore. It isn't fair! I only did what I had to! I just couldn't pretend any longer! Please!"

"I don't understand you, Mom," I said. "You don't seem to have any problem accepting the other gays around here. Why can't you accept Donny?"

"That's easy, Matt," Donny said. "Some of her best friends are homosexuals. She just wouldn't want her son to marry one!"

"Matt, do you think we could put her in one of the little cedar chests?" Elizabeth said. "We could bury her out next to the sycamore by the back fence."

"Oh, for God's sake, Elizabeth!" I screamed. "Just roll it up and put it in a coffee can or something! Jesus!"

"Matthew!" everyone shouted.

Elizabeth ran out of the room.

"Oh shit," I muttered, and went after her. She had locked the door, and when I got back to the living room, everyone had gone.

I looked at the cold, dry, uneaten dinner on the table in the dining room. I looked at the Tiffany lamp on the mantelpiece, the lamp Donny had seen the colored streams of light coming out of. I lay down on the couch, wishing I had someone to hold me. I fell asleep, trying to remember that warm feeling I used to get when Panther Piss would curl up on my stomach and purr us both to sleep.

12.   A Dance To The Solstice

I used to look forward every year to putting out the Festival Edition of the Clarion. It's the official guide and program for the week's events. We usually do twenty pages with front page color. It includes the agenda for the Founder's Day Program with texts of the speeches and we do complete bios of the artists with descriptions of the paintings they're offering that year. It lists each Solstice event with background information on the instruments, dances and songs and the names of the participants.

As I said, I used to look forward to putting out the Festival Edition of the Clarion. This year changed all that. Pat and I had to work sixteen-hour days for the entire week and a half prior to the opening. None of the new artists got biographies and photos to us on time. Several of the ad mats were late. The family was driving me nuts. And our usual corps of volunteers was missing. Josh used to be the biggest help, but in his new capacity as hotel manager, he couldn't get away from work this year. Gwen couldn't help because Doc was running late clinic hours. Donny was useless. Even Pat's son, J.D., who had been our office boy for five years, had more important things to do, he said, now that he was fourteen. One of those "things he had to do" brought us all to a screeching halt a week before the festival.

It was Thursday, June 14, Flag Day. Pat and I had just gotten finished with the regular weekly edition of the paper and were gearing up to devote our full attention to the Festival Edition. We were in the middle of a short coffee break before tackling the artists' bios, when Jack called:

"Are you sitting down?" Jack asked.

"No," I replied.

"Then do."

"Okay, I'm sitting. But before you start, isn't there someone else you'd rather make this call to? I'm not up to whatever it is."

"Nope, you're the one."

"Then do it."

"It's Donny."

"I'm not surprised."

"He's, uh, well, I was working on my final inventory for the year and, uh, when I went to check out the sports equipment, I, uh, found Donny and J.D. in the shed. Donny was, uh, blowing J.D."

"Oh, that's terrific. Where are they now?"

"Donny's here in my office."

"And J.D.?" I asked. Pat was out of her chair and on her way to grabbing the phone out of my hand. I waved her down.

"I sent him home and told him to wait there for his mother. He was a little shook up getting caught like that, so I think he'll do it."

"I'll tell her," I said. Pat was tugging on my sleeve.

"I called Eddie. She hung up on me," Jack said.

"She what?"

"Yeah. She listened right up to the good part, then hung up without saying a word."

"Is Donny fighting you?" I asked.

"No, gentle as a lamb."

"Is he drunk?"

"Yes."

"Can you take him to Mom's? I'll meet you there."

"Okay."

"I'll talk to Pat and be right there. Sorry 'bout this, Jack."

"Not your fault. See ya there," he said and hung up.

Pat was ready to pounce as I lay the receiver back in its cradle.

"What happened? Are they all right?" she asked.

"No one's hurt. It wasn't an accident or anything," I stalled.

"Did they get into a fight?" Pat asked.

"No. More of a, uh, it was, he . . ."

"Matt!"

"Jack walked in on Donny and J.D. in the equipment shed at school and Donny was going down on J.D. and Jack's taking Donny to my mother's house where I'm going now to do God knows what and he sent J.D. home to wait for you."

"To do God knows what," Pat added as she sat back down in her chair.

"Exactly. I think I'd rather stay here and edit these lousy bios," I said. "Pat, I don't know what to say, I . . ."

"Don't. You've got Donny to worry about. Let me worry about J.D. I've had lots of practice."

"What will you say to him?" I asked.

"What will you say to Donny?" she asked.

"I don't know."

"See how it works? I don't even know what I feel. If Jack hadn't caught them, would one blow job in a school shed make any difference in their lives? I think not. But, we're going to make a big fuss over this, so it probably will make a difference."

"There is the question of age."

"J.D.'s pretty mature for his age," Pat said. "We've talked considerably this past year about sex, gay and straight. He's asked a lot of questions about sex with girls and about sex with boys and I've been quite frank with my answers. From some of the things he said, I don't think this was his first experience with another boy, although I'm pretty sure it's his first with Donny. I'll go home and we'll talk and he'll be honest with me about it, but I think the major concern here is why Donny would turn to a fourteen-year-old boy at this particular time. Aren't he and Josh seeing each other?"

"It changes every ten minutes. I'd better get over there. It's not fair to leave Jack in the lion's mouth."

"Good luck," Pat said.

"You too."

They were all sitting in the living room when I got to Mom and Dad's house. Jack and Donny were on the sofa, Eddie in the chair nearest the kitchen, Carl opposite. No one was speaking. I was greeted with a mixture of relief and resentment.

"Thanks a lot," Donny said to me.

"What'd I do?"

"You told him to bring me here!"

"It's your home!"

"Bullshit!"

"That's enough of that!" Carl said. "In fact, that's enough, period. You two jackasses are tearing this family apart and I want it stopped. Now!"

"Tell *her*," Donny said.

"I'm telling you both," Carl shouted. "Donny, what you did with that boy was wrong and you're going to have to answer for it. Jack, here, says he'll work with you, and he has experience and training with kids, so I want you to start talking to him every week—hell, every day—until you get yourself straightened out. And Edwina, he's our flesh and blood. You have no right to treat him the way you been doing. He can live here with us if he wants to. And he can come here and be welcome even if he doesn't live with us. And we will treat him as our son!"

Eddie stood and walked to her bedroom door.

"Is that understood?" Carl asked.

Mom opened the door, went into the bedroom and slammed the door.

Donny jumped up from the couch and bolted out the front door.

"See why I stopped trying, Matt?" Carl said and then walked out the back door, presumably to his workshop.

"Well, Jack." I said.

"Well, indeed!" Jack said.

"I'll go after Donny," I said.

"I'll be at the school if you need me."

Donny was easy to find. He went straight to his room at our house. The room that was once the guest room, and more recently had been my den, after my former den became Elizabeth's art studio.

The next morning, I went to check on Mom. She was still in her bedroom and wouldn't talk to me. Carl was in his workshop making a miniature cedar chest and didn't want to be disturbed. When I got back home, Elizabeth was waiting for me at the front door.

"He won't come out of there!" she said.

"So, leave him in there. Mom won't come out of her room either. Maybe we'll get some peace."

"Amelia has called three times," Elizabeth said. "Eddie's been taking care of her, and now Amelia's sitting there in her wheelchair waiting to be fed."

"Well, I don't have time," I said.

"And I do? Are you aware that, in addition to my regular responsibilities at the festival, that I've had to take Amelia's on as well? I'm not going to have a minute to myself till this damn thing is over and now there's three generations of your family laid up and waiting to be taken care of! You know your father can't do a thing around the house other than make coffee. They'll all starve!"

"Let 'em!" I said.

"Don't be ridiculous. We'll have to figure out something, someone who isn't doing anyth . . . Caroline!"

"Aunt Caroline?"

"She can look after the whole damn bunch of them! She doesn't do anything all day except walk from one window to another in that creepy old house of hers. She's perfect for the job."

"But she doesn't come out of that creepy old house of hers, either. What am I supposed to do? Abduct them all and leave 'em on Aunt Caroline's porch with a note saying, 'Please look after these people?'"

"No, dummy. Just go explain to her how much she is needed during this *family* crisis. She'll do it for you."

"She doesn't even know me! We've never been introduced, not since I learned to talk, anyway."

"It's worth a try," she said. "Go do it. Tell Hugh you want to take her groceries to her today."

"You do it."

"I'm just an in-law. Besides, it's your family, not mine. And I have to get to the hotel for a meeting. Bye. Good luck!"

"I have to go to work, too!" I yelled after her.

I felt like a complete fool standing on Aunt Caroline's porch with my little basket of food. Little Red Riding Hood about to face the mean ol' wolf.

"Hi, Aunt Caroline," I practiced. "I'm your nephew, Matthew, your sister Edwina's son. Remember? I was three years-old when you locked yourself up in there."

I knocked lightly on the screen door, hoping she wouldn't hear me. The door opened. I couldn't keep from staring at her. She was a very old woman. She was only four years older than Mom, but she looked as old as Amelia. Her hair was white and was braided and coiled on top the way Gramma Ginny used to do it. Her dress looked almost new, but the style was very fifties.

"Hello, Matthew," she said. "Won't you come in? I've been expecting you."

Speechless, I followed her into the living room. The place was spotless: not a speck of dust on anything; all the glass and wood shined; the dark, rich colors in the upholstery and rugs stood out like new. There was a small, handmade, paper banner over the mantel: "Welcome Home, Donald!"

"Would you like some tea, Matthew?" Aunt Caroline asked.

I nodded, still unable to speak.

"Find yourself a seat there and I'll be right back. It's already steeping in the kitchen. Go on, sit down."

I sat on the long, blue couch in front of the fireplace, staring at the banner which would've welcomed my Uncle Donald home from the war, if he had come home from the war. It gave me the willies, so I looked down. On the low coffee table in front of me was a Ouija board with the marker pointing to *yes*, and a crystal ball which was sitting on the fiery tongues of three medieval dragons. I leaned forward and gazed into the crystal, half-expecting to see something.

"See anything?" Aunt Caroline asked as she placed the tea tray on the table, startling me.

"Don't be disappointed; it takes a lot of practice," she said, pouring. "How do you like your tea?"

"Black."

"Oh, you *can* speak! Wonderful! Now we can talk."

"I'm sorry."

"Don't be silly. Here, drink your tea. Cookie?"

"Yes, ma'am."

"Ma'am, indeed. You call me Aunt Caroline. Hear?"

"Yes, Aunt Caroline."

"That's better, Matthew. Now eat that cookie. It isn't poisoned." She laughed as though it might have been.

The chocolate chip cookies tasted just like Mom's.

"Did you make these?" I asked. "They're excellent."

"Thank you."

"You said you were expecting me?"

"Dear Hugh tells me everything when he brings my groceries."

"But Hugh didn't . . ."

"Thank you for bringing them today. That was very sweet of you."

"You're welcome."

"Would you like me to tell you about your future?" she asked. It was probably just a reflection from outside or something, but the crystal ball flared.

"Uh, no, no thank you. I don't think I could handle that information right now. Aunt Caroline, would you . . ."

"Yes."

"But I . . ."

"I'm sorry," she said. "I interrupted you. When you get old and you don't have much company, you tend to jump ahead. You were about to say?"

"Would you consider helping us out for a few days? Amelia's in a wheelchair; you probably know that. I mean, Hugh probably told you, and she can't take care of herself, and Mom, who was helping Amelia, well, she isn't feeling well either. Carl can't cook and Donny's in bed, too. The festival's coming up, so Elizabeth and I—she's my wife, if you didn't know already—we can't, don't have the time to . . ."

"Yes, of course, I'll help out the family. It's so sweet of you to ask me. Amelia can have the little room off the kitchen and I'll put Donny in the room next to mine, and . . ."

"But . . ."

" . . . and Eddie, and Carl, too, I suppose, in the master bedroom. I've never used it . . ."

"I'm afraid you don't understand, Aunt Caroline."

"Oh?"

"What I, what *we* had in mind was that you'd sort of *drop in* on them."

"You mean leave this house?"

"Yes."

"Good heavens, I couldn't do that!"

"Oh."

"I never go out. Haven't you noticed?"

"Well, of course."

"I haven't been out since—since—when was that? I'll have to look that up." She went to the built-in bookcase that ran the length of the back wall of the room and started running her finger alone one shelf of books. "You can help if you like," she said.

I joined her at the bookcase. Two entire shelves were filled with fat volumes of bound yellow writing pads. They were bound in those covers one might use for manuscripts or theme papers, with just a top and bottom and the bendable, metal spikes that adjust to whatever thickness. The outer edge of each was marked with a year and each year was bound in a different color, in repeated sequences of ten, so that all the years ending in "one" were yellow, the "two" years were yellow-green, "threes" were green, "fours" blue-green, "fives" blue, etc. The first volume was labeled 1932—1943, then they ran yearly from 1944 through 1983.

"What are these?" I asked.

"My journals," she replied, moving her finger back and forth under the middle fifties.

"You wrote all these?"

"Yes, I like to keep up on things. But so much happens every day, it's difficult to remember everything, so I write it all down every night before I go to bed. That way I don't have to remember it all, I can just look it up. Of course, I have to remember approximately when something happened to be able to look it up without reading everything from the beginning. I keep meaning to do some kind of an index, but it seems like such a huge task, I put it off, year after year. What year were you born?"

"Nineteen-fifty-five."

"Yes, of course. Well, it would've been after that, because I remember you as a baby. I'll take 1957 and you look in 1958."

I took 1958 off the shelf, knowing it was the right year. It was the year Baby Caroline died. It was the year Aunt Caroline retired into her house. I didn't tell her I knew it was the right year. I didn't want her to know that I knew anything about it, and I wanted to see inside one of those books.

I opened the journal. Each day had it's own page. The handwriting was exemplary.

> Thursday, November 6
> I couldn't bear to go to the baby's funeral today, so I held my own little private service here. The very thought of that child being dead makes me want to die, too, and I knew if I saw her in that awful little cedar chest they put her in, I'd fall apart. They probably think I killed her, but God is my witness. He knows I didn't harm that poor baby. He knows I loved her with my very soul. And He knows I didn't have any pills that day, or weeks before. But I don't blame Edwina for being upset. I had told her so many times that I was off them, naturally she might think I was lying. But it didn't seem to make either of us feel any better that she wasn't able to find any pills when she searched the house.

The whole town went to the
funeral in Escondido, and when the
last of them drove away, I put on
my black dress and that little black
felt hat with the veil and I went
out to the old burned-out garage,
ashes of so many memories. I had
planned to say a little something, a
prayer for Baby Caroline, but my
heart, my soul, was too burdened
with sadness and confusion to
speak. I tried to picture her in my
mind as she looked that night in
her crib when I put her down to
sleep. Those gorgeous big brown
eyes and that precious smile of
hers. I didn't cry. I came back in
the house.

"It was in 1958," I said, clearing the lump from my
throat, and replacing the book on the shelf.

"Yes, that sounds right. So, you see, I couldn't possibly
go out after thirty . . . after all those years."

"What if I helped you?"

"How?"

"We could do it a little at a time. Start with the back
yard, say; that's private, no one can see back there. Then
maybe the front porch."

"I don't think I can."

"Please try. We need you."

"Just the back yard?"

"Yes."

"You won't leave me?"

"No. Here, take my arm."

She clamped both of her hands onto my forearm and we

inched our way through the kitchen to the back door. She was shaking and I was beginning to doubt the wisdom of my methods.

"Are you sure they couldn't just come here to stay for awhile?" Aunt Caroline asked as we neared the door.

"They can't."

"It's so bright out there," she said, ceasing her miniscule steps.

"Here, use my sunglasses," I said, handing them to her.

She let go of my arm just long enough to put the sunglasses on, then resumed her grip. I opened the door and stepped out onto the small stoop, leaving my arm and Aunt Caroline just inside the door.

"I'm afraid," she said.

"I know."

We stood there, silently, for several minutes, she inside, me outside. Her short, shallow breaths were beginning to make me feel uneasy. I put my other hand on top of hers and gently rubbed her fingers. She faked a smile. I didn't have to fake my smile: Her bravery made me feel good.

She put one foot out onto the stoop next to mine, took a deep breath, and brought out the other foot. She sighed. She giggled. I laughed out loud.

It took us another half-hour to get from the stoop out to the lawn, but our time was well spent. She talked. She talked about Donald, her Donald, Little Donald. How she had waited for so many years, refusing to believe he was really dead—they never sent the body home—then finally losing hope. She talked about Hugh. How he had been such a good friend all these years, bringing her the groceries, and little gifts from time to time, sitting around with her in the evenings talking, telling her everything that was going on in Beech Grove. Her outside source for the journals. She talked about how much Hugh missed Gloria. She talked about the things she missed: the creek, the hotel, her family, the feel of grass under her bare feet. She kicked off her shoes. She let go with one of her hands, then let the other slide down my forearm until we were holding hands. We walked circles around the lawn. Then sat in the shade of one of the pines, still holding hands.

"Will you go with me at the beginning?" she asked. "If I do it, that is."

"Yes, to get you started, but then I have a lot of work to do. You would have to be on your own after that. That's why we need you. None of us has the time."

"I understand. Would I have to be out all the time?"

"No, just to make sure everyone's all right. Amelia will be the hardest. Although I understand Mom worked out some kind of system with her, for leaving things out for her, you know, where she could reach from the wheelchair."

"Would I have to go today?"

"No. Tomorrow, though. One day of fast will probably do them all good anyway."

"You mean they're not eating?"

"I was exaggerating. Donny's at our house. Carl's with mom. I can look in on Amelia on my way home from the paper tonight. Of course, there's no one at our house with Donny, and Carl can only make coffee, and Amelia . . ."

"You made your point. I'm a selfish, stupid old woman, who would let her family go hungry because she is too afraid to leave her house."

"I'm sorry. I didn't mean that."

"Yes you did and you're quite right. And just as soon as you figure out a way to get me out the *front* door of this creepy old house, we'll get started."

She stared at me, awaiting my solution.

"Well?" she asked.

"I'm not an expert on these things," I protested.

"You've done fine so far. Don't give up now."

"Thanks."

"You're very welcome."

I pulled up a weed.

"I must have Hugh speak to J.D. about his gardening," Aunt Caroline said. "The weeds are taking over."

"You might consider speaking to J.D. directly."

"I might."

I pulled up another weed.

"I think we'd better go back in," she said. "I'm feeling strange all of a sudden."

We practically ran to the door, hand in hand.

"More tea?" she asked, calmly, once we were safely inside.

We sipped our tea, then ventured out to the back yard again, pulled a few more weeds, and returned again to the kitchen, for still more tea. I had to go to the bathroom before we went out weeding for the third time.

I declined tea on our next trip inside.

It was time for the front porch.

I opened the heavy, wooden door and we stood, arm in arm, looking out through the screen door. We caressed each other to keep up our courage. I opened the screen door. We stepped out onto the veranda. We sidled over to the rattan sofa and sat together. We watched a scrub jay chase a squirrel off the grape stake fence which ran along the side of the property. We watched a dog run down the hill in pursuit of a rolling tennis ball. Fortunately, no human beings came along.

We took a breather, just inside the door, for a few minutes, then returned to the porch sofa. We counted some of the hardier weeds in the front lawn. We tiptoed down the steps to the grass and pulled a few of those weeds, vowing to speak firmly, and directly, to J.D. about his gardening skills.

Aunt Caroline, no longer clinging to my hand, yanked out a particularly healthy dandelion, then shouted: "I know! I'll pretend to be somebody else! I'll masquerade as something!"

"Masquerade?"

"Yes! A costume, that's what I need. I must have something in the house I can use. Let's go look."

We rummaged through her closets, rejecting a host of possible combinations, none of which gave her the protection, the anonymity, she needed.

I found a gypsy costume in a box on the top shelf of the closet in the master bedroom.

"Look at this!" I shouted. "It'll go great with your Ouija board and crystal ball!"

She loved it. It came with a choice of veils.

"I can even pick my mood," she said, first trying on the blue veil, then the red, changing to the green and finally settling on the black one, but sticking the others into her handbag in case her mood should change while she was out.

She dragged me out the *front* door, but then came to an abrupt halt at the edge of the front lawn, the edge of the road, the edge of the world.

"You'd better lead from here," she said.

"My pleasure."

I introduced her to her Aunt Amelia, her adoptive mother.

I introduced her to her other nephew, Donny. And to her niece-by-marriage, Elizabeth.

I introduced her to her sister, Edwina. And to her brother-in-law, Carl. And I left her there.

She called me three times at the paper that afternoon and twice at home that night. She was doing fine, she thought, but she was beginning to wonder if maybe the gypsy outfit might be a little too much for people? Would they think her batty? I told her I certainly didn't think so. That, in fact, I loved her costume. That Elizabeth loved her costume. That we loved her.

Elizabeth went out before breakfast the next morning, and when she returned, Aunt Caroline was on her arm, wearing a peach leisure suit and very large, but attractive, designer sunglasses.

People stared as my legendary Aunt Caroline—the old lady who moves from window to window in her creepy old house—as my darling, brave aunt made her rounds that next couple of days.

Hugh called me three times to thank me for getting "that dear, sweet woman back out into the world where everyone could enjoy her charming company!" He offered me free drinks for the rest of my life. I told him I didn't think I'd live very long if I took him up on his offer.

Aunt Caroline called me at the Clarion from each of her stops to let me know how everyone was doing. Amelia was cranky, Caroline said. Eddie and Donny were still in bed, she said. Carl was making those awful little chests, she said. But everybody was eating fine, Caroline said. And dinner was in the oven when Elizabeth and I got home in the evenings.

I didn't see Donny or talk to him until about four o'clock in the morning on Saturday, when he woke me with his screams. I ran to his room and turned on the light. He was fighting some invisible assailant, screaming about blood and knives. I sat on the bed and grabbed his shoulders.

"Donny, wake up!" I shouted over his screams.

"Don't kill me! Please don't kill me."

"Donny, it's me! Matt. It's all right. You're dreaming. Donny, Donny."

"He had a knife," Donny said, still not completely awake. "He was pushing it into my stomach. I could see the blood start to come out."

"He's gone, Donny. He's gone. You're safe."

"He was hammering on the end of the knife. I couldn't really feel the blade, but it was in me. I saw it!"

"Stop it!"

"Matt?"

"Yes."

"Jesus Christ!"

"It's over."

"It was . . . it was that guy, Jake," Donny whispered.

"Who?"

"You know. The one who shot . . ."

"You know about that?"

"Yeah. No thanks to you."

"I didn't tell you that part of the story because I knew it would give you nightmares."

"Right as usual," Donny said.

"How'd you find out?"

"Elizabeth."

"Goddamn her!" I said.

"She thought I knew already. That's why Mom hates me, isn't it? Because a queer killed her father."

"I don't know. To me, it seems so remote, so very long ago. But I guess to her, it was yesterday. She ought to know better than to blame you or any other gay person. It may be based on that, but I think a lot of it has to do with your defiance. She had set her mind to . . . you challenged her authority. She probably wouldn't have reacted so strongly if you would've just quietly had an affair, or whatever, instead of flaunting it in her face that night at the bar."

"So you think it's my fault?" Donny asked.

"Not your fault, exactly. I just think it can be patched up, if you'll tell her you're sorry."

"You want me to apologize to her? For being gay?"

"Not for being gay, damnit! For making a public event out of it. For defying her that way."

"You can forget it."

"You can take her the music box."

"You can forget that thing, too," he said.

"Goddamnit Donny! I don't understand you. You just keep fucking up. Then, when we talked about it, you seemed to be getting it together. Then you turn right around and fuck up again!"

"Well, I don't understand it either. But I know I ain't apologizing to her. I didn't do nothing to apologize for!"

"It's time you grew up, Donny. Time to act like a man. We don't always get everything the way we want it. Face it, kid, it's life."

"You face it. I don't want it."

"You have no choice, my friend. I want you out of that bed this morning. You have an appointment with Jack and you're going to keep it. We're all too busy around here to be looking after you night and day, so you're gonna start looking after yourself. As of now. You can live here, if you want, but you're gonna have to get a regular job of some kind, you're gonna have to see Jack as often as he thinks it's necessary, and you're gonna have to start acting like a civilized human being! Now! You got all that straight?"

He just stared at me.

"Then you think about it, boy! You got a couple of hours till daylight!"

I went back to bed.

The alarm assaulted me at 6:30. I hit it and rolled over. Elizabeth hit me. I hit her back and rolled over. She put her feet in the middle of my back and shoved me off the side of the bed. I cursed her under my breath, then went out to the kitchen to start the coffee. I cut my finger on the edge of the coffee can. I had a glass of the orange juice Aunt Caroline had fresh-squeezed the day before. It was full of pips; I spit it into the sink and went to take a shower. Then, determined not to let the day continue as it had started, I went back into the kitchen and poured three mugs of coffee. I put on a big smile and took one cup to Elizabeth in bed along with a friendly kiss. I took the other cup to Donny. He wasn't in his room. There was a note:

Matt,

 You were right. It is time I started looking after myself. And so you don't send search parties after me, I'll tell you where I'm going. I'm going up to the pond. Just for a few days to think things over. I'll be okay. I'll keep a fire going all night and I have my hunting knife. I can fix up the old tree house we started and sleep in it. Don't come up there! I'll go away if you do. I need to be alone, so please do this for me and then I'll see you in a few days.

Love,
Donny

I called Josh and woke him up.

"Do you know what time it is?" he growled.

"Yeah, I know. Wake up. Donny's gone!"

"So what?"

"He's gone up to the pond."

"Ooooh, how terrible. 'ittle Donny gone up to the big bad swimming hole all by hisself. Matt! Have you lost your mind?"

"Yes! He says he's going to stay up there."

"Big fucking deal."

"When's the last time you stayed up there at night?"

"He's a big boy now, Matt. Leave him alone. And leave me alone. I don't need this."

"I thought you loved him," I said.

"This is funny," Josh said.

"What's funny?"

"I didn't hit on Donny all those years because he was your little brother. Now you're trying to push me into marriage with him."

"I didn't say anything about marriage."

"You want me to take responsibility for him. In our situation, that amounts to marriage."

"You think I should just leave him up there?"

"Yes. If he can't hack it, he'll come running home," Josh replied.

"I don't know."

"I do. Bye."

I ran to Mom and Dad's house. Aunt Caroline was cooking their breakfast.

"Good morning, Matthew," she said, cheerfully. "Would you like some breakfast?"

"No thanks. Oh, thanks for the orange juice, by the way."

"My pleasure," she said. "Would you like me to look into your future this morning."

"I'm living it, thank you. Where is everybody?"

"I'm afraid Edwina's still in bed and Carl . . ."

"Carl is in his workshop. I'll start with him."

I ran out to Dad's workshop. As I walked in the door, he was taking a swig of Jack Daniels.

"At seven o'clock in the morning?" I asked.

"You got a better idea," he said.

"Dad, our fucking family is disintegrating as we speak. That shit's not going to help anything."

"But it does, son. It does."

"Well, it isn't helping Donny, who is, at this very moment, setting up a homestead at the pond, confident in his ability to withstand the rigors of nature."

"Good for him," Carl said.

"Sure. But will the furry little creatures who live up there feel the same way about it? We've had more than a few adventurous campers come bleeding into the clinic after tangling with the wild dogs or the bobcats up there."

"He knows enough to stay away from them," Carl said. "Leave him be, Matt."

"He needs us."

"It's too late for us to help him. We're the ones who let him get this way. He doesn't trust any of us anymore, because we let him wander off into his head, thinking he was all alone in this world. Now he is. Maybe we all are."

"He needs to know that we love him."

"He wouldn't believe it."

"It's worth a try!"

"It's not up to us now. He's in God's hands."

"You're drunk."

Dad's hand went automatically to his hearing aid, and the click signaled the end of our conversation.

I went back into the house.

"How's your father this morning?" Aunt Caroline asked. "Do you think he'll want breakfast soon? Everything is getting cold. I gave your mother hers already. She ate so well."

"I'll go congratulate her," I said.

"That's a good boy," Aunt Caroline said as she went back to washing dishes.

I didn't knock.

"I don't recall hearing a knock," Eddie said as I barged into the room and stomped up to the side of her bed.

I banged on her nightstand with my fist.

"There's your knock!" I shouted.

"Matthew Mark Russell, if you don't get out of here this minute," Mom started to say.

"I'm not leaving until we talk," I interrupted. "What the hell is wrong with everybody around here? All of a sudden, the seams are coming apart! I don't remember you ever staying in bed, even when you were sick. Dad's drinking before breakfast. Donny's going crazy. We used to be such a happy family, the ideal family, I thought."

"That's your problem, Matt," Eddie said, pulling herself up and leaning back on the headboard. "You only saw what you wanted to see in this house. The ideal. Your ideal. I'm not saying we were ever really unhappy, this unhappy, but these things have always existed. There have been many mornings over the years where I had to drag myself out of this bed, forcing myself to deal with another day. Your father and I haven't had a week in all the years of our marriage without at least one good spat, usually over his drinking. Donny and I haven't been friends since he was seven years old. And if I recall correctly, you never liked him much, until about a year ago. Now you're his champion. Why, Matt? Why now? Oh, you were always such a bright boy, reading all the time. A very bright boy, maybe too bright for us, huh? But, if you stop to think about it, son, you never had much to do with us as a family. You ate with us, that was about it. Now, you want to get involved. You want to bring us all together, make us closer, heal our wounds. You've got a wife. Go start your own family. But pay attention—pay *close* attention—to where it's going as the years pass or things will go too far before you even know they're happening. Go Mattie. Go have your own family."

I couldn't speak. The tears were welling up in my eyes and at the back of my throat. My skin was on fire. I turned and walked out of the room. I left the house without saying good-bye to Aunt Caroline.

"You look terrible," Elizabeth said when I got home.

"Thanks."

"Pat's been calling."

"I don't care."

"Well, don't snap at me!"

"I didn't."

"What are you going to do about Donny?" she asked.

"Nothing."

"I didn't do anything. Don't yell at me!"

"Just leave me alone. Okay?"

"No I won't," Elizabeth shouted. "I will not let your family come between us like this! I can accept the fact that you have to work long hours before the festival; so do I. But that leaves us precious few minutes together and you're giving them all to them and not me! You didn't even come to Panther Piss' funeral!"

"Oh Queenie, for chrissake . . ."

"I'm serious! Not about the cat—yes, her too!—you and I have to come first."

"We do," I said.

"We haven't been lately. And I'm not putting up with it another day. Let your family work out their own problems. We have ours. You didn't cause all this to happen. And you can't cure it!"

"Don't tell me what I can do. Damn, Elizabeth, I don't want to fight with you. I don't ever want to fight with you again. I want to make love to you. I want to—I want to have a baby."

"Well, *you* go right ahead and have one," she said.

"Don't tease. I mean it."

"I'm sorry. I think I'm probably ready, too. But, you're upset right now. We can talk about it when you're feeling better, when some of this pressure goes away."

"Can we make love anyway?"

"Only if you unplug the phone," she said.

"I'm unplugging. See? Un-plug!"

Mercifully, the Festival Edition of the Clarion consumed all my waking hours for the next three days, even with J.D. there at Pat's side. He balked at first, but when he got caught up in it, he worked as hard as his mother or I did. We put the paper to bed early on Tuesday evening, for Wednesday's festival opening.

Josh was waiting outside for me when I locked up.

"Hello, stranger," Josh said.

"Hey Josh."

"Get it finished?" he asked.

"Finally!"

"I'm sorry about the other morning. I wasn't awake and I was pissed at Donny."

"I hope he's okay. I should go up there."

"He's okay," Josh said.

"How do you know?"

"I went up there."

"When?"

"Day before yesterday."

"How was he?"

"He loves it up there. He's living like a savage. Runs around naked all the time. He's got that old tree house made into a little nest for himself. He picks berries and nuts, even got a jackrabbit with that knife of his."

Josh said he'd gone up there late Sunday afternoon, planning just to make sure Donny was okay, and not be seen. He walked the last part of the dirt road so Donny wouldn't hear the motorcycle. When he got up near the pond, he circled around to the top of the slope on the upside of the pond where the creek comes out of the rocks and found a hiding place in the brush and watched.

Donny was in the tree house when Josh first got there. Suddenly, he leapt from the tree, hitting the ground with legs apart and both arms out, a knife in one hand. Donny sniffed the air. He bent over into a crouch and took slow, apelike steps around in a circle between the tree and the water, stopping every third or fourth step to sniff again. He snarled. A bird squawked from the tree behind him and Donny swung around, knife poised. He screamed and ran toward the tree, scaring the bird into flight. He began to laugh. He threw his knife into the trunk of the tree and fell to the ground, rolling in the dirt and laughing. He sprang to his feet, assuming the ape stance again, pounded his chest and let out a Tarzan yell. Then, he began to laugh and jump around like a chimp. Then back to rolling in the dirt again and howling. And as suddenly has he had begun, he stopped. He lay out spread-eagle on his back in the dirt, looking up and the sky, and grinning.

"Hey Josh! Wanna play?" Donny shouted.

"How'd you know I was here?" Josh asked him.

"I'm a wild animal and animals can smell you humans sneaking around our lairs. You might as well come down. Your spy game has been found out!"

Josh climbed and slid down the hill to where Donny was lying on the ground.

"Hi!" Donny said.

"Hi," Josh said. "Looks like this place has cheered you up a little."

"I was just playin'. Wanna play?"

"Maybe. Can we talk first?"

"In the water," Donny said, leaping up and diving belly flop into the pond. "Get naked, Josh! I ain't talkin' to no humans in clothes!"

Josh stripped and jumped into the water.

"Okay, here I am," Josh said. "Let's talk."

"Gotta catch me first," said Donny, diving under the water.

Josh went after him, caught him easily and dragged him up onto the bank at the shallow end of the pool. Donny rolled onto his stomach and began thrusting his hips into the mud.

"Look! I'm fucking Mother Nature!" Donny cried. "And they said you can't fuck Mother Nature!"

"That's *fool* Mother Nature," Josh said, laughing with Donny. "Now, can we be serious?"

"No! I never wanta be serious again! I wanta have fun. I wanta laugh. I wanta have a good time. I wanta fuck. I wanta have a fuckin' good time," Donny howled.

"You . . ." Josh tried.

"I wanta be happy, like everybody else. See, I don't fuck up when I'm up here by myself. I don't disappoint anybody. This is paradise, Josh! My paradise! There's no school, so I can't be a lousy student. There's no parents, so I can't be a lousy son. There's no jobs, so I'm not a jobless bum. There's no girls, so I'm not a queer. There's no lovers, so I can't be lousy in bed."

"I never said . . ." Josh began.

"There's no lovers here, I said, so I can't be lousy in bed! I don't have to worry about gagging because I don't hold my mouth right, someone once said. I don't have to worry about being too tight because I don't know how to relax right. I don't have to worry about coming too soon—boy, I can't come soon enough! See, Josh? I only have to please me. And I do."

"I didn't mean to criticize, Donny," Josh said. "I thought you wanted to learn."

"I did, but not every goddamn second! But it's okay now. All that's gone. See? It's like this mud on my dick. All I have to do is wash it away and it's like new again, just waiting for you. Wanna play now?"

I didn't stop Josh from telling me the details that time, but he spared me the embarrassment anyway. He said it was different for them that day. He said it was the first time he had thought of them as one.

"Why'd you leave him up there?" I asked Josh.

"He was so different, so confident. I guess he charmed me. I didn't feel worried about him when I left. He was really okay, felt good about himself for a change. And he definitely wasn't ready to come back into this."

"I can't blame him for that," I said. "Did he say anything about when he thought he would come home?"

"Soon is all he would say."

"I hope so," I said.

"Me too," Josh said.

This year's festival was the biggest we've ever had. More music. More art. More craft. More audience. In fact, attendance was remarkable. But then, Elizabeth had talked the Executive Council into placing four times the usual number of ads in newspapers and magazines. And just about every art group, large and small, in Southern California participated, bringing with them their own followers.

Some people just drove out for the day, but most stayed in town or nearby. I know that quite a few got rooms in Escondido and then commuted each day. I heard that the campground about ten miles down the highway was booked solid for the duration of the festival. Our hotel was overflowing, with many guests doubling up, even strangers. And a lot of Beech Grove residents rented out their spare bedrooms (or their kids' bedrooms) to our cash-spending festival guests.

The Summer Solstice came earlier than I ever remember its coming: 10:02 P.M. on June 20. But then, before Elizabeth created our Solstice Celebration, we didn't open the festival by the Sun, we opened it on Founder's Day and Mom's birthday. Elizabeth said that if the actual solstice was at 10:02 P.M., so must be the opening dance. So, the Founder's Day Program was scheduled for nine, with a short break before Elizabeth's big number, this year without Pan.

I hated that the Festival was starting without Donny. And without Eddie, who was still in bed, or so I thought, anyway. We all crowded at the street side of the lawn for the speeches. Aunt Caroline wheeled Amelia up onto the speaker's stand for her annual *Praise Leonard* offering. Amelia and her adopted daughter, Caroline, looked enough alike to be twin sisters. I looked around to see if others had noticed, and apparently they had, because there was considerable buzzing going on. I spotted Mom way in the back with Carl. I waved. She waved back!

"Elizabeth, Mom's here," I said.

"I know," Elizabeth said.

"How'd you know?"

"I got her to come."

"How?"

"Secret."

"Tell me."

"Are you sure you want to know?"

"I was until you said that," I said. "Yes. Tell me."

"I told her I was pregnant," Elizabeth said calmly.

"Elizabeth!"

"It worked. She's here."

"But you shouldn't lie to her."

"I wasn't lying."

"What?"

"I said I . . ."

"I heard you. Besides, you can't know yet. It's only been a few days and . . . hey wait, you said we should talk about it later; and the pill? Did you . . . ?"

"Seven weeks ago, yes."

"You did?"

"Uh huh. Then, the night Josh got into the fight and we gave each other rubdowns. Remember?"

"Oh yeah! And you really are pregnant?"

"Uh huh."

"Oh."

"Oh? Is that all you can say?"

"Yes."

"Aren't you happy?"

"Yes."

"Then?"

I kissed her. Three times. Maybe four. Then I ran over to Mom and Dad and kissed them a couple of times. I found Josh at the beer booth and kissed him. I dragged him up to the front of the crowd so we could watch the dancing together. I put my arm around his shoulders. I smiled a lot.

I felt a little sorry for Elizabeth that Donny wasn't there to dance Pan. She had created a spectacular effect on the great lawn for this opening dance. There was a huge, canvas sun at one end, flooded with spotlights. The rest of the lawn was lit with torches made from the bottoms of oil drums. There was a torch every ten feet in a circle around the lawn.

When the speeches were finished, all the lights were turned out except the spotlights on the sun, which seemed to double in size in the darkness. The torches cast eerie shadows across the lawn and on the surrounding buildings and greenery.

A bugle sounded. Everyone quieted down. I could see Elizabeth off to the side getting her musicians and dancers ready to come out.

The bugle sounded again. One brigade of the children walked slowly and silently out to the very center of the great lawn.

The bugle sounded. The second brigade of kids marched out onto the field, circling it twice before positioning themselves between the torches. This group carried musical intruments.

The bugle sounded. The children in the center burst outward to form a large circle just inside the ring of torches.

The bugle sounded one last time. The musicians began to play. The dancers began to dance with their arms casting shadows in kaleidoscopic patterns on the grass. Then, as the music began to build, the dancers moved in small circles in front of the torches. Their circles grew and overlapped one another. Their movements became larger and more animated. It was very pretty, but it didn't have the emotional pull or fervor like the year before, when the children danced with Pan.

A flute called from behind the three oaks at the far end of the lawn. My pulse quickened. Had Elizabeth found a new Pan? Had she somehow, gotten Donny down out of the hills

to surprise us? I looked for her and found her, but she didn't
see me.

The children seemed as surprised as I was. They all
froze, staring at the oak trees.

The flute called again. Donny leapt out from behind the
trees! The children screamed and chased after him as he ran in
leaping strides, weaving in and out of the torches.

The audience went wild.

Donny was stark naked! His body was a deep reddish-
brown. His tan line had disappeared completely. His lean
muscles gleamed in the firelight. His hair was wild and he had
a full beard. He was a faun. He was Pan, even without the
phony horns and the glued-on hair. He was beautiful.

Donny soared in a high arc across the face of the bright
sun. The children chanted as their silhouettes pursued him
through the light. He ran out to the middle of the ring of
torches, gathering the children around him. There were black
streaks on his arms, stomach and chest, which seemed to be
lengthening as he raised his arms and began to spin. The
children started to clap and play their instruments, first
slowly, then louder and faster as Donny turned faster and
faster. He let out a steady, low moan which increased both in
volume and pitch with each successive spin.

Suddenly, Donny stopped. The music and clapping
stopped. Donny turned to the sun. He jumped straight up in
the air, released a terrifying scream, then fell to the ground.
The kids piled on top of him, screaming, with arms and legs
flailing. I remembered my impulse of the year before to run
out there and rescue him. Then Elizabeth was at my side, her
fingernails digging into my arm.

"Something's wrong," she said.

Josh and I ran as fast as we could out to the lawn and
started pulling kids off the pile. Their hands were smeared
with blood. Some were crying; some were laughing, thinking
this was all part of the game. When I picked J.D. up, he stared

at his bloody hands for a second, then put them to his face. I handed him to someone. People were pouring onto the field by then and the large floodlights were turned on. I screamed for the doctor. I screamed for for anybody to help. I was really scared. Josh and I pulled the last two children away. Donny was covered in blood.

"Hi, Matt," Donny said. "Where's Josh?"

"I'm here," Josh said. "What happened to you?"

"Bobcat."

Doc Weston was bending over Donny, "They're animal scratches all right."

"Will he be okay?" both Josh and I asked.

"Oh sure," Doc said. "We'll take him up to the hospital in Riverside and . . ."

"Can you treat him here?" Eddie asked as she pushed her way through the onlookers. "Will you people please move back so he can get some air! Can you fix him up, Bill?"

"Yes, but he's going to need around-the-clock care for a couple of days."

"Then we don't need a hospital, do we?" Eddie said.

"No," Doc said.

"Good. Just bring him home. Bring my son home."

13.   Mother and Son

J osh carried Donny home.

Doc said the only reason Donny's cuts had begun to bleed again was the physical exertion of the dance, and once Donny lay quietly on the grass for a few minutes, the bleeding stopped.

Josh put one arm under Donny's knees, the other under his back, and lifted him slowly. Eddie walked on one side and Doc on the other. Carl, Elizabeth and I followed. All the way home, Mom fussed at cleaning Donny up. She picked blades of grass from his hair. She brushed loose dirt from his shoulders and upper arms. She moistened a handkerchief in her mouth and wiped the blood, the sweat and the tears from his face.

Josh didn't falter once, not up the steep driveway at Mom and Dad's house, not up the steps, and not as he maneuvered the doorways to Donny's room. He lay Donny on the bed and sat beside him as Eddie and Doc cleaned Donny's wounds. Doc showed Mom exactly how he wanted the bandages done, gave Donny a couple of shots, and left. I had thought to leave with him, but as I started toward the front door, a feeling of dismay, of anxiety, came over me and I stopped abruptly. Elizabeth took my hand, kissed me on the cheek and told me to sleep well.

Carl was standing behind me. He put his hand on my shoulder. "Come on, son," he said, and led me to my old room. The easel and unfinished painting were gone. So were all of Mom's sewing and houseplant things. My room looked just as it did the day I left for college. The twin beds had fresh sheets, which were turned down as though company had been expected.

"Dad?" I asked.

"Your Aunt Caroline said she thought we might be needing the beds, so she fixed up the room before she left this afternoon. Get some sleep now. He'll be all right. Doc says so."

"Thanks, Dad."

He turned to leave, but then hesitated in the doorway. "Shall I leave the door open a little?"

"Please," I said, remembering those many nights as a very young boy when he used to have to carry me back to my room after I had run crying to their room in the middle of the night, frightened by a sound, a shadow, a dream.

I undressed and crawled between the cool sheets, then gazed out the open window, listening to the night sounds. An owl kept watch in the avocado tree just across the driveway from my window. Crickets, frogs and a mockingbird sang in harmony. I could hear Carl puttering in the kitchen. I heard Josh come out of Donny's room and walk the few steps along the hall to my door. I watched him come into the room, closing the door behind him, but leaving it open just a crack. He leaned over me, gave the top of my head a quick rub, then undressed and went to bed. He gazed out the window, listening to the sounds of the night. We could hear faint voices from Donny's room, sometimes coming through the open window, sometimes from the hall. Our mother cooing over our little brother.

Eddie sang to Donny, a song about pretty little fireflies you could hold in your hand:

In the dark, out in the dark,
   lights go on and off.
Twinkling lights, like twinkling lights,
   shine the little fi-re-flies.

In my hand, here in my hand,
   now I'll peek inside.
Twinkling lights, like twinkling lights,
   see the little fi-re-flies.

Day will come, yes day will come,
   you must fly away.
Twinkling lights, like twinkling lights,
   hide, you little fi-re-flies.

Night will fall, then night will fall,
   come on back to me.
Twinkling lights, like twinkling lights,
   my pretty little, pretty little fi-re-flies.

The hot sun was beating down on my forehead. A fly was digging at my hairline. I brushed it away, but it came back. I hit at it; it buzzed and redoubled its efforts. I shook my head furiously, then opened my eyes. I wondered why I was in my old room. Then I remembered. I sat up. The blanket was on the floor, the sheet rumpled at my feet. The sun was coming in through the wrong window, which meant it was afternoon.

The desk chair had been pulled up to the side of the bed and on it were my blue corduroy shorts and a note:

> Dear Sleepyhead—
>   Elizabeth brought the shorts
> first thing this morning. She said to
> tell you to enjoy your first day of

vacation and that she'd see you at
the festival this afternoon.

Sure hated to pass up that
beautiful hard-on you were waving
in the air this morning, but the
hotel is packed and I'm a busy man
these days.

See you tonight.

Love,

Josh

I pulled on the shorts, stuck Josh's note in my pocket and
wandered out to the kitchen. Carl was at the sink, washing
dishes.

"Morning," I said.

"Afternoon," he corrected.

"Any coffee?" I asked.

"In the coffee pot."

"Oh yeah." I poured a cup and sat at the kitchen table.

"Guess you were a little tired," Carl said.

"What time is it?"

"Two."

"Jesus. How's Donny?"

"Good. Very good. Thanks to the mother hen in there.
Stayed with him all night. Then only left him long enough
this morning to get him food. You want something to eat?"

"You cooking?" I asked.

"No, but your mama made cinnamon rolls."

"I'll take two."

"There's only one left."

"I'll take it."

"Donny ate five. After breakfast."

"I guess he's all right then," I said.

"I think he's more shook up than actually hurt."

"I would be, taking on a bobcat."

"You goin' to the festival today?" Carl asked.

"Yeah. Elizabeth is revealing those two secret paintings of hers at noon. I told her . . . Jesus Christ! Did you say two o'clock?"

"Yep."

"I'm in trouble! Did Elizabeth bring me a shirt?"

"In the closet in your room. And she said it was okay if you were late."

"But what if somebody bought one of them? Or both of them? I'll never get to see them."

"Slow down, boy," Dad said. "They'll be there when you get there."

"But . . ."

"They're already bought, and they ain't goin' nowhere."

"Have you been up there today?" I asked.

"I went with Elizabeth this morning," he said, grinning.

"So you saw the paintings."

"Uh huh."

"What are they like? What are they of? What—who . . . ?"

"You'll see."

"Dad!"

I ran to the bathroom for a quick piss and to splash water on my face and hair. I was about to rinse with mouthwash, when I noticed a new toothbrush in the rack with my name on it. I brushed, then ran to my room and put on my shirt.

"Don't forget Donny!" Carl called from the kitchen as I passed the door.

"Oh shit! I almost forgot!"

"That's why you spent the night. Remember?"

I ran into Donny's room. He was propped up against the headboard with half a dozen pillows, his torso and arms covered with fresh bandages. Eddie was sitting in her bentwood rocker next to the bed, book in hand.

"Morning," I said.

"Good afternoon, Matthew," **Mom** said.

I kissed her on the cheek. "Hi, **Donny**. How are you today?" I kissed him, too.

"Mama's reading 'Wind' . . . 'Wind' . . ."

" 'The Wind in the Willows,' " Eddie said.

"With Mister Toad," Donny added.

"I'm sorry I can't stay," I said. "I was supposed to be at the festival hours ago."

"Give our love to Elizabeth," Mom said, as she went back to her reading.

In past years, the artists were each assigned a different shop in which to display their work, so when I left Mom's, I headed for the little row of shops that faced the great lawn. They were all art-free. I started up toward the hotel to find out where the Art Festival was, only to discover upon turning around that I was looking right at it. No wonder Elizabeth accuses me of not paying attention, I thought. She had told me weeks earlier that she was renting tents this year, and there they were, all over the great lawn.

The ring of torches and canvas sun were preserved in the center, then fifty or so bright, white and blue canvas tents lined the perimeter, with the food and drink booths slightly apart at the near end.

As I walked out on the lawn, a group of children were just finishing a dance in front of the canvas sun, and I remembered that Elizabeth had told me something about little music and dance interludes running throughout the four days of the Art Festival. It was very crowded, and I couldn't see Elizabeth, so I just started going from tent to tent.

Amelia was sitting in her wheelchair in front of one of the first tents I came to. It was the only tent with flaps covering the front.

"You're looking very well today, Gram," I said.

"Thank you, Matthew. How's Donny?"

"He's doing fine. Do you know where my wife is?"

"All the way around on the other side."

"Thanks. What's in this one?" I asked. "It's the only one closed up."

Amelia smiled and pointed to the colorful, hand-painted sign behind her. It said: "*Madame Caroline—Psychic Readings.*"

"Aunt Caroline?"

"One and the same," Amelia replied. "She's good, too. Knew all about Donny and the bobcat, and your new baby, and that you and Josh were going to sleep in your old room last night. Did you? Sleep at your mom's last night?"

"Yes."

"Isn't that wonderful!" Amelia cried, doing a little cha-cha-cha with her wheelchair, dangerously near my bare left foot. "You have to have her tell your fortune. You know what she wants to do? Everything we make on her readings is going into a fund to turn her house into a little Beech Grove Museum and Art Gallery. She's moving in with me, next week, I think. Imagine! Our own museum with the beech tree memorial going in behind it. And we'll do a rose garden with little white benches and fountains out front, as sort of a formal entrance. Caroline saw it all in her crystal ball. You have to go in for a reading, Matt. There's someone in there right now, a tourist, but you can be next. It's only ten dollars, but it's for charity."

"I'll come back," I said, trying to catch my breath. "I'd better find Elizabeth first. I'm late."

"Are you ever! Wait'll you see!"

"Pardon?"

"Go on. But come back."

I walked away, slightly dazed. I could hear Amelia playing carnival barker to the tourists, offering amazing revelations through palmistry, Ouija and crystal ball readings, all for charity, of course.

As I came around behind the canvas sun, I spotted a

crowd in front of one of the artists' tents. I had a sinking feeling it was Elizabeth's display they were crowding around. I inched my way up to the front. It was Elizabeth's, all right.

It was the largest showing she had ever put together. There were five or six paintings that didn't sell last year. There were nine new pieces that I'd seen already, all landscapes. There was her annual remake of "Red Ball Under a Beech Tree," a guaranteed sale every year. This year's version had a little piece of yellow yarn hanging from a twig on one of the lower branches, as compared to last year's green yarn.

But the sensation, the pièces de résistance, were the two newest, the two secret paintings, boldly displayed on easels out in front of the tent.

The first was Eddie. It wasn't photographic in nature, but it was extraordinarily lifelike. It was a large painting and it showed Mom from the waist up, sitting in her bentwood rocker with a book in her hands. But she isn't reading; she's looking off to one side. She's looking at something special, judging by the expression on her face, the look of love in her eyes. I know the pose: there is a photograph on my dresser with Mom sitting in her rocker like that. I took the picture myself, ten years ago. But the face in Elizabeth's painting was not the face in the photograph. It was Mom's face as I had seen it that very morning in Donny's room. The painting was titled: "Eddie."

The other painting was of a young man, naked and without a face. His body was brown, his muscles lean, but relaxed. His skin glistened with sweat as though he'd just completed excercising—or dancing. His head was cocked to one side and back a little. One hand was on his hip, the other resting loosely on his thigh. The knee of that leg was bent forward, his heel slightly raised. His balls were drawn up tight in the sac; his penis was semi-hard and stuck straight out and a little to one side. There was a long scar on the side of his penis. The painting was titled: "The Scar."

I stared at the scar.

"My God, he's beautiful!" a man next to me said.

I looked up.

"Oh hello!," the man said. "Jerry! Look who I found!" he called to his companion.

"Have we met?" I asked.

"On the beach, in Long Beach. A couple of weeks ago. I'm Craig. This is Jerry. You're *his* brother, aren't you?" Craig said, pointing at "The Scar."

"Yes. Matt." We shook hands.

"Is *he* okay?" Craig asked. "We saw that spectacular dance last night. And then everything happened so fast, we didn't know if it was part of the show or what!"

"He's fine. Resting," I said, trying to catch Elizabeth's eye. She was busy listening to praises from her fans. Too busy to rescue me.

"Did your wife paint *this*? It's wonderful," one of them said.

"Yes."

"I'd love to buy it, but it's sold," Craig said, pointing to the little sticker in the lower right-hand corner of the frame. "Do you suppose she would do another one for me? I'd love one. Does she take Visa?"

"I'll go ask," I volunteered, and ran to the back of the tent to hide behind Elizabeth. I pulled at her smock. She ignored me. I pulled again.

"What are you doing?" she asked, turning quickly. "Oh, there you are."

I threw my arms around her and kissed her.

Craig and Jerry were waving at me from out front.

"Who's that?" Elizabeth asked.

"Fans. They want to know if you'll paint a nude Donny for them. And if you take Visa. I can't believe you did this. Who bought . . . ?"

"I'd better go talk to them," she said, and walked away from me in mid-question.

" . . .*that* one, anyway?"

Twenty-seven people shook my hand and congratulated me for having such a talented and daring wife. I accepted their praises with all humility, all the time wishing my talented and daring wife would get back to me. Finally, she did.

"What'd you tell them?" I asked her.

"To come early next year. You didn't tell me they were the ones we met on the beach."

"You met. I didn't meet anyone on the beach. Never mind them. You painted Donny in the nude!"

"Obviously."

"When?"

"Before last year's festival. Remember when he was around the house all the time?"

"Yeah. Helping with housework, you said."

"Helping around the house is what I said."

"Why didn't you show it last year?"

"I just finished it. I was going to put a face on him and never could decide whose, so I finally decided not to put one on him at all. Now, no one, except maybe his closest friends and relatives, will know it's Donny."

"They knew."

"Who?"

"Craig and Jerry."

"Eye for detail I guess."

"Detail is right. Did you have to put the scar on . . . there? It wouldn't . . ."

"It wouldn't be 'The Scar' without it, now would it?"

"Has Donny seen it? Has Mom seen it?"

"Donny has. Eddie hasn't. She hasn't seen hers yet either. I wanted to surprise her for her birthday."

"Oh my God, when is it? It's today! But you sold both of the paintings. The stickers. Who bought them?"

"Will you settle down. Carl bought them."

"Dad?"

"Uh huh."

"That one too?!" I said, pointing at "The Scar."

"Yes."

"For Mom's birthday?!"

"No, silly, just hers. He bought the other one for Josh and Donny."

"He did?"

"Will you stop with the question marks, please? Carl bought both paintings, weeks ago. He came by the house one day when I was working and saw them, loved them and bought them. Both paintings will remain on display until the festival closes on Sunday evening, at which time "Eddie" will go home to Eddie and "The Scar" will go home with Josh. Tonight after dinner, I will tell Eddie, or Carl will tell Eddie, that we have something, a painting, for her and that she will get it on Sunday night. That should cover it."

"Are we having dinner with them tonight?" I asked.

"You're doing that again. Questions. Of course we are."

"Our house or theirs?"

"I give up. Theirs. Donny still has a couple of days in bed."

"Do we have a gift? I mean, if Carl is actually giving Eddie the painting, then we gotta have something."

"The music box," Elizabeth said, impatiently.

"Oh yeah. Where is it?"

"Sitting on the library table in our living room, gift-wrapped and ready to take over there."

"I didn't see it."

"You weren't home last night!" she screamed, and everyone turned to look at us. I quickly kissed her to let them know everything was all right.

"What time is the festival over tonight?" I whispered.

She clenched her teeth and spit out, one word at a time:

"Nine, but some of the Sunday night bunch will be taking over for me around six. I will meet you at home at six-fifteen. Now, will you please go bother someone else?"

"Can I ask one more question?" I asked.

"It may cost you your life."

"Did you see Aunt Caroline?"

"I even had a reading," Elizabeth replied.

"Really?"

"Did *you*?"

"Have a reading? I mean, no."

"Why not?"

"It's silly."

"Who says?"

"Stop that!" I said.

"Go see her."

"Maybe tomorrow. I'll see you at six-fifteen, right?"

We had Eddie's birthday dinner on the foot of Donny's bed. Carl made a family-size, plywood bed tray just for the occasion. Donny sat cross-legged at the head of the bed. Mom, Dad, Elizabeth and I pulled chairs up around the foot and sides, with Mom, at Donny's insistence, as close to Donny as was physically possible. Josh was late.

Carl made a stew he had learned how to cook during— but had not made since—his days in the navy. It was suspiciously good, especially sopped up in large chunks of french bread. Dessert—("You have to have birthday cake," Elizabeth had said)—was chocolate cake which no one, except Donny, ate. Eddie didn't want birthday candles, so Donny insisted on blowing out what seemed to be an endless series of those long, wooden fireplace matches, filling the room with sulfured smoke.

Donny's room felt different, as I sat there letting my mind wander, waiting for the match ceremony to end.

Apparently Mom had straightened up a little, as she would have put it. The usual disarray of junk had been neatly arranged about the room. There were no cutoffs, T-shirts, socks or underpants lying around on the floor, over lamp shades or half-under the bed, a first for Donny's room. His rock magazines and comic books were stacked in uniform piles on the two bottom shelves of the bookcase. His cassettes had all been returned to their racks, in alphabetical order by artist. His souvenir button collection was mounted on a large, felt-covered board hanging over the chest-of-drawers. The buttons with four-letter words were conspicuous by their absence, and there had been a lot of them in Donny's collection. The bumper sticker collection was displayed on cardboard strips which formed an arch around the window: The Cars, Mötley Crüe, AC/DC, Grateful Dead, Duran Duran, Pink Floyd, Billy Idol, KISS, Iron Maiden, Judas Priest, Queen, Quiet Riot, Black Sabbath, Twisted Sister, Rolling Stones, ZZTop, Yes. It took me awhile to figure out that Mom had used what she considered to be their "last names" in deciding the order. Donny's posters, an almost story-like sequence of science-fantasy art, had been rehung in story order starting to the right of the hall door. They continued around the room and ended just left of the door, rather than just having been thrown at the wall in no particular order and haphazardly affixed with oversized chunks of masking tape, their former condition. Mom had respected Donny's individuality, his personality, in her redecorating efforts (except for the buttons with dirty words), but, being orderly, the room was no longer Donny.

"Can we stop with the matches now?" I asked, trying to rid my mind of the impulse to mess up the room.

"We didn't sing Happy Birthday to Mama," Donny said, blowing out one more match.

"You know how lousy we sound," I said.

"'Lizbeth don't," he said.

We sang. Out of key, except Elizabeth, with each ending at a different time. Josh walked in on the final sour note.

"That's awful," Josh said. "Sorry I'm late. The hotel's a madhouse. Happy Birthday!" He produced a bouquet of flowers from behind his back and handed them to Mom with a kiss on the cheek.

"Thank you, Josh. They're beautiful," Mom said.

"What'd I miss?" Josh asked.

"Dad's navy stew and Elizabeth's chocolate cake," I said.

"Can we do Mama's presents now?" Donny asked.

"We should let Josh eat something first," Eddie replied.

"That's okay," Josh said.

"Wine?" Elizabeth offered.

"That, I'll take."

"Presents now?" asked Donny, squirming.

"Yes Donny," Carl said.

"Me first," Donny said, then reached under his pillow and brought out a large, hand drawn card. Donny had made his own version of the festival poster. It read:

Beech Grove's Annual
Founder's Day Program
ART FESTIVAL
and
Summer Solstice
CELEBRATION
AND MOM'S BIRTHDAY!!

"Oh Donny, it's lovely," Mom said. "I know, we can put it on the refrigerator door so everyone can see it."

"You don't have to," Donny said, with a most uncharacteristic shyness.

"I'm next," Carl said, handing Eddie one yellow rose and kissing her. "I've got another present for you. That is, Elizabeth and I have another present for you, but you can't have it until Sunday night when the festival is over. We want everyone to see this masterpiece before we give it to you."

"Carl, please," Elizabeth said, with a most uncharacteristic modesty.

"One of Elizabeth's paintings?" Eddie asked. "Oh, thank you both. I can't wait to see it."

"Oh damn! Elizabeth, I'm sorry," Josh blurted. "I meant to come to your unveiling today, but we got so busy."

"It's okay, Josh."

"I'll be there tomorrow, I promise."

"This is such a wonderful surprise," Mom said.

"It will be," I muttered.

"Donny should be able to go out by Sunday," Mom continued. "We can all go to the festival together, after an early dinner."

"Surprise is the right word anyway," I was still muttering, despite Elizabeth's repeated kicks to my shin.

"What, Matt?" Mom asked.

"I said, we have another surprise for you. It's from me, Elizabeth, Josh and Donny." I gave her the box.

"What is it?" Donny asked.

Eddie methodically removed the ribbon and the bow, then each piece of tape, careful not to tear the colorful, beclowned wrapping paper.

"Mama, hurry up!" Donny fidgeted.

Eddie slowly removed the paper and folded it. She peeled the tape off the flaps and lifted them individually in sequence. She tugged gingerly at the tissue stuffing.

"I can't stand this!" Donny cried.

Mom took the music box in her hands. "It can't be," she said.

"It is," we said.

Mom set the music box on the table next to the bed and turned it on. As it began to turn, and as the petals began to unfold, Mom began to cry. Then Donny began to cry.

"Let's have coffee in the living room," Carl suggested.

"Yes," Mom said, "Donny needs his rest."

"Mama?" Donny said, reaching for her hand.

"Get some sleep now, dear. I'll be right out there if you need me." Mom kissed Donny on the forehead and tucked him in as we all filed out to the living room.

Either Carl had his hearing aid turned off or he was lost in worried thought because he didn't say another word all evening. Josh paced, his conversation jumping from one subject to another, never actually settling on any one thing. Elizabeth was staring at me with a puzzled expression on her face. Mom served the coffee and refused to talk about Donny, which pissed me off because I wanted to talk about Donny. I thought his reactions were as much emotional as physical and that they should be dealt with accordingly, but Mom kept stopping me in mid-sentence, or, worse yet, getting up to run off to Donny's room when he called "Mama!" every five minutes. And Mama went.

"Can't you see what he's doing?" I said.

"Go home, Matt," Eddie said.

"But this is . . ." I started blurting out.

"Good night, son!" Mom interrupted me, trying to keep me from getting into trouble with Elizabeth.

It was too late. Elizabeth was glaring at me.

"Good night," I said.

"Good night," everyone said.

"Mama," Donny said.

Elizabeth and I walked home in silence. And, in silence, we went to bed. I tossed and turned and sweated. And mumbled obscenities to myself. Elizabeth ignored me, until I got out of bed and started to put my clothes back on.

"What are you doing?" she asked.

"Going for a walk."

"For a walk? Or back *home*, as you called it?"

"No. I'm going for a walk, plain and simple. I need some air. I need to think."

"Matt, what is happening to you?"

"I'm not sure."

"Honey, I know you're worried about Donny, but Doc said he'd be fine and Eddie's with him around the clock."

"That's what I'm worried about."

"What?"

"You saw them tonight. It's like—he's like a little kid."

"And what are you?"

"I?"

"Did you talk to Josh last night?" she asked, saving me the embarrassment of trying to come up with an answer to that last question.

"No, we just went to sleep. Mom sang Donny a lullaby."

"And?"

"Nothing. I just don't remember that ever happening before."

"Are you coming back here tonight?"

"I . . ."

"Stay there tonight, then. But get it worked out, Matt. You can't live there; this is your home now."

"I know."

"Just remember it. I'm going to sleep now. You send me a postcard from time to time and let me know how you're getting along."

Everyone was already in bed when I got to Mom and Dad's house. I tiptoed into my old room. Josh was in the other twin bed, sitting up against the headboard and staring out the window.

"Hey Matt."

"Just like the old days, huh?" I said, starting to undress.

"Not quite, but it's eery."

"Déjà vu."

"Yeah. Are you all right?" Josh asked.

"Why does everybody keep asking me if I'm all right? Donny's the one that got hurt and the one who's reliving his past. Shit, I'm just showing a little concern—for a change, according to some people—and you all jump on my back!"

"Feel better?"

"No."

"Wanta talk?"

"No. Yes."

Silence.

"Anything?" Josh said.

"Confusion?" I guessed.

"Jealousy?"

"Huh?"

"You heard me," he said.

"Of Donny?"

"With your mom like that."

"You really think so?"

"I'm asking you."

"Maybe," I said, not knowing whether I really was jealous or just vulnerable to suggestion in my confusion. "Time to sleep."

"It's no big deal, Matt. Don't go nuts over it."

"I'll try."

"G'night."

"G'night."

My sleep was fitful, filled with a myriad of dreams, none of which I could remember. I woke up once thinking I was late for school. Another time, I awoke thinking I was in bed with Josh—but I wasn't.

Josh had gone to work before I got up the next morning. Mom was having breakfast with Donny in his room, so I ate with Dad at the kitchen table.

"Goin' to the festival today?" Carl asked.

"I don't know. Probably not."

"Wanta help me in the shop?"

"No. Thanks anyway."

"I wasn't askin' as a kindness to you, Matt. I could use the help. The orders are comin' in faster'n I can build the damn things."

"I'm not up to it, okay?"

"Don't bite my head off, boy. I was just askin'."

"Sorry. I don't feel well. Really."

"You oughta get out for some fresh air."

"I will. Later."

He went out to his workshop. I washed the dishes, then went to the den and plopped down on the sofa.

And stayed there most of the day. I went in once to see if Donny wanted to play checkers or something, but Mom was reading to him. They were cuddled together in bed and they as much as told me to get lost. I took a stack of Donny's Adventure Comics and went back to the den, stretched out on the sofa and read the comic books.

Dad came in sometime in the afternoon and harrassed me until I finally went outside just to get away from his nagging, which apparently was his plan all along. I walked toward the hotel, at first thinking I'd wander around the festival for awhile, but then changed my mind and ducked into the general store when I saw Elizabeth and Jack standing near the soft drink stand in the first row of tents.

I bought a pack of cigarettes. I had not had a cigarette since college, since Elizabeth threatened to not marry me if I didn't quit, since the day Elizabeth showed me a preserved, dissected lung from someone who smoked too much. I walked back to Mom and Dad's house, playing with the cigarette pack, but not opening it. Then opening it, smelling it, but not taking any out of the pack.

Dad was back at work when I got to the house. Donny was napping. Mom was in the kitchen, making coffee.

"Did you have a nice walk, dear?" she asked.

"It was okay."

"What are you doing with those?"

"What?"

"The cigarettes. Are you smoking again?"

"No, I just bought them to, uh, to smell."

"Give them to me, before you get tempted."

"Don't worry about me. You've got enough to worry about."

"What's that supposed to mean?" she asked.

"It means what the hell is going on?"

"Don't you talk to me in that tone."

"Okay, Mother. What is—why is Donny acting like that?"

"Like what?"

"Like *what*!"

"Keep your voice down."

"Like a child, that's what."

"Because he needs to. You do the same thing whenever you get sick, even a little cold. So does your father. It's a male trait."

"Funny, Mom. He's not just seeking a little attention, he's regressing."

"He is not regressing. You and your college psychology. Right now, he doesn't have a care in the world, not a worry. And that's apparently what he needs to get well. You know, Matt, sometimes the pressure just gets too great and we need to get away from it, to escape. Now, *you* stop acting like such a baby and help me with this coffee."

Her hands were shaking, so I took the pot from her and finished pouring the coffee.

"Matt," she said.

"Hm?"

"I didn't get a chance to thank you for the music box."

We hugged.

Mom took her coffee to Donny's room along with a cup for him. I took my coffee to the den, plopped down on the sofa, grabbed a comic book and lit a cigarette.

Josh showed up after dinner. I was back in the den again because Mom was reading to Donny again and Carl was out in the workshop again.

"You still here?" Josh asked, grinning.

"Yeah."

"Elizabeth's gonna be pissed."

"Elizabeth's state of mind is really none of your business, is it?"

"Yessirrrr."

"What's that?" I asked of the shoebox he was holding.

"A present for Donny."

"What is it?"

"Come and see."

I followed him to Donny's room. It was a frog.

"Goddamn he's big!" Donny cried.

"Donny!" Mom scolded.

"Well, he's huge!"

"And he's going outside."

"Mom!"

"Frogs are not indoor pets."

"I'll keep him in the box."

"And what's he supposed to eat?"

"I'll catch flies for him."

"You can't get out of bed."

"Matt'll do it."

"He will not," I said.

"Asshole!" Donny said.

"One more of those and you're getting your mouth washed out with soap, young man," Mother said.

"Jerk, then," Donny said.

"He's built to catch flies," I said. "Let him find his own food."

"Mama?" Donny pleaded.

"Matt will catch some flies for tonight, then he goes out tomorrow."

"Jesus Godda . . ." I started to say.

"I have enough soap for you, too."

The phone rang.

"I'll get it," I offered, and went out to the den to answer it.

"Matt?" Elizabeth said on the other end when I picked up the phone and sort of grunted into it.

"Hi Queenie."

"Is that any way to answer the phone?"

"You knew it was me, didn't you?"

"Yes."

"Then it was sufficient, wasn't it?"

"Are you coming home?"

"Why don't you come over here?"

"Because I don't want to come over there."

"Then don't."

"Are you coming home?" she asked again.

"I have to catch flies."

"Matt, I'm worried about you."

"But I do. Josh gave Donny a stupid frog and Donny won't let it go outside to feed itself, so I have to go out and catch its goddamn dinner."

"I don't mean that. I mean this whole thing. You shouldn't be living over there."

"It's my family, my brother! Where should I be?"

"*Here*. From which you could visit *there*. We live very close. Remember?"

Silence.

"Matt?"

"What?"

"Are you coming home?"

"I don't know yet."

"When do you think you might know?"

"You don't have to get sarcastic. I won't know till it's time to leave."

"Don't bother!" she shouted, then slammed down the phone.

"Told you she'd be pissed," Josh said as he came up behind me.

"You're a real prophet."

"I gotta get back to the hotel. I left a bunch of paperwork undone and we've got an early staff meeting. Guess you'll be looking after things here tonight?"

"Don't you start in on me."

"I'm not. Hope you sleep better tonight."

"Sorry if I kept you awake."

"No problem," he said. "What you need is some exercise to tire you out and make you sleep better. Maybe the fly-catching will do it."

He ran out the door before I could hit him.

I went outside to catch the frog's dinner. It was too late: the flies had all gone to bed. I filled a jar with assorted gnats, mosquitos and some funny-looking, super lightweight, fuzzy black things and took them into the frog.

"Where's Mom?" I asked.

"She said she was tired, went to bed," Donny said.

"No wonder."

"Huh?"

"Nothing. Here's some bugs."

"Thanks."

He emptied the jar into the shoebox and replaced the lid.

"How are you feeling?" I asked, sitting on the edge of the bed.

"Okay, I guess."

"Do they itch?"

"A little."

I pulled out the pack of cigarettes and lit one. "Want a cigarette?"

"No. I thought you quit years ago."

"I did."

"I can see that."

"Shouldn't you be out of bed, walking around a little?"

"Mom said not yet."

"Whatayou say?"

"Whatever Mom says."

"You mean *Mama*."

"What's the difference?" Donny asked.

"The way you've been saying it, that's the difference."

"I don't understand. What's the matter?"

"You."

"Hey, I didn't do anything. Wasn't my fault the fucking bobcat got me."

"I'm not talking about that."

"Then what are you taking about?"

"This—this *Mama's Boy* game you're playing!"

"I'm not the one playing. It's her. She wants to . . . to baby me."

"And you love it."

"It's okay."

"Sure it's okay. You get to lie around while she waits on you hand and foot, tiring herself out so she has to go to bed at nine o'clock."

"Matt, don't be mad at me."

"I'm not mad at you! I just want you to stop this game you're playing. And *grow up*! You can't cling to your mommy for the rest of your life!"

"I notice you've been hanging around a lot lately."

"That's because I . . ."

Mom's voice hit me on the back of the head the way the

flat of her hand used to do when I was a kid. I jumped to my feet.

"That's because you what, Matthew?" she asked, daring me to answer.

I did not.

"I think you'd better leave," she said. "Come back when you're feeling a little less selfish. Come back when you're ready to apologize, when you're ready to grow up, yourself."

"It's okay, Mom," Donny said.

"It is not okay!" she screamed. "Matt, what the hell were you thinking of? Donny is sick. And he doesn't need—we don't need your opinions on the matter!"

Mom sat on the bed and put a protective arm around Donny's shoulders. I left the room. Dad was standing in the living room shaking his head as I walked to the front door, and out.

Elizabeth didn't say a word as I crawled into bed. She put her hand on my chest, kissed me on the shoulder and snuggled up against my side.

The phone woke me up at seven the next morning. It was Josh.

"Are you out of your fucking mind?"

"Morning, Josh."

"He's sick, for chrissake! Why don't you just take a baseball bat to him and finish him off good? What a lamebrain stunt to pull, Matthew! If I didn't have a goddamn meeting in a few minutes, I'd come over there and use a bat on you! I may do it anyway. Are you listening?"

"Yeah."

"Well?"

"What can I say? You're right."

"What're you gonna do about it?"

"I don't know."

"I suggest you think of something. Soon!" he screamed. And hung up.

I pulled the sheet over my head. Elizabeth pulled it off.

"You want a muffin with your coffee?" she asked.

"Is it Sunday already?"

"No, Saturday."

"Oh. I guess so."

"Cigarette?"

"No. How'd you know?"

"Stench, darling. Stench. On your breath, on your hair, on your clothes. And there's a pack sitting right there on your night stand."

I threw them away.

"When I said I wanted you to come home last night, I didn't mean you should get yourself thrown out," Elizabeth said.

"You know about that too, huh?"

"Josh called the first time at six-thirty."

"How did he know?"

"Donny called him this morning."

"What a network."

"What did you expect?"

"Exactly what I got."

"And?"

"And I'm going. Right now."

"Take a muffin with you."

I didn't go in the house. I went around the side and scratched on the screen of Donny's window. He was alone in the room, eating breakfast from a lap tray.

"Hi," I said.

"Hi," he said.

"Can I come in?"

"Doors locked?" he asked.

"No. I just didn't know, you know."

"I know. Just yank the screen. It comes right out."

I pulled the screen off and climbed through the window.

"Want something to eat?" Donny asked.

"I've got a muffin here someplace." I dug the bran muffin out of my pocket. It was emaciated.

"Here, have some of my toast. She made enough for an army." He patted the bed for me to sit next to him.

"Aren't you mad at me?" I asked, sitting on the bed. "Everybody else is. Well, most everyone anyway."

"No. We all do stupid things sometimes."

"Thanks."

"But you usually don't, so I figure you got a lot of free ones coming."

"Something to look forward to."

"Nobody's perfect, asshole."

"I'm learning that."

"About time."

"I'm sorry."

"Don't."

"I have to. It's none of my business if you . . ."

"Are you starting again?"

"Okay, but I would like to understand."

"So would I, brother. All I know is that she likes me now and I don't want to spoil it."

"It's not going to disappear just because your wounds heal."

"I don't know that."

"Believe me."

"I'm scared, Matt."

"Of what?"

"I don't know. Everything."

"Like what?"

"Like losing everybody again—Josh, Mom, you," Donny said, sliding his hand across the sheet toward me.

I took his hand. "You ain't gonna lose us."

"I did before."

"Maybe you didn't really have us before, but you do now. It's called love, Donny. Sometimes its real hard to find, but once you do, it sticks pretty good. And we're all afraid of losing it. Some of us get stupid at times, but nobody's going away this time."

Donny pulled my hand to his mouth, my fingers folded into a fist, and I could feel his warm breath between my fingers. I leaned down to him, my forehead resting on his.

Mom's voice clobbered me on the back of the head again. Donny bit into my knuckle.

"That's better, you two," she said, cheerfully. "You want some breakfast, Mattie?"

After breakfast—melon, sausage, eggs, home-fries and biscuits—I babysat while Mom and Dad went to Escondido for a day of shopping. Donny and I played checkers, read to each other, listened to music and told each other every dirty joke we could remember.

Mom made a huge dinner that night, which we ate on Donny's bed. Then, at nine, I went to the festival to help Elizabeth close up and the two of us went for a long, slow, romantic walk, ending up on our front porch where we made love on top of our new Union Jack afghan. It was the afghan Elizabeth's mother worked on for five years in the hope that she would be able to give it to her daughter as a divorce present. Then last month, my mother-in-law called, as she does every month, to find out if it was time to send the present. Elizabeth was in a particularly brassy mood that night and told her mother that she could burn the damn thing as far as we were concerned and that if Mother was only going to call to hear divorce news, she could just bloody-well stop calling altogether! The afghan arrived special delivery a few days later with a lovely note addressed to the both of us, wishing us love and happiness—and promising to come for a long visit, finally, after all these years. I asked for a divorce— in jest, of course.

On Sunday morning, Eddie missed the service, the first time ever, as far as anyone could remember. Even the week Mom had taken to her bed, Aunt Caroline said she had dragged herself to the service, then came home and went right back to bed again. Eddie didn't go to service that Sunday morning because she wouldn't leave Donny and she wasn't letting him out of bed until dinner and the festival.

On Sunday morning, Josh came over and had waffles with Elizabeth and me. We ate on the veranda, picnic style on the Union Jack afghan. The hotel was still jammed with guests, and Josh was on call, but he was determined to take the day off. We didn't go to the service either, so we had all morning to sip our coffee and savor our waffles. Elizabeth made them special with fresh strawberries and cream, which I managed to spill all over the afghan.

The family Sunday dinner was set for one o'clock to give us more time at the festival afterwards. We cleared up our brunch mess at our house, then went on over to Mom's about noon. Eddie, Carl and Donny were sitting on the front porch when we arrived.

"Hey, look who's out of bed," I said, sitting next to Donny on the porch swing.

Josh pulled two chairs around from the side porch for Elizabeth and himself.

"S'posed to hit a hundred again today," Carl said.

"So I heard," Josh said. "I don't know how those people can stand the hot springs on days like this."

"Josh!" Elizabeth teased. "As manager of the Beech Grove Hot Springs Hotel, I would think you'd be more positive about the use of your own facilities."

"I guess, but that water's too hot for me in the summer. I'll take the pond anytime. Ooops."

We all looked at Donny to see if he reacted to the mention of the pond, but he was playing with the frog.

"Help me get dinner on the table, Elizabeth," Mom said, moving toward the door.

"Sure."

They went inside. I reached over to touch the frog. Donny pulled it away.

"I just wanted to see it," I said.

"No."

"C'mon Donny! I didn't get to look at it the other day."

"No."

"What's the matter with you? I thought we were friends again."

"Matt," Josh said.

"Give it to me," I yelled. "Don't be so damn selfish!" I grabbed for the frog.

"MATT'S TRYING TO TAKE MY FROG!!" Donny screamed.

"Matthew, for God's sake!" Carl said. "Leave the boy alone. What's wrong with you?"

"Oh, keep your damn toad!" I said.

"I guess I should have brought Mattie a frog, too," Josh said, laughing.

"Oh shut up!" I said, and went into the house.

"What was that all about?" Mom asked.

"Nothing."

"Something wrong with Donny's frog?" Elizabeth asked, leading.

"No. Apparently you were eavesdropping."

"I thought maybe you wanted one, too."

"Drop it, huh?"

"I have a Kermit doll in my closet. Want me to run home and get it for you to play with?"

"Oh shut up," I said, and went into the dining room to set the table.

Sunday dinner was a very large, tender pot roast, with

the vegetables cooked around it in the roasting pan. Waldorf salad. Three kinds of pickles. Two kinds of olives. A giant loaf of homemade bread, fresh from the oven. Peach cobbler.

Josh and I did the dishes, then we all trooped off to the festival.

Mom had a new dress. It was white, ankle-length with long sleeves, a frilly collar up to her chin, and more frills at the wrists and around the bottom. Mom had a new hat, a big, floppy white one. Mom had a new parasol, also white. Mom looked very different, as if she were dressed up in some kind of costume.

Mom led our little parade, with her parasol in one hand, Donny in the other. Elizabeth and I followed, then Josh and Dad.

We strolled up the road toward the festival, nodding and waving to neighbors on their porches. Donny kept tugging at the crotch of his safari shorts.

"Do you have to go to the bathroom," Eddie asked.

"No. They're too tight."

We made our entrance onto the great lawn.

"Isn't that sweet," I heard a woman say to her husband.

"What?" the man asked.

"That woman and her son, walking hand in hand."

"Oh, he's probably retarded."

"Sh!"

Josh and I both laughed. Elizabeth elbowed me and glared at Josh. We stopped laughing.

"Can I have a Coke?" asked Donny.

"Later," Mom said. "Oh look, there's Amelia!"

"Edwina!" Amelia called from her wheelchair in front of Madame Caroline's. "Look at you! That dress is absolutely stunning! Caroline! Come out here! Your sister and her . . . uh . . . entrourage have arrived!"

Madame Caroline popped out through the flaps, in full gypsy regalia. "Be right back, honey," she said to someone inside the tent. "You just keep concentrating on the dear departed. Oh Eddie! Amelia, do you believe this? Our little Edwina in a summer dress! Oh, and look at the rest of you! You're all so pretty! Especially you, Donny. But that's what everyone at the festival's been saying, haven't they? Oh dear, did I let the cat out of the bag? I hope not. I must get back to this poor woman. Lost her husband and her parakeet in a fire. She's bound and determined to contact one of them if it takes all day. I hope you like Elizabeth's paintings, Eddie. Keep an open mind, will you? Matthew, you still haven't come in for your reading yet."

"Boopsie!" the woman screamed from inside the tent.

"She's made contact!" Caroline said. "I'd better get back in there before she loses it."

"Is Boopsie the husband or the parakeet?" Elizabeth asked, setting off a round of giggles.

"Sh!" Caroline scolded, between giggles. "Some people take this stuff seriously. Coming!" Madame Caroline disappeared through the flaps from which she had come.

We continued our tour of the tents. Up ahead, I could see Elizabeth's tent, staffed with Jack and Dennis, Kurt and Terry, Rae and Gloria, Pat and Gwen.

"There seems to be a party going on at that booth," Eddie said as we approached.

"Sure does," I said.

"My helpers," Elizabeth explained.

"Oh, is that your tent?" Mom asked.

"Yes."

"I'm so excited. I don't know if I'm quite ready."

"You're gonna love them," Carl said.

"*I'm* not ready," I said.

"Them?" Eddie asked.

"There are two new paintings, special paintings," I began.

"And you'll love them both," Josh interrupted. He'd run

out first thing on Friday morning to see Elizabeth's surprises. Then spent most of the day dragging people away from other tents to see "Eddie" and "The Scar." He didn't seem at all worried about Mom's possible reaction.

The Regulars, each with a paper cup of beer in hand, were standing in front of the easels as we walked up to the booth. Everybody kissed everybody. Dennis went for more beer. I tensed.

Jack was standing in front of the painting of Eddie. "Ready?" he asked her.

Mom nodded. Jack moved aside.

Eddie just stood there, overwhelmed. She stepped back a little and cocked her head, then stepped forward and leaned in for a closer look. She turned to Elizabeth, smiled, then threw her arms around her.

"Thank you, thank you. It's, it's . . ."

"Beautiful," Donny said.

Then Mom hugged and kissed Dad. All I could think about was that it was rapidly approaching the time to look at "The Scar," which was, at that moment, still hidden behind Gloria and Rae.

Dennis returned with a tray of beers and passed them around. "Has she seen "The Scar" yet?"

"The scar?" Mom asked.

Aunt Gloria and Rae moved aside.

"Oh my!" Eddie gasped.

"Don't you like it?" Donny asked, but Eddie was too busy looking at the scar to hear him.

She blinked her eyes a couple of times, then stepped back and cocked her head. She stepped forward again and leaned in. She studied the colors and nodded. She examined what was just the shadow of a face and twisted her mouth off to the side. Her eyes followed the smooth lines of the boy's muscles from the shoulders down to the calves of his legs. Her eyes twitched, she puckered and she wrinkled her nose and brow.

"Mom?" Donny said, leaning in next to Mom's face. "Don't be angry, please."

"Angry? Oh no! This is a wonderful painting. Elizabeth, it's the best thing you've ever done. I love it!"

The sigh that was heard 'round the world.

"But it says 'sold.'" Eddie said. "Has someone bought it already?"

"Me," Carl announced, then quickly added, "for Josh."

"Oh good, I wouldn't want—I mean, something like this, something this special, should stay in the family. Don't you think?"

"Yes I do," Elizabeth said, smiling.

"You won't put it in the hotel lobby, will you Josh?" Mom asked.

"No ma'am," Josh answered with a grin.

"Oh good."

Donny tugged on Mom's new white summer dress, "Can we go home now?"

"Soon as I get my new painting."

"I'll bring it," Josh offered.

"Thank you, Josh. We can go then," Eddie said, taking Donny's hand.

"Can I have a Coke now?" he asked.

"Oh I guess so. Come on. See you all at home."

Eddie and Donny walked off hand in hand. Donny took the parasol from Mom and held it over her head for her.

14.   He Would A-Wooing Go

O what a week it was.
       I got to play bartender at Respighi's. Mom would not go to work. She said a bar was no place to raise a son. I was on vacation, no Clarion for two weeks, so I got to play bartender. I was lousy. I could make all the normal cocktails, but the fancy ones and the blender ones were beyond my capabilities. Fortunately, there weren't too many exotic drinkers around that week, so I didn't have to run to the mixology book or bother Hugh too often. What I couldn't do at all, even with all the suggestions people had to offer, was remember more than two drinks at a time. The service was very slow that week at Respighi's.

   O what a week it was.

   Elizabeth came to the bar every night to keep me company. And to nag me about my inability to remember more than two drinks at a time. We had a nice week together. We slept late every morning, made special breakfasts-brunches and lazed on the veranda till noon. Then, in the afternoon, she'd paint (she started next year's version of "Red Ball Under a Beech Tree" the day after this year's festival was over, saying she wanted to get it out of the way) and I went for walks or played pool at Respighi's with Josh. Elizabeth and I talked about the baby, our baby. Or rather, I talked about our baby; Elizabeth said she didn't want to start making a big deal out of it so early.

O what a week it was.

Josh was bored to death: The masses had evacuated the hotel and Mom was consuming all of Donny's time. Josh would show up on our porch at the very moment we were about to start eating our crêpes or waffles or blintzes, so we would, of course, invite him to join us. Josh would offer to do the dishes in return for the meal, which would make Elizabeth feel guilty, so she'd insist that he not do them alone, meaning I had to help him, while Elizabeth returned to her studio to paint. Then Josh and I would go for a walk and/or play pool at Respighi's until five when it was time for me to play bartender.

O what a week it was.

The Sunday Night Regulars thought it was so "cute" that I was tending bar, they came in every night. And every night, they would try to convince me they were eligible for the discounted drinks. On Tuesday, they said they were all the guests of Pat and Dennis, the two artists in the group, and, thus, I should give them Art Night special prices. On Wednesday night, they said they were Pat's guests, she being the only mother in the bunch, and that I should give them half priced drinks for Mom Night. On Thursday, they all wore bowling shirts. On Friday, Kurt and Terry came as father and son, and the others wore green visor caps, for Dad Night, aka Poker Night. On Saturday, Music Night, they carried beat up, old musical instruments, which I recognized as being the ones that had been collecting dust for years in the front window of Kurt's Junque Shoppe. I held out all week, then gave them all their drinks free on Sunday Night. Sunday night was Queer Night at Respighi's, and we had one hell of a party.

O what a week it was.

Aunt Caroline moved in with Amelia that week, leaving most of her furniture behind to give the new Beech Grove Museum and Art Gallery "a homey touch." Besides, there was no room at Amelia's for any more furniture. She still had all the choicest pieces that they had appropriated from the other houses when the family found Beech Grove fifty-two years ago. Most of us offered to help with the move and with setting up the Museum, but Amelia and Caroline wanted to do as much as they could on their own. So, once Dad got the new wheelchair ramp built at the Museum, the two women were on their own. They moved things on Amelia's lap in the wheelchair. When they had larger items to cart around, they put a piece of plywood over the arms of the wheelchair and put whatever had to be moved on top of that, usually blocking Amelia's view so that she was constantly nagging Aunt Caroline about her "driving." Going down the ramps, Caroline would be braced and pulling backwards with all her might while Amelia leaned on the brakes. Going up the ramps, Aunt Caroline would turn around backwards and push the chair with her shoulders, digging in with her heels, while Amelia puffed. They conned each Beech Grove artist into donating one painting to the Art Gallery and they scoured the town looking for relics to put in the Museum. They found the hotel's 1932 register and the original bell from the reception desk. They found an old pool cleaning brush and a device for holding mud under one's chin. In Amelia's garage, they found a grave marker which said: "Here lie Matthew and Mark, the Delaney Twins. Born on February 29, 1896. Died on July 24, 1932."

O what a week it was.

Carl made little cedar chests all week, other than the afternoon he spent putting a wheelchair ramp on the Museum steps. Those little boxes were the hottest selling item at the festival. Fifty-three of them were sold and a hundred more were ordered. They sold for seventy-five dollars—Dad got fifty and the school got the twenty-five. Dad's contribution to our community. Miss Blankenship had run the booth and put her heart and soul into selling the cedar chests. She even made up a little sign listing possible uses for the chests: Sewing Box,

Little Girls' Keepsakes, Fine Lace, Sweaters, Planter Box, Cassettes, Make a Lamp, Button or Coin Collections, Doll Crib, and so on. She didn't know about burying baby sisters or squashed cats in them, or that probably would have been on her sign, too.

O what a week it was.

Eddie and Donny spent every waking hour together. They were starting all over again with each other. Donny's second childhood only lasted a couple of days, but not his dependency. Other than to sleep, he didn't leave Mom's side all week. It was as if he was trying to relive his life, or something, like he wanted to make up for all the things he'd missed, first time around.

They cleaned house together, the spring cleaning type of cleaning, top to bottom, inside and out. And when they finished at Mom's they came over and cleaned our house. They washed and ironed clothes together. They sewed on buttons, darned socks, mended rips in everything, and they made baby clothes. They cooked, first together, then Donny alone. They invaded Dad's workshop and Donny taught Mom how to make a miniature cedar chest. They walked together up in the hills. They swam together up at the pond—in bathing suits. They made daily rounds of the Beech Grove shops and even took a bus trip to Escondido for a day of shopping. It was nauseating.

They read together. Every night. One word at a time until Donny didn't stumble or hesitate anymore. They started with Dr. Seuss and worked their way up to *Moby Dick* by the end of the week. I couldn't figure out what Donny was doing. Josh said not to worry.

They listened to music together. First it was Prokofiev's "Romeo and Juliet," then the Rolling Stones. Prokofiev's "Classical Symphony," then The Doors. Piano concerti, then Queen. "Cinderella," then Pink Floyd's "The Wall." Neither became particularly fond of the other's music, but their battle of the bands became a thing of the past.

They took art lessons together, from Elizabeth. Eddie finished her painting of the Cinderella Music Box. Donny painted a series, a suite if you will, of frogs. Amelia and Aunt Caroline insisted these new works of art, "Cinderella" and "The Frog Suite," hang in the Beech Grove Museum and Art Gallery.

Eddie and Donny studied sex together. On the shopping trip to Escondido, Mom bought every book this one shop had which dealt with homosexuality. Their favorite was "The Joy of Gay Sex." They also liked "Gay Spirit," although Mom thought it was too risque. They gave four stars to "The Hite Report on Male Sexuality," but burned "Everything you always wanted to know about sex* but were afraid to ask" because it said two men couldn't live together happily. Eddie thought that was nonsense, so she threw the book into the fireplace and built a fire around it, on a hundred-and-two degree afternoon.

And together, Mom and Donny supervised the final preparations for Beech Grove's new, and only, beech tree, our "Arboretum."

The big day, the planting and Dedication Day, was the following Monday, July 2. Hugh and the Sunday Night Regulars had been working on the site for a week. All the debris had been removed and the canopy had been strung between the two pines on either side. The old garage foundation had turned out to be unmortared adobe bricks rather than cement, so they dug up the bricks individually and used them to make a low wall around the arboretum. The hole had been dug. All that was needed was the proper soil and the beech tree, both of which Professor Dhunwhit was bringing.

When Eddie started her research on the project, her first contact was Professor Dhunwhit at UCR. Oddly, he was delighted to help; he just happened to be looking for a home for a beech tree that he'd been nurturing at the University. A new building was going in, he told Mom, at the one spot on the whole campus which was ideal for his beech tree. He thought Beech Grove would make a nice home for his beech tree, provided he had control of the planting and supervision over the tree's formative years.

Professor Dhunwhit was late. Half the town of Beech Grove was standing out there wilting in the hot summer sun, and the professor was nowhere in sight. We—the actual work crew, consisting of me, Josh, Donny, Hugh and the Regulars—leaned on our shovels, cursing and sweating. The others, the spectators, fought over the limited and transient shade. Then, as Amelia and Aunt Caroline were refilling everyone's lemonade glasses, the roar of a large truck announced the professor's arrival.

It was a very old and delapidated dump truck. One of the front fenders was missing. There was a hole in the muffler and very little paint. It listed to one side and it either had bad brakes, or he didn't know how to use them, because the truck came barreling around the corner at the bottom of the hill, roared up the slope, careened into the driveway and didn't come to a stop until it slammed into the large mound of dirt in front of the hole.

Professor Dhunwhit jumped down from the cab, brushing dust from his suit and patting sweat from his brow with a handkerchief.

"My, but you people live out in the middle of nowhere. Dhhewnit's the name," he said, lighting his cherry scented pipe. "It's not Duhoonwhit, nor Donut. Dhhewnit. Sorry I'm late. Forgot where this place was."

"No problem," Eddie said. "No problem at all. We were just having some lemonade. Would you care for some?"

"Oh, no thank you. Best get on with the task at hand, don't you agree? As you can see, I have the soil here, so all we have to do is dump it in there and . . ."

"Think we better turn the truck around first," Hugh said.

"Oh, surely. One of you boys do that, would you?"

Josh volunteered. Donny climbed on the back.

"Hey! Where's the tree?" Donny asked.

"I think it's in here," Josh called from the cab. He leaned out the window with a small coffee can in his hand. A foot-long twig was sticking out of it. "Is this it?"

"You be very careful with that, young man," the professor said, taking it from Josh.

We all stared at the little, tiny beech tree.

The professor held the can up triumphantly. "Behold!" he said. "A beech tree for Beech Grove!" He waited for the applause, but none came.

We all stared at the nine-foot long, nine-foot wide, nine-foot deep hole he had instructed be dug.

Eddie started to speak, but then put her hand to her mouth. She closed her eyes for a second. Carl moved to her side and took her arm. When she lowered her hand, she was braving a smile.

"Hey Mom!" Donny yelled from the truck as Josh turned it around slowly. "Got any flowers you want planted. Got lots of dirt up here!"

Mom sobbed aloud.

"That's enough out of you!" Carl shouted.

"I was only kidding," Donny said, then buried himself in the truckload of loam.

"Better get out, Donny!" Josh said. "I'm gonna dump her!"

"Go ahead!"

He did.

I grabbed Donny's arm as he slid by and yanked him aside. The soil filled the hole and left a three-foot high mound above the ground.

"What do we do with this hill?" Hugh asked.

"King of the Mountain!" Donny screamed, leaping to the crest.

"Not for long!" Terry cried, and attacked.

"Boys! Boys!" the professor said. "You've got the right idea, but it has to be more organized. We need as many people as we can get on the mound to tamp it down."

"You're kidding, right?" Carl asked.

"Without proper equipment, one does what one must," the professor replied. "Everyone up!"

What a sight we were: two dozen of us, huddled together on top of that mound, hopping up and down in unison. But we flattened it. The onlookers applauded us. Amelia and Caroline rewarded us with a bonus glass of lemonade.

The professor walked over to the middle of the planting site with his coffee can. He pulled a small home-gardening trowel out of his jacket pocket and made a small hole in the dirt. He yanked the little beech out of the can and stuck it in the hole, pushed some dirt on top of the roots, tamped it with the heel of his hand, then stood back to admire his handiwork. "Lovely," he said. He glanced up at the canopy, some fifteen feet overhead, and added: "That will have to be lowered. Who has the water?"

We had planned a little family dinner at Mom's that night to celebrate the new arbortum. It was a very quiet dinner. Elizabeth and I cooked, Josh and Donny served, Eddie and Carl sat silently at their respective ends of the table. Once everyone was seated, I poured the wine, then raised my glass to toast; no one followed my lead.

"Oh come on! It's not that bad. In a few years, it'll—well, the dedication plaque looked nice anyway, don't you think?"

Silence.

I sat. I picked at my food like the others were doing.

Donny giggled. I glared at him. He stuck out his tongue at me, then stood, raising his glass. When no one looked at him, he picked up his spoon and banged it on the side of his glass. We gave him our attention. He cleared his throat, then:

"Professor Donut did it in the arboretum with a trowel!" He sat down.

That was the end of that meal. We all got stomach aches from laughing and couldn't eat. Eddie and Donny both got the hiccups.

We had coffee on the veranda.

"Mom?" Donny said, once we were settled on the front porch.

"Yes dear."

"I want to start seeing Josh again."

Josh grinned, a little embarrassed.

"I think that would be very nice."

"Can I go home with him tonight then?"

"Don't be ridiculous. It's fine if you want to date—uh, see each other, but you're not going home with him. And he can't stay here either, so don't ask."

"Motherrrr," Donny whined.

"And don't whine. We discussed the rules for seeing other boys and there'll be no more arguing about it."

"Should we leave?" I asked.

"This is family. Sit still," Carl said.

Eddie continued: "You can see Josh as much as you want. He can come for dinner every night if he wants. You can visit him at the hotel. When he's not too busy, that is. You know how you can get under foot. In fact, now that I think of it, you could work for him at the hotel if he needs you. But when you go out at night, I want you home, alone, by eleven. Is that clear?"

"Yes, Mama."

"You know what you should do? Since I'm going back to work, and Matt won't have to work the bar for me anymore, the four of you should double date. My, I think that's a splendid idea!"

"Mother, really," I said.

"I think it sounds like fun," Elizabeth said.

"You do?"

"I'd even be willing to forget the curfew if you're with Matt and Elizabeth," Eddie said.

"Please Matt?" Donny pleaded.

"What can we do?" Elizabeth said. "A picnic! A Fourth of July picnic! And we can stay for the fireworks!"

"Okay Matt?" Josh asked.

"I guess so. But where?"

"Lake Perris," Josh said. "You can rent boats and sit out on the water for the fireworks."

"I want to go there," Donny said. "Then I want to go to a drive-in."

"A what?"

"A drive-in movie. I've never been to one."

Elizabeth beamed: "Spilled sticky Cokes, popcorn in your lap and between your teeth, XLNT Tamales, hot dogs with mustard on your shirt! God, what memories!"

"Steamed windows," I said.

"I don't know." Eddie said.

"Matt! Why'd you say that?! Now she won't let me go!"

"You can go, Donny, but only with Matt and Elizabeth."

"I don't want to be his goddamn *dueña*," I said.

"Watch your mouth," Carl aid.

"What's a, what's a . . . ?" Donny tried to ask.

"*Dueña*. Chaperone. Nanny. Babysitter."

"Matthew, I want to do this," Elizabeth said in one of her irresistible tones, threatening in nature.

"Okay," I said. "Fireworks at Lake Perris on Wednesday. The drive-in on Saturday. Everybody happy now?"

"Thank you, Matt," Donny said.

"Just go easy on the steamed windows please," Eddie said.

"We'll see . . ." said Donny, teasing.

"Don't you get persnickety with me," Eddie said.

"What?" we all cried amid a burst of laughter.

"Oh!" Mom said. "The images that just flashed through my mind! That wonderful woman!"

"Who?"

"Esther."

"The chocolate cake lady?"

"Yes. The chocolate cake lady."

Lake Perris is quite large, for a small lake. It could almost accommodate the thousands of cars, trucks, campers and boats, along with the attendant thousands of people, trying to take advantage of the lake facilities on Independence Day.

"Where is the motor?" I asked of the boat that Josh rented.

"See those long, thin pieces of wood with the flat part on the end?" replied Josh.

"It's a hundred and three!"

"Sweating is good for you."

"My sweat glands are just fine, thank you. It's heat stroke I'm thinking about."

"Then don't help out. The three of us can handle it," Elizabeth said, trying to shame me.

"Good," I said, sitting up front. "Let's go!"

"You're going to let us do your share of the rowing?" Elizabeth asked.

"You said you could handle it."

"I thought it would help you see your responsibilities."

"I know what you thought. It didn't work."

"Of all the . . ."

"Hey guys," Josh interrupted. "We're out here to have fun. Remember?"

"Sure. Let's go," I said. "Who's going to row first?"

Elizabeth screamed and started to hit me. The people in the boats on both sides of us turned to look. I smiled and waved. They looked away immediately.

Josh and Donny each took an oar. Elizabeth sat in the back of the boat, refusing to talk or even look at me. We found a small shaded cove and dropped anchor. The anchor was a coffee can filled with cement.

"I'm hungry," I said.

"Only oarsmen, oarspeople, get to eat," Elizabeth gloated, as she opened the picnic basket.

"I'm an oarsperson. Or, I will be, all the way back to the dock. By myself. Just, please, give me some food!"

"You promise?"

"I promise!"

Mom made the lunch. Five pieces of chicken each. At least a gallon of homemade potato salad. Carrot and celery sticks. Homemade rolls. Pickles. Olives. Oranges. Apples. Bananas. Fudge brownies. A case of ice-cold beer.

We ate every bit of it. It took us four hours to do it, but we ate it all.

We napped. Josh and Donny curled together in the front of the boat, Elizabeth and I in the back.

At dusk, I rowed us out to the center of the lake to await the fireworks show. I rowed, not because of my promise to do it alone, but because when Elizabeth helped me, she kept putting her oar in too deep so that she couldn't move it, and we went in circles; so, I rowed alone.

The fireworks were shot off from a barge and all the boats lined up, at a safe distance, around it. The lake was jammed with boats. The shoreline was jammed with bodies.

It was at least eighty-five degrees and clear. The stars were brilliant, while the moon shone on the smooth surface of the lake. Then skyrockets filled the sky with patriotic bursts of color and, unfortunately, great clouds of smoke. There was a good breeze blowing, though, so the smoke cleared quickly.

Josh stretched out at the front of the boat and Donny sat between his legs, leaning back into him. They locked arms across Donny's stomach. Elizabeth and I mirrored them at the other end of the boat.

"Fags!" someone shouted from a nearby boat.

"Hi!" we yelled back, smiling and waving. They left us alone. It was too beautiful a night to let anyone spoil it for us.

When we got back to Beech Grove, when we got back to Mom and Dad's house to drop Donny off, he didn't want to get out of the car.

"C'mon, Donny, don't mess things up," I said. "You'll see Josh tomorrow."

"I don't want to be alone," Donny said.

"I've got an idea," Elizabeth said. "I need some paper and a pencil."

We rummaged through the glove compartment of the station wagon till we finally found a pen and a little scrap of paper.

"What are you going to do?"

"We are going to camp out tonight. The four of us. In our back yard. Thought we should leave Eddie a note, so she won't worry about Donny."

We camped out. It was so warm we didn't need anything over us, so we opened our two sleeping bags out side by side, and all slept in our bathing suits. However, we didn't sleep. Most of the night was spent telling dumb jokes and trying to scare each other with ghost stories and false alarms about wild animals lurking in the trees just beyond the lawn.

Donny told us about the bobcat.

"I had been so careful," he said. "I kept the fire going all night. Never went more than ten feet from the treehouse or the pond at night. I figured I was safe in the daytime. Anyway, I was playing monkey or something, and I must've attracted his attention with all the jumping around. I heard a noise in the brush, but I didn't think anything of it. Suddenly, he was right there in front of me. Between me and the water, or I'd've jumped in real fast. He just looked at me. I stared right into his eyes, trying to show him I wasn't scared of him. He didn't believe me.

"He was beautiful. He looked like he could be someone's pet cat, you know. He was super clean. I could see a dozen different colors in his hair. And muscles! Shit, I'd love to have muscles like his. He was strong. But his eyes are what got me. He didn't look mean at all. I mean, he looked at me like he was gonna just hop up on my lap and start purring, wanting me to pet him.

"He started moving closer to me, one paw at a time. I don't know if I didn't move because I was too scared, or if he hypnotized me, but I just stood there and watched him creep towards me, those friendly eyes staring into mine. Shit, he was probably thinking about dinner, huh?

"Then I jerked. I don't know why. My body just tensed up all of a sudden. Maybe he wouldn't have jumped at me if I hadn't done that, but I didn't do it on purpose anyway, so there was nothing I could do about it.

"I thought about my knife just as his front legs hit me in the chest. I fell backwards and he was right on my stomach, his teeth trying to get to my throat. His claws dug into my chest and arms. I got him by the throat, and started choking him, but shit, he just tightened his neck muscles, hard as a board, and my fingers weren't doing nothing. I worked my hands up underneath his jaw and pushed my thumbs as hard as I could into the soft skin at the top of his throat. I must've hit something, because he let out a yelp and took off into the woods. I washed—well, you know the rest."

No one wanted to sleep after that story, so we made coffee and sat on the porch for awhile, snuggling and sighing about what a beautiful and balmy night it was.

It was equally balmy the night we went to the drive-in movie, so we went in our bathing suits. We thought we were being so daring, going like that, but everybody at the movie was in swim suits or shorts.

Josh and I got the snack bar detail. Elizabeth wanted one of everything. So did Donny.

"I don't know why those two don't get fat," I said, after placing our very large order at the counter.

"Metabolism," said Josh.

"Mom said something about not letting Donny eat a lot of junk, but I don't want to tell him what to do."

"You know what she said to me tonight when I picked Donny up?"

"What?"

"You mother really knows how to hurt a guy. She said, 'Josh, I'm so happy it's you Donny wants to be with, because you understand what I'm trying to do for him. You know, not wanting him to be, uh, promiscuous like they said in one of those books. It just helps me so much knowing I can trust you.' That's what she said! Trust! What a terrible thing to say to someone."

"Yeah. I'm so glad Elizabeth's mother never trusted us."

"Why am I doing this?" asked Josh.

"Doing what?"

"This! Home by eleven. No overnights! There are people at the hotel right now that I'd bet my last dollar were, as your mother would put it, promiscuous. I could be fucking my brains out every night instead of holding hands in a movie."

"God! You don't suppose you're in love."

"Oh, shut up and carry some of this stuff. What are we going to do with all this food?"

We went to see "Bounty." It was fun seeing the movie, after having visited the ship in Long Beach. Josh, Donny and Elizabeth went on and on about how gorgeous Mel Gibson was. They stuffed popcorn down my trunks when I pointed out his bad complexion to them.

There is something instinctively erotic about drive-in theaters. We actually fought over who got the back seat. I could understand Josh and Donny, they were undergoing a strange phase in their relationship. But Elizabeth and I lived together, slept together—and we still fought for the back seat at the drive-in. Josh and Donny won.

"We promise not to look," Donny said.

"Just shut up and watch the movie," I said. "And I mean watch the movie. Mother will ask questions."

"Speaking of Mother," Josh said to Donny, "how long does she expect us to play this game?"

"I don't know," replied Donny.

"It better not be much longer."

"Don't you want to keep seeing me?"

"Yeah. That's not the point."

"Do you two have to have these personal conversations in public?" I asked.

"In the first place," Josh said, "this isn't public. It's just you. In the second place, double dating was not my idea in the first place. And in the third place, shut up and watch the movie. Okay?"

"Okay. Jeez."

"Donny," Josh continued their conversation, "I'm just not used to all this . . . restraint."

"I don't like it either, but what am I supposed to do about it? I can't go through another fight with her. Don't you understand, Josh? I just can't, now that we've made up finally."

"Then let's talk to her about something more, uh, more permanent."

"You'll have to do the talking. I've gone through too much these last weeks to risk setting her off again."

"Fine. We'll do it tomorrow."

"What are you going to say?"

"I don't know."

"Why don't you tell her you're pregnant and have to get married," I suggested. Both Donny and Josh whacked me on the back of the head.

"Elizabeth," said Josh, "do something with him."

Her hand slid down the front of my trunks, fingernail into flesh.

"Ouch!" I screamed. "Watch the fingernails!"

"Foul!" Josh cried from the back seat.

The people in the movie were running around half naked, and we were half-naked sitting there in the station wagon, so it wasn't too difficult to get into an amorous mood. Had our windows not been rolled down, we would've steamed them up. I didn't think adults could neck so—so fervently. Then I remembered why I always hated drive-in movies and why I always hated double dates. You get all worked up, then there you are: out in public with people walking by the car and with another couple in the car with you. And, unless you're extremely free-thinking about going all the way in front of other people, which I never was and am not, you are suspended in a very uncomfortable position.

That's when the whispering starts:

Oh God.

What are we going to do?

You could . . . you know.

What about you?

And from the back seat:

We can't.

Why not?

Your mother.

I won't tell.

She'll know.

Well, Elizabeth's doing it!

DAMN!

The four of us camped out in the back yard again that night, but this time we did sleep. Just as I was dozing off, I heard the biggest sigh from the other sleeping bag. Then: "We are definitely going to have a talk with your mother in the morning."

15. One Yellow Rose

When you live in town the size of Beech Grove, you get used to the fact that everyone knows everything. What you do not get used to, however, is when everyone knows something before it happens.

The entire community was at the Sunday Service the next morning, thanks to Aunt Caroline. She didn't tell them why they had to be there, just that they had to be in attendance. The *reason* for them to be there hadn't even happened as yet. The *reason* for them to be there happened as we were walking to the service.

We walked in couples: Mom and Dad, Elizabeth and I, and Josh and Donny. Donny kept poking Josh, and whispering, *Ask her, ask her.* Josh finally got his nerve together and stepped up his pace to catch up to Mom.

"Eddie, uh," Josh stammered.

"Yes, Josh?"

"Uh, Donny and I want to . . . that is, we'd like to, uh . . ."

I translated for him: "Mom, Josh and Donny think it's time for their relationship to move forward."

"They do?" she said to me. "You do?" she asked Josh.

"Yes, um, we do."

"In what way?" Eddie asked.

"Mother!" said Donny, turning red.

That time Dad interpreted: "I think Mother would like to know your intentions."

"Are we passing through some kind of time warp?" I asked.

"Matt," Elizabeth scolded, pinching my arm.

"Don't do that."

"My intentions?" Josh asked.

"Yes," Mom said.

"Well, I, uh, I don't . . . I guess we . . . I don't think I know what to say to that."

"I thought you had your speech all planned out," I said. That time I got knuckles in the ribs.

"This is stupid," Donny said. "We want to live together."

"I don't think so," Mom said.

"Damnit! What do you expect from us?"

"I expect you to get married," Mom said, calmly.

"What!"

"Shotgun wedding! I told you!" I cried out. "And don't hit me."

Elizabeth didn't hit me. From the smile, and from the far away look in her eyes, I think she was already making plans for the wedding.

"You're kidding," said Carl.

"I don't mean a wedding in the traditional sense, but I think before two people try to make a life together they should make an open expression of their commitment to each other. Just living together is too flippant, too casual, and much less likely to last. Sharing a life with someone is very difficult; it requires real commitment to help it endure the bad times. It's as important as the love you feel for one another and it will only make your love grow stronger. Believe me."

"Josh?" Donny asked.

"Yeah. I like it—a lot. How about you?"

"It's kinda scary," Donny said.

"See? It's already become more important in your mind," Eddie said, smiling.

"I guess so," Donny said. "I want to do it."

"I need a drink," Dad said.

"I'll buy," I said.

"Both of you, keep still," Eddie said. "Next Sunday all right?"

Josh and Donny nodded, a little dazed by what they had just agreed to.

"Fine," Mom said. "I think we should have it on the great lawn, over by the oaks. There'll be shade there. We can have it as part of the service. Maybe put flowers between the trees and . . ."

"Sounds like a wedding to me," Dad said.

"Hush," Mom scolded. "Elizabeth, could you design robes for them? Something special."

"Robes?"

"Something biblical. White, I think, for both. And sandals or bare feet?"

Josh grew pale.

"Bare feet," Elizabeth joined in the planning. "Do you think rings are appropriate?"

"I'm not sure; we can discuss that and, oh dear, the meeting is starting without us. We'll have to finish later."

The meeting was on the great lawn, in the shade of the three oaks at the far end. We sat behind Jack and Dennis, off to the side. Amelia was reading something, which I couldn't make out because she was mumbling and stopping every other word to find her place.

But it was Aunt Caroline, standing next to Amelia, that everyone was watching. They all wanted to know why Caroline had told them to be there that morning in particular.

They didn't have to wait long. When Amelia finished, or rather, when Amelia paused so long that we assumed she was finished, Mom stood.

"Everyone!" Eddie shouted to get their attention. "I have an announcement to make!"

The crowd buzzed. *This must be it.*

Donny and Josh shrank a bit behind Elizabeth and me.

"Next Sunday morning," Mom continued, "I would like to invite you all to a very special event. My son, Donny, and Josh Bowen have decided to share their lives with one another and, as a favor to me, they will make a declaration of their commitment in a small ceremony as part of next Sunday morning's service."

Jack and Dennis whipped around, beaming. Rae and Gloria leapt to their feet and started making their way around to us. Amelia sat upright in her wheelchair: "Your son is marrying a man?" she screamed.

The entire town came to its feet, blocking Amelia's view. She pulled furiously at her wheels, but the chair wouldn't move. "Caroline, push!"

Aunt Caroline reached down, released the brakes, then wheeled Amelia over to where we were standing. "Have you gone mad, Edwina?!"

"Amelia, please calm down," Mom said. "It's not a marriage, a wedding. We just . . ."

"I won't allow it!" Amelia ranted, her face getting beet red.

"Let me," Josh said, moving in front of me and squarely in front of Amelia. "Amelia, I guess I've always been a little afraid of you. Seems like most people around here are. And I never cared enough about anything to fight with you over it. This I care about and I'm willing to fight you this time. Donny and I love each other . . ."

"That's sick," Amelia interrupted.

" . . . we love each other, and we're going to stand up here next Sunday morning and say what we feel. If you don't like it, you don't have to attend!"

By then, people were shaking hands, patting backs, hugging and kissing.

"Oh, I'll be here" Amelia said, "to stop this, this sacrilege, this disgusting, perverted . . ."

"Hey!" Josh cut her off. "I guess you have the right to feel anyway you want, but that doesn't mean we have to listen to your bigotry! Do what you will, you will not stop us!"

Those close enough to hear, applauded. Amelia started puffing violently. Doc and Caroline took her home.

The congratulations continued.

"What about a shower?"

"I think it'd be a bachelor party."

"We'll combine them."

"Saturday night."

"At Respighi's."

Hugh and the Sunday Night Regulars went all out for the party on Saturday night. Flowers everywhere, even one in Gordy's hair. He was staying on to help out with the bar. Crepe paper streamers everywhere, even hanging from the rotating ceiling fans in whirlpools of bright colors. Champagne everywhere, even in the kids' punch bowl. We took up the entire wing of the hotel, including the restaurant, the bar and the veranda; even the single-lane bowling alley had flowers and streamers in it. All the tables in the dining room had been pushed back to the walls and were loaded with food, pot luck from the cooks of Beech Grove. Hugh paid for all the booze and refused to take contributions from the rest of us. Instead, he put one of Dad's little cedar chests on the bar and told us to fill it with money for Josh and Donny. We did. They had asked us not to bring gifts, but we wouldn't let them turn down the box of cash.

Eddie had wanted a live band, but we couldn't find one on such short notice, so we danced to the music from the juke box. Hugh even had speakers installed in the dining room and out on the veranda so more people could dance.

Poor Josh and Donny had to dance with every woman at the party, and quite a few of the men. They got wise after a while and started demanding a glass of champagne from each dance partner. After a few glasses of bubbling courage, I even danced with them, the three of us at one time. The idea caught on. All over the place, people were dancing in groups of three, four or five, always with glass in hand. My favorite group was Eddie, Elizabeth and Caroline. (Amelia didn't come to the party.) We were all a little high, but my mother, my wife and my aunt were sloshed. They did a cha-cha to Bette Midler. They did a tango to Barry Manilow. They did a bunny hop to Michael Jackson. They hopped out to the veranda.

When they didn't hop back in, I grabbed Dad away from Aunt Gloria, and we went looking for our stray dancers. We searched the spa facilities first, much to the dismay of the young couples we stumbled over in the dark out there. No sign of Eddie, Elizabeth and Caroline. We checked the great lawn and the row of shops across the way, and still came up empty handed. We were about to go back inside when we heard shouting from down the road. It was very distinctly Gram Amelia's voice.

"What the hell do you think you're doing? I'm calling the sheriff if you don't stop immediately!"

"Don't get your spokes in an uproar," we heard Eddie say. `

Carl and I ran. There was a very loud banging sound as we approached Amelia's. Amelia was sitting up on the porch in her wheelchair, jerking back and forth, waving her arms in the air, and cursing.

Eddie, Elizabeth and Caroline were dismantling the wheelchair ramp.

"I'll get there somehow!" Amelia shouted. "This is not going to keep me from stopping this perverted wedding!"

"Eddie!" Carl screamed as we ran up to the steps. "What the hell are you doing?"

"Keeping this old witch from spoiling everything tomorrow! Tha's what!"

"You're drunk," Dad said.

"Maybe."

Elizabeth threw her arms around my neck and just hung there.

"So are you," I said to her.

"Mos' definitely."

"Me too!" Aunt Caroline announced proudly.

"You can't trap a person in a wheelchair in a house," Carl said. "What if there was a fire? What were you thinking of?"

"Donny! Tha's what I was thinking of! If she gets out, she'll ruin everything! So, she ain' gettin' out!"

Mom took her hammer and starting whacking away at the ramp again. Dad started to move toward her, but she stopped suddenly, before he got to her.

"That's better," Dad said.

Eddie just stood there for a second, a very strange look on her face. She dropped the hammer. Dad held his arms out to her, but she didn't come to him.

"Eddie?"

"Mom?"

Eddie sat on the steps.

"Are you okay?"

Carl sat beside her and put his arm around her. "Is it your heart?" he asked.

Mom nodded.

"I'll get Doc," Elizabeth said and ran off toward the hotel.

"Just be still," Dad said to Mom.

"O Lord," Amelia said.

Aunt Caroline walked up the porch steps and behind Amelia's chair. She put her hands on Amelia's shoulders and rubbed gently.

I sat on the other side of Mom. She took my hand.

"Mama . . ."

"Shhh," she said. "Look." She was looking up towards the hotel. Donny and Josh had walked out to the great lawn, at the far end by the three oaks, and were standing there in each other's arms, swaying back and forth to the faint sounds of the jukebox inside.

Mom slumped into Dad's arms.

The lights from the hotel made beautiful streams of color as Elizabeth walked me up to the lawn. Josh and Donny were still dancing as we walked up to them.

"Hey Matt, Elizabeth," Josh said.

"Great party, huh?" Donny said. He was facing the other way and couldn't see our tears.

Josh could. "Matt, what's wrong?"

Donny turned around, looked into my eyes.

"Mama's dead," I said, starting to choke again. "She's dead, Donny. Our mama's dead."

He didn't say anything. He inched his way over to me and leaned his head into my shoulder, his arms folded across his chest between us. I grabbed him and held as tight as I could.

The four of us walked arm-in-arm to Mom and Dad's house—Dad's house. Doc Weston was sitting on the front porch. Mom was on the couch in the living room. Elizabeth and I sat with Doc while Josh and Donny went inside.

"Where's Dad?" I asked.

"Workshop."

We sat silently. I watched Josh and Donny through the open window. They walked up to the couch, then Donny took Josh's hand and knelt in front of Mom. He closed his eyes for a second, then opened them and got to his feet. They came back out on the porch.

"I'll take care of all of the details," Doc said. "I think you should go talk to Carl."

We could hear Dad's power saw and we walked out to the workshop.

"Dad?" I said, once we were inside.

He just nodded and continued his work.

"What are you doing?"

"She needs a coffin, son. Your mother needs a coffin."

"We can buy her a coffin, Dad. You don't have to make it."

"Yes I do. She asked me to. So, I'm makin' it. You know she wants to be buried here in Beech Grove, don't you?"

"Can we do that?"

"We're gonna."

"But, what if it's against the zoning regulations or something?"

"Doc said he could fix it up, but even if he couldn't, it's what she wanted. And it's what she's gonna get. Run along now. I've got work to do."

Sunday Service was cancelled the next morning; Josh and Donny's vows were postponed until the funeral.

Instead, everyone brought food to the house. I had allowed myself to forget that odd little custom, and I was loitering over my coffee on Sunday morning, when Elizabeth announced: "We'd better get over there."

"Where?"

"To your mom's—to your dad's house."

"Why?"

"They'll be bringing food."

"Oh damn, you're right."

We went.

Josh and Donny were already there, sitting at the kitchen table with Carl, sipping coffee. They hadn't brought food. Elizabeth and I didn't bring any food. We joined them for coffee and waited for the others to arrive.

They brought food and consolation. Mostly food. Rae and Gloria brought some kind of casserole dish with foil over the top. They also brought Gloria's father, Randolph. He brought a loaf of french bread. Jack and Dennis brought a pie, something with meringue. Hugh, the only sensible one in the bunch, brought a mixed case of booze. Pat and Gwen arrived with a casserole of some kind in a Corning Ware dish with a glass lid on top. Miss Blankenship brought a casserole with no top, proudly displaying the spinach, noodle and cheese contents. Doc and Gordy somehow came as a pair, sharing their offering of a chocolate cake. Kurt and Terry brought assorted cookies. Aunt Caroline arrived, pushing Amelia in the wheelchair. In Amelia's lap were a pie and a casserole with steamy cellophane on top. Amelia was upset because Caroline had to push her all the way up the steep driveway and around to the back door where there were no steps. Even Deputy Sheriff Michael Pilsudski showed up at the door with a casserole his mother had made for him to bring over. He couldn't stay, he said. Had to patrol his section of the county.

Rae and Gloria took charge of the food. Hugh took charge of the bar.

We ate a little. We drank a lot.

They mumbled awkward condolences. We mumbled awkward thanks.

Everyone shared little remembrances. And gossiped.

We did this for several hours.

Then Rae and Gloria divided the leftovers—almost everything was leftover—into Tupperware servings and stored them away, some in the fridge, some in the freezer. Then everyone left.

I said I thought the ritual was stupid and that it made me feel worse.

Carl said he felt better.

Elizabeth agreed with Carl. Donny agreed with me. Josh was undecided.

Carl went into his bedroom and returned with a piece of wood. "Matt," he said, "you take this over to Caroline tomorrow. I forgot to give it to her. Your mother wanted it to hang in the new museum after she—after she died."

He handed me the board with the Yellow Rose verse on it. I hadn't seen it since the day we scattered Grampa Leonard's ashes around the old garage.

As we were leaving, Dad stopped Donny and Josh at the front door. "Donny, I sure would appreciate it if you and Josh would move in here with me. Hate to be all alone. You can even have the big bedroom up front. I'll get our—I'll get the things out of there tonight. Or tomorrow. You can move in anytime. Okay?"

Donny looked to Josh. Josh nodded and smiled.

"Thanks Dad," Donny said.

I took the wood-burning to Caroline the next morning, right after breakfast. As I was walking up Amelia's driveway, I heard a yoohoo from down the road. Aunt Caroline was standing out in front of the Museum, waving to me.

"Good morning, Matthew," she said.

"How's Amelia?"

"She'll be all right, bless her soul. Didn't want to get up this morning, but she'll be fine by tonight, you wait and see."

"Mom wanted you to have this for the Museum," I said, handing her the piece of wood.

"Come inside. I have something for you, too."

I followed her up the steps and into the living room, or rather, the Leonard Briggs Room of the Beech Grove Museum and Art Gallery.

"Would you like some tea?" Aunt Caroline asked.

"No thank you."

"Here, sit down."

I sat on the couch near the fireplace. On the coffee table in front of me were the Ouija board and the crystal ball. I gazed into the crystal, half-expecting to see something.

"See anything?" Aunt Caroline asked.

"No."

"Want to?"

"I'm not sure."

"I peeked already. Want to hear?"

"Yes."

"Well, first off, you're going to get another one of those awards. At least, there's some kind of banquet and I could see you being handed a plaque. Couldn't really tell when or exactly what, though. Sorry. And, let me see, oh yes, you and Elizabeth are going on a trip, looks like a long one with jet planes, the big kind, and I'm pretty sure that's later this year because . . ."

"But what about the baby?"

"Oh, that's not for a year-and-a-half yet."

"But she's already expecting!"

"Oops."

"Oops what?"

"I wasn't supposed to tell."

"Tell what?"

"I think you'd better ask Elizabeth."

"I think I'd better. Now!" I jumped up too quickly and knocked the Ouija off the table. "Shit, is that bad luck or anything?"

"Naw. Damn thing lies anyway; no substitute for a crystal. But wait, I didn't give you what we came in here for."

Aunt Caroline went to the bookshelf and took down a cigar box. She handed it to me.

"I'll want this back, but I thought you'd like to read through these letters sometime. This belonged to Eddie's and my father, our real father, Mark. It has some lovely letters from Esther and a couple from Mat—*Leonard*. But the special—oh you're going to love this—the special thing is that our father wrote a poem for our mother, that was Sarah, and it's the same one he burned into that piece of wood, only that was just the last verse. This original has two other verses. Guess he didn't have time to give them to her. Anyway, it's perfect for Donny and Josh. I know you'll agree. So, give it to them and tell them it's from the whole family; going back a long way. And you tell them to read it to each other as their vows. Will you do that for me, Matthew?"

"Of course I will. Thank you for . . . for everything."

"ELIZABETH!"

"WHAAAT?"

"WHERE THE HELL ARE YOU?"

"UNDER THE TABLE!"

"WHICH TABLE?"

"DINING ROOM!'

"Oh, there you are. What are you doing?"

"Lost a button."

"Come out of there."

"I haven't found it yet. Wait a minute."

"Then I'm coming down there."

"Come ahead."

"What is all this stuff under here?"

"Sewing stuff."

"What's it doing here?"

"No room anyplace else."

"Amazing. Elizabeth, talk to me about babies. Talk to me about this baby, darling, the one in there now. There is one in there now, isn't there? Crazy old Aunt Caroline says it ain't there. Her crystal ball says it ain't there. Normally, I wouldn't pay much attention to such nonsense, but things have been a little strange around here lately, so it seems worth considering. What do you say about all this? Is it there? Or is it not there?"

Silence.

"I'll try again. Mrs. Russell, Mr. Russell—that's me, the

future father of your baby, *if* you have one in there—would like to know *if* you really have one in there."

"No."

"Hm. You had a miscarriage?"

"No."

"You had an abortion?!"

"No!"

"What's left?"

"I lied."

"Terrific."

"Not *lied* in the traditional sense of the word."

"You'll have to explain that one to me."

"You remember I was telling you about the philosophy of creative visualization, 'imagining creates reality'?"

"Yes."

"Well, that's what I did."

"You *imagined* yourself pregnant?"

"Yes, knowing that eventually the imagining would become reality."

"I read those books you gave me, and there's nothing in there about lying to your husband!" I shouted.

"Settle down before you bump your head," she said.

"I'll settle down when I've made you understand that deception was not nice!" I bumped my head. "Okay, I'll settle down. But you'd better re-read this philosophy you are trying to live by. It is not deception. It is concentrated imagining. And faith. Belief."

"I was afraid I couldn't convince myself if no one else thought I was pregnant."

"You lacked faith."

"I guess so. But I've been off the pill for almost a year, and nothing had happened, and . . ."

"A year? More deception!"

"I was afraid you'd be mad."

"This is a partnership. Or was."

"It still is."

"Jesus, Elizabeth, what are you trying to do to me? For years, I thought we agreed that we didn't want to have any children, then all of a sudden you're pregnant, and I'm supposed to accept it and like it. Then you're not going to have a baby! I feel like I'm on a fucking roller coaster. What am I supposed to be feeling at this moment?"

"Oh honey, I'm sorry. I shouldn't have lied to you. You said you thought you wanted us to have a baby, but it was right after the upset with your mother and you didn't sound very sure. I thought if you got used to the idea that we actually were going to have a baby, then when it really did happen, you'd be sure and, uh . . .."

"Happy?" I guessed.

"At least not against it. Not angry with me."

"I'm not angry with you. Just confused. It would—it *will* make me happy. But! We do it together, creative imagining and all. Okay?"

"You're sure?"

"Very. Maybe we would help it out a little?"

"I wasn't planning an immaculate conception."

"I mean now."

"Under the table?"

"Why not?"

"But your mother . . .."

"We owe her a baby."

"You're right."

We stood just inside the low, adobe wall, forming a complete ring around the arboretum. We held hands.

Carl. Lifelong friend, husband, widower.

Matthew. Her oldest son.

Elizabeth. Her daughter-in-law.

Hugh. Friend and partner in business.

Amelia. Aunt and adoptive mother.
Caroline. Sister.
Jack. A special friend.
Dennis. Friend.
Gloria. Friend since childhood.
Rae. Friend.
Kurt. Friend.
Terry. Friend.
Gwen. Friend.
Pat. Friend.
J.D. Friend.
Gordy. Friend and fellow bartender.
Doc. Her physician and friend.

The rest of the town of Beech Grove formed larger circles behind us and Professor Dhunwhit stood off to the side, holding the temporarily homeless beech tree in his hands.

Mom lay in her cedar chest in the very center of the aboretum. Her casket was open. She was wearing her white summer dress, the one with the frilly cuffs and collar.

Two long wooden poles and two ropes lay across the grave under the casket.

On a lace doily, on a small handcarved oak table, sat the Cinderella Music Box, silent with its petals closed.

Josh and Donny joined our circle. Having abandoned the idea of robes, they wore white cotton shorts and white cotton shirts with long sleeves and no collars. Their feet were bare. Their bodies were brown. They each carried a yellow rose. Donny gave his rose to Dad.

Carl stepped forward and placed the rose on Mom's chest. He kissed her on the forehead and closed the lid. Then he, Doc, Hugh and I lifted the cedar chest with the ropes while Jack and Kurt removed the support poles. We lowered the casket into the hole. Each of those in the center ring threw a handful of the loam soil into the grave, then we filled the hole. Professor Dhunwhit replanted the beech tree.

We returned to our places in the circle, again holding hands.

Josh and Donny stepped to the center.

Aunt Caroline started the music box. As it began to turn, we heard the bright chiming of Prokofiev's "Cinderella." The petals began to unfold, revealing the dancing porcelain figure.

"Today is for Eddie," Josh said. "We all love her very much. We will miss her dearly."

"This poem was written by my grandfather for my grandmother," Donny said. "It meant so much to Mom, we would like to share it with you."

Josh and Donny turned to face each other. They held the rose between them.

Josh spoke first:

> Love is the essence of life . . .
>   love is this blossom I hold.
> With our love, we are as one . . .
>   together, our lives unfold.

Then Donny:

> Love is the nature of man . . .
>   our ray of life from the sun.
> This flower comes from my heart . . .
>   this rose unites us as one.

Then Josh and Donny spoke together:

> Give me but one yellow rose . . .
>   it will be our life's bouquet.
> Give me but one yellow rose . . .
>   for it is our love today.